Beneath a
Rising Moon

***

Keri Arthur

PIATKUS

PIATKUS

First published in the US in 2003 by ImaJinn Books,
a division of ImaJinn, USA
First published in Great Britain as a paperback original in 2008 by Piatkus
This paperback edition published in 2008 by Piatkus
Reprinted 2008, 2009

A CIP catalogue record for this book is available from the British Library

ISBN 978-0-7499-0877-5

Typeset in Times by M Rules
Printed and bound in Great Britain by Clays Ltd, St Ives plc

Papers used by Piatkus are natural, renewable and recyclable
products sourced from well-managed forests and certified
in accordance with the rules of the Forest Stewardship Council.

Mixed Sources
Product group from well-managed
forests and other controlled sources
www.fsc.org Cert no. SGS-COC-004081
© 1996 Forest Stewardship Council
FSC

Piatkus
An imprint of
Little, Brown Book Group
100 Victoria Embankment
London EC4Y 0DY

An Hachette UK Company
www.hachette.co.uk

www.piatkus.co.uk

One

The music swirled through the darkness, its beat rich, seductive. Night cloaked the ballroom, a mantle challenged only by the occasional flicker of a torch burning high on the rough-hewn stone walls. On the dance floor, couples swayed to the music, their bodies so close they almost seemed one. Heat and sweat mingled with the growing odor of lust and longing. Scents that stirred her senses, made her hunger.

Neva Grant looked uneasily over her shoulder. Though the moon was lost to the clouds that crowded the night sky, she could feel its presence. Feel its power.

The full moon was too close. She shouldn't be here. Shouldn't be doing this when the wildness within was so close to the surface.

But she'd made her promises. She intended to see them through, no matter what the cost.

She let her gaze roam the dance floor again. Somewhere down there, a killer lurked. A man who was using this secluded, exotic retreat as his own private hunting ground.

A man she had every intention of finding. And slaying.

She raised her glass and finished the last of her wine. The alcohol slithered warmth through her body, and perspiration beaded her skin. Hunger rose, flashing white-hot through her veins. She closed her eyes, took a deep breath.

Not tonight. Please, not tonight.

But the pulsing need suggested it was already too late for such prayers. The wildness had woken. It would not remain leashed for long.

Maybe she shouldn't bother even trying. The killer seemed to be choosing the more adventurous of this wanton crowd. Unleashing the wildness might be the quickest way of attracting his attention.

Bile rose up her throat, and she swallowed heavily. While she had no real choice about what she had to do tonight, she wasn't about to give the wolf within free rein. She wasn't like any of the hunters who danced on the floor below. Her world was one of sunshine and restraint, of trying to live normally.

These people rejoiced in the night and the power of the moon. They came to this mansion for the freedom and the safety it offered, seeking to sate the moon-spun lust surging through their veins. That was why most of the men were naked. Why most of the women wore little more than wisps of material that covered everything and yet left nothing to the imagination. Only their faces were concealed. Once the moon's spell had faded and daylight returned, they would fade back to their packs, picking up their lives where they'd left off, not knowing the face of any of those they'd chosen to mate with the previous night.

Unlike her pack, these wolves were free spirits, exhilarated by the thrill of the chase, by the excitement of capture and possession. The belief of one mate, one life partner, had never touched these dark halls.

But for her promise, she would not be here tonight.

She put aside her glass, then adjusted her ornate mask and made her way down the stairs. The deeper shadows that lined the walls were filled with hunters in various stages of mating. She forced her gaze away, even though the wildness within yearned to watch. Hungered to join them.

Her stomach turned again. God, she hated this place.

Hated everything it represented. Given the choice, she'd rather burn the Sinclair estate to the ground than be walking its halls. She wasn't a prude, far from it—she'd given in to the power of the moon more than once herself. But if it wasn't for this place, if it wasn't for the wanton and careless behavior of its guests, her twin sister would not now be lying in the hospital close to death.

Tears stung her eyes, and she took a deep breath. *Don't think. Just do.*

She moved onto the dance floor, inching her way past the slowly dancing couples. Her pulse throbbed in time to the music's heavy beat, and the deep down ache got stronger.

She clenched her fists and made her way towards the rear exit. She'd spent most of her adult life fighting the worst of her desires, and she would not give in now. Not fully, even here in this place of dark freedom.

And yet at the same time she knew she'd do whatever she had to—even unleashing the wildness—if in the end it led her to the man who'd attacked her twin.

She'd studied the files in Savannah's office before she'd come down here this evening. The killer had struck three times, each time near dawn and just beyond the boundaries of the Sinclair mansion. The victims were always alone, though forensics had, not surprisingly, found evidence to suggest each victim had taken more than half a dozen lovers the night of their deaths. Savannah and the other werewolf rangers who patrolled the Ripple Creek Reservation—which was the mountain homeland of the four Colorado wolf packs—believed the killer was shadowing his victims as they left the mansion, attacking once they were well clear of any help. But they had no proof of this, nothing more than scents and suspicions—neither of which were admissible in court—human or werewolf.

Savannah had been following one such scent when she'd been attacked by a silver wolf. Only the fact that she'd been in wolf form herself had saved her. The winter coat of their tribe was thick, and the silver wolf had been unable to gain any true grip around her sister's throat. But even so, her wounds were multiple and life threatening.

Neva had shared the last, terrifying moments of her twin's horror. And while she'd never wanted to go through something like that again, it was the link between them that had in the end saved her sister. Savannah had siphoned Neva's stronger psychic abilities and used them to finally fend off the wolf.

Neva closed her eyes and took a deep breath. Even now, her sister's pain edged Neva's consciousness. When she'd left home this evening, the doctors still weren't sure if Savannah would survive. Even *she* couldn't say with any degree of certainty. Savannah was hanging on to life by the slenderest of margins, and it wouldn't take much to snatch the lifeline away.

Which is why Neva had touched her twin's unresponsive mind and made a silent vow: She'd hunt down the killer and finish what her sister had started, if Savannah found the strength to live.

It may have been foolish, but it was better than sitting at home waiting for the worst.

Of course, she was no ranger. Far from it. She had no idea how to load a weapon let alone shoot, and she only had a wolf's natural skills when it came to tracking. But she was far from defenseless. Like most of the wolves of her tribe, she rated high in telepathy, but she was also almost off the scale when it came to empathy. The two abilities combined could be a deadly weapon if one knew how to use them properly—as the wolf who'd attacked Savanna had found out.

So far tonight, Neva had kept her shields well up. Skimming the minds of hunters when the moon bloomed was far too dangerous and would attract the kind of sexual interest she was trying to avoid. Besides, she might just alert the killer she was here, seeking him.

The rangers believed it was probably one of the Sinclairs behind the killings, but they were a large and closed-mouthed pack and had yet to provide the rangers with any real help. And while the Sinclairs were all silver wolves, they did not have a monopoly on the coat. Even in her pack, which were primarily golden-coated, silver could be found.

She'd never find the killer roaming the outskirts. It was doubtful if even the rangers could. It had to be done from within the Sinclair stronghold. And there was only one way she could achieve that. Goose bumps skated across her skin, and she sent a silent prayer to the moon for strength.

She'd spent a good part of the day studying the Sinclair lineage. The wolf she'd chosen to seduce was the pack leader's third son. By all accounts he was the wildest of them all, but he was the only one who'd been away when the first two murders were committed. Safe—or as safe as any of the Sinclairs could be.

She'd also spent time studying the mansion's floor plans before coming here, and she had talked to Betise, a regular customer at her family's diner. Though barely thirty-six, Betise had been attending moon dances at the mansion for a good twenty years and knew the place almost as well as the Sinclairs themselves. It had been Betise who told her that Duncan Sinclair rarely joined the dance before mid-night, and that before then he could usually be found close to his rooms on the west side of the mansion.

She hurried out the rear doors. The night breeze stirred her flimsy skirt. Its touch was cool against the fever-kissed skin of her thighs. She glanced skyward again, judging the time by the position of the moon she could feel, not see. Close to midnight. She had to hurry. She tugged the delicate material clear of her bare feet and ran to the back of the mansion.

A cherub-filled fountain came into sight. She slowed, scanning the windows until she found his. Her heart was beating so fast it felt as if it would tear free of her chest, and she knew its cause was fear, not exertion. She'd never done anything like this before. Didn't know if she even had what it took to attract, and hold, a wolf with Duncan Sinclair's experience.

But she had to try. It was the safest way to gain full access into the mansion.

She could only smell one wolf in the rooms above, and there were no others in the immediate area. Betise's information had certainly been accurate. If she pulled this off, she was going to keep the woman supplied with free coffee for the next year.

She walked over to the fountain and stripped off the flimsy excuse for a gown. Then she stepped into the icy water, avoiding the worst of the water-tossing cherubs as she turned her attention to his window.

Everything she'd learned about him suggested he liked a chase and preferred his mates to be sexually adventurous. While she could never claim to be that, she was a wolf and the moon was high. And Betise had offered more than a few tips.

But she couldn't exactly send out a blatant invitation to the man. The rules of the moon dance said no names, so she had to be a little more devious. The Sinclairs were the only other wolf pack who were strong telepaths, so she just had to make it seem he was catching her thoughts.

Lord, I ache tonight.

She kept her mindvoice breathy, wistful. For several tense seconds, nothing happened, then his presence stirred and walked across to the windows. She dipped her fingers into the water and wet her neck, letting the cool droplets dribble between her breasts.

Hunger surged through the night, a force so strong it almost knocked her over. His need for the dance was high. Very high. The thought churned her stomach, but she was here now and would not back away.

She let her gaze roam the windows until she saw him. If his shadow was to be believed, he was big. Bigger than she'd expected. She cupped another handful of water, sipping it quickly to ease the dryness in her throat.

Why do you ache? The moon is high and the night free.

His mind voice was rich, husky, and stirred her senses with longing. She clenched her fists. She had to remain in control. She couldn't let the wildness free.

Perhaps I am choosy.

You can be choosy as many times as you like on a night such as this. Amusement swam across her senses, warm and sensual.

Perhaps I long for a more careful seduction once the initial fire has passed.

His silhouette stirred. She caught the brief glimpse of a muscular arm before the shadows closed in again. *A difficult request when the moon rides high.*

So it would seem. She arched her back, stretching her arms skywards. The emotive swirl of his thoughts became a wall of heat. He wanted her, of that she was certain. Whether he would take her was unclear. He hadn't yet moved from his dark hideaway.

Perhaps I should go home. The moon, it seems, offers me no comfort tonight.

He hesitated. *Perhaps we should talk on the matter.*

The bait had been taken. Now to snare him fully. But the elation that ran through her was tempered by the knowledge that true victory would mean spending the rest of the week in this man's bed. But it was a small price to pay when her sister's life hung in the balance.

She considered him a moment longer, not wanting to seem too eager. *You are little more than a shadow to me. I cannot discuss possibilities with someone I cannot see.*

The French window opened, and he stepped out onto the balcony. Her heart slammed into the wall of her chest, then it seemed to drop somewhere in the vicinity of her toes.

He was tall, close to six foot, if not over, his build quietly powerful, but lean like an athlete's. His hair was dark and long, full of unruly waves that brushed his shoulders. His face was that of a dark angel's—beautiful, and yet somehow sinister. And while it may have been true that the eyes were the mirror of the soul, this man's were shuttered and painted black. There was nothing to be read in his expression—or the lack of it. If not for the sensation of hunger that burned between them, she would have thought him uninterested.

Do you like what you see?

She gave a disinterested shrug. *Looks are not the measure of the man.* Even though *this* man's looks were stirring her in ways no man ever had before.

A wise statement for one so young.

She raised her eyebrows, a smile teasing her lips. *And that is a very condescending statement from one so young.*

Amusement touched his sensual mouth. He crossed his arms and continued to regard her in that disinterested yet oddly disturbing manner of his.

I have squeezed many years of living into this young body, believe me.

So his reputation had suggested. Had she any other choice, she would have stayed far away from this particular wolf and his wild, hungry ways. But he was the only Sinclair the rangers did not have under suspicion and, therefore, her safest route into the Sinclair stronghold.

Ah. Then perhaps you have little interest in one less well travelled. She picked up her gown and pulled it on. The sheer material clung to her damp breasts and caressed her aching nipples. Again his need swam around her, a blanket that smothered, leaving her breathless.

I did not say that.

No. She hesitated and stepped free of the water, then raised her gaze challengingly to his. *I intend to leave. But if you can find me before I depart these grounds, we shall . . . talk . . . more on this matter.*

She turned around and walked away, not looking back. Yet his gaze burned into her back as surely as his hunger sent a fever blistering across her skin. He would come for her, she was sure of that.

Now all she had to do was pray she could hold his attention for more than just this night.

Duncan Sinclair moved through the crowd, silent as a shadow. Unnoticed, unseen. The music pounded through his veins, a heavy, throbbing beat that matched the need in him.

He'd had no intention of joining the dance tonight. He'd wanted nothing more than to complete his task here and leave as quickly as possible. But his intentions had flown out the window the minute he heard the wanton, wistful thoughts of the female.

He let his gaze roam the darkness. There was still a wealth of unclaimed women ready for the taking, but most of them were long-time participants of the dance, as jaded as the night itself.

Not so the wolf who'd played in the fountain outside his rooms. There was a freshness about her, a vibrancy, which suggested she was very new to the mansion and the dance.

She was here somewhere. He could sense her. She was a teasing hint of sunshine in the darkness, a caress of warm shyness that taunted the outer edges of his mind.

He wanted her. God, how he wanted her.

He continued on through the crowd and made his way out the rear doors. The night breeze rifled cool fingers through his hair, but it failed to ease the fever pulsing through his body.

She was close. The musky scent of femininity stirred the air, mixed with the gentle tang of jasmine. He walked through the strand of Aspens that divided this section of the house from the main gardens, his strides long, eating the ground. If she was indeed leaving, she would have do so through one of three gates. The closest gate to his room lay behind the summer house. He made his way past the grand old pavilion, but her scent didn't linger near the gates. She hadn't come this far yet.

He backtracked to the summer house and there he found

her. Stopping in the shadow-filled pavilion, he once again drank in the sight of her. She was small and delicately built—not what he usually chased, that was for sure. Her hair was a silky wave that brushed her hips, and deep gold in color. She still wore the mansion's gown, and the gossamer fine material hid little. He hungrily surveyed the lean length of her, from the proud thrust of her breasts to the dark gold triangle of hair between her thighs, then down the long length of her legs to her toes and back up again.

Her mask was heavily ornate and hid most of her features. But even from where he stood, he could see her eyes. They were the green of a newborn leaf, rich and exotic.

The heat in his loins became an ache that almost consumed him. He had to have her. Now.

He moved out of the shadows. Uncertainty flickered in her beautiful eyes, then she came towards him. Her gaze boldly traveled the length of his body, seeming to linger on the hard evidence of his excitement before finally rising again to his face. Her nipples were puckered, straining against the gossamer restraints of her gown, evidence of the desire he could clearly smell.

She entered the pavilion and stopped in front of him. The musky scent of her desire grew stronger, fueling the already raging need in him. But he wasn't the only one aching with the needs of the night and the moon.

"So you found me."

Her voice was huskier than before, but still as smooth as silk, as rich as velvet. Despite the heat that surged between them, her gaze was cool. Wary.

"Yes."

He touched her cheek, running his fingers down to the

warm fullness of her lips. She trembled under his caress, but didn't back away.

"So you wish to discuss the matter further?" she asked.

"No. What I wish is to dance with you."

The words were little more than a formality. She'd basically consented to his advances back there in the fountain.

Panic flitted through her eyes, making him wonder just *how* new she was to the mansion and its ways. Certainly he'd never seen her here before, but he'd been away for nearly ten years.

She swallowed convulsively. "Indeed?"

He moved his hand down the long line of her neck. Her pulse was a wild flutter under his fingertips. "Indeed."

"And what of my desire for a more lingering seduction once the initial fire had gone?"

He let his hand drift down to her breasts and gently rubbed one firm nub through the film of her dress. She shivered, her lips parting a little, as if she couldn't suck in enough air.

"I think that could be arranged."

She closed her eyes briefly. "One night holds no interest for me this phase."

"But you have not yet tried the goods and cannot say whether one night or more will be enough." He leaned close, his mouth capturing hers, gently demanding.

For the briefest of moments, she froze, her lips hard and unyielding under his. Then she sighed and seemed to melt toward him, deepening the kiss, opening her mouth, letting him explore more fully.

Heat shivered through his soul, and the urgency increased tenfold. He wanted her as he'd wanted no other in his life, and the effort of holding back, of not taking her right then and there, had every muscle trembling.

But she had yet to say yes. Until she did, he couldn't fully take her. There were rules, even here in this mansion some called a den of debauchery.

He slid his hand down her waist and found the slit in her skirt. Touched the silk of her thigh and worked upwards. He cupped the triangle of her curls then gently delved her moist heat.

Her moan shuddered through him, testing his strength, his will. He delved deeper, sliding through her slickness, until her muscles pulsed around one finger, then two. She pressed against him, riding his hand with increasing urgency. Her skin was feverish, flushed with desire and need.

A need he understood only too well.

She grabbed his shoulders, fingers trembling, nails digging deep.

"By the moon." Her voice was little more than a fractured whisper. "Please . . ."

Her plea raged across his senses, almost destroying his control. Yet at the same time, an oddly primeval sense of power surged through him. She was his for the taking, whether she'd admitted it yet or not.

He stroked harder, faster. Her body shuddered against his, her skin glossy with perspiration. He kissed her ear, ran his tongue down the long line of her neck. She tasted of honey, desire and sunshine—and he knew then she was a wolf who played in the daylight more often than moonlight. They lived in two different worlds, but right then, he didn't care. She'd stepped into his realm, and he intended to take every advantage of it.

He took a nipple into his mouth, sucking hard through the gossamer material. Her shuddering reached a crescendo, and her cry of pleasure sang through the night. A wave of primitive power surged through him, yet he knew he could take her higher, deeper, than what she'd yet tasted.

He slid his fingers free of her and began undoing the ties of her gown. Her eyes, darkened by a mix of pleasure and surprise, flew open.

"Dance with me." The ancient yet formal words of binding slipped hastily off his tongue, his voice little more than a hoarse whisper. "Let your body join with mine and rejoice in the power of the divine light."

He slid the gown from her shoulders and let it fall to the ground. Her skin was pale gold silk and glowed softly in the darkness. Her breathing was quick, sharp, every intake seeming to shudder through her entire body.

He pushed her back until she was trapped between the wall of the pavilion and him. The heat of her washed across his senses, and the wild beat of her heart was a siren's song that fueled his urgency to greater heights. It was all he could do to simply stand there, his body pressed hard against hers, seeking and yet not entering.

"This night," he continued raggedly. "And the remaining nights of this phase."

An odd mix of apprehension and elation ran through her eyes. She took a deep breath, then released it in a shudder. "This night," she whispered. "And the remaining nights."

Mine. With savage exaltation he surged into her. Groaned in bliss as her muscles contracted against him. God, was there a sweeter sensation on this earth? He slid his hands down her hips and cupped her buttocks. "Wrap your legs around me."

His demand was little more than a growl, but she seemed to understand him. Her legs wrapped around his waist, and her arms slipped around his neck. His movements became hard, fast. Hot flesh slapped against hot flesh. There was nothing gentle about this mating. Couldn't be, with the heat of the moon riding them both so fiercely. Gentleness would come later, once the initial urgency had gone.

He claimed her mouth, kissing her ferociously. Passionately. Their tongues dueled, explored, the rhythm echoing the thrusting of his hips.

The red tide rose, becoming a wall of pleasure he could not deny. His movements quickened. Deepened. Her gasps reached a second crescendo, and her cries echoed across the silence as her body bucked against his. He came—a hot, torrential release whose force tore a shout from his lips and sent his body rigid.

He couldn't say how long they stood there like that, bodies locked together, the night air gradually cooling their fever-kissed skin. It could have been minutes, or it could have been hours.

It could have lasted an eternity, and he wouldn't have cared.

He breathed in the scent of her—the sweet flowery tang of jasmine mingled with the more evocative musk of femininity and sex. He couldn't remember a time when he'd felt more satisfied, more fulfilled. And yet there was so much more to come. This delicate beauty had agreed to be his, not only tonight, but for the remainder of the week. They had the time to explore each other more fully. It was a thought that sent a jolt of primitive pleasure coursing through his veins.

He kissed the pulse point in her neck. Felt the still erratic flutter under his lips.

"Do you have a name?"

It was a question he had no right to ask. No names, no faces. Those were the rules set by his ancestors long ago, rules he'd abided by up until now. But if she was new to this place, she might not be aware of them. There was something about this woman that intrigued him in a way no other had, and he had no intention of simply letting her walk away in the morning without some means of finding her should she decide not to return. Not after he'd sampled the delights she had to offer.

Tension crept through her limbs. She was still trembling, but he couldn't say whether its cause was his closeness or something else.

"Neva." Her breath whispered past his ear, a heated touch that stirred barely sated embers. "Yours?"

"Duncan."

She unwrapped her legs from his waist, and he carefully lowered her to the ground. Though her gaze met his without qualms, the rush of color through her pale cheeks suggested she was not as bold as she was making out.

She tucked silken wisps of gold behind her ears. "Do you come here often?"

"Not recently. You?"

"My first time." Reluctance filled her voice, and the red bloom in her cheeks grew. "I wasn't sure if I was doing the right thing or not."

He was glad she'd taken the chance. Glad it was he who'd heard her wistful thoughts. He touched a hand to her cheek. "And now?"

A smile teased her lips. "I'm more uncertain than ever."

"Then I shall endeavor to prove your decision to come

here was no mistake." He leaned forward, needing to taste her again.

Her eyes widened slightly, and her uncertainty surged, crowding his mind. Despite her promises, she still wasn't sure about him. Not that it really mattered now. While it was a female's right to pick and choose as she pleased, once she had said yes to mating, the male had the right to enforce it. And he would do so, if that's what it took to keep her by his side these next few nights.

Her mouth was warm and sweet under his, and as the kiss deepened, the moon's heat began to burn through his veins again. But this time, he would take his time, pleasure her more fully.

A howl sang through the night, the cry of a wolf in trouble. But not just any wolf. His brother.

What? He broke off the kiss and stepped back. The night was silent for several seconds, then the howl came again. A long, demanding note.

René was either out of range, or simply too angry to hear any mind contact.

"Trouble?" She rubbed her arms, her eyes haunted, sad.

He touched a hand to her cheek and wondered what she sensed. Even though he could feel only anger, the golden wolves were powerful telepaths. She was probably picking up a whole lot more than he—but she wasn't from his tribe. He had no right, no desire, to involve her in any way. Even when it came to something as simple as a question.

"I'm afraid so. Will you wait here, or would you prefer to go to my rooms?"

She hesitated, and her reluctance washed around him. She didn't want to face the moon-hungry pack again, and of that he was fiercely glad. He wasn't in the mood to fight

tonight, though he would if another tried to usurp his claim
on her.

"Here."

He touched her lips, outlining their kiss-swollen sweet-
ness. "I won't be long."

She nodded, her gaze searching his, green depths filled
with uncertain wariness. "Be careful."

He raised an eyebrow, but again restrained the urge to
ask what she sensed and called instead to the wildness
within him. His body became liquid, flowing from one
shape to another, then he was on all fours and running
through the trees.

He found René just outside the main gates. At his
brother's feet lay the mangled, bloody remains of what once
had been a woman.

Two

The minute he left the shuddering began. Neva slid down the wall, hugging her knees close to her chest, taking deep, careful breaths. It didn't help the churning in her stomach. Didn't help the deep sense of loathing coursing through her.

Everything she'd believed in, everything she'd been taught, had simply slipped away under the raging of the moon and the smooth skill of his hands. And he'd proven her as wanton as any of those in the hall below, despite the high ideals she'd spouted half her life.

A sob tore up her throat, followed quickly by bile. She scrambled to her feet and raced out to the nearest tree, where she lost what little she'd eaten for dinner.

When there was nothing left to lose, she made her way back to the pavilion and sat on the steps.

Moons, what was she going to do?

She closed her eyes and leaned her head against the wall. It wouldn't have been so bad if the whole episode had been nothing more than a quick, heated mating in which there'd been little pleasure. That was all she'd been expecting, and something she could have survived. But this man's touch was like no other—his caress sang across her skin, his kiss seared her mind. And his scent invaded every pore, claiming her just as surely as his body had.

Lord, even thinking about him made her ache. And it was *that* fact, more than anything, that frightened her.

Duncan Sinclair was the wildest of the wild. His ferocious appetite for women and sex was renowned through all the packs—a fact she'd been well aware of when she had set out to seduce him. But she simply hadn't expected her own intense reaction to the man. Her cheeks flamed as she remembered the way she pressed against his hand, wanting, seeking, so much more than just his fingers. She'd howled in pleasure when he'd thrust into her, for moon's sake. *Howled.* She, who'd once sworn to give no wolf the satisfaction of her cries until she met the one destined to be her life mate.

Duncan wasn't that. Could never be that. By all accounts, the longest he'd ever stayed with a mate was one phase of the moon—which was the second major reason she'd chosen him. A phase gave her enough time to hunt down a killer then get out.

But after one, all–too-brief dance, she very much suspected she wouldn't *want* to leave after a week of his caresses. A chill ran down her spine. What if she become so addicted to the fever of his touch that she came back, night after night, hungering for something he would no longer give? What if she became just another rabid seeker of pleasure, like so many others in the hall below?

She took a deep breath and tried to calm the frantic direction of her thoughts. One night of pleasure—or two or three—would not make her a slave of the moon. She was stronger than that. It was stupid to believe the touch of *any* man could so totally destroy her beliefs in such a short space of time—no matter how good that man's touch was. Her fear, her uncertainty, were little more than the shock of discovering she was as capable of yielding to the wanton fever of the moon as anyone else here tonight.

It didn't *mean* anything. Not unless she let her fear and vague sense of humiliation override common sense.

She'd come here to do one thing—to find and destroy the man who had attacked her sister. As long as she kept that goal uppermost in her mind, she could survive anything.

Even Duncan's touch.

She pushed to her feet, retrieving her gown and quickly donning it. Though it hid little, it at least offered the illusion of clothing. Better than running around naked—especially if she came across another hunter in the forest.

She couldn't risk using telepathy, simply because skimming the mind of a hunter like Duncan was dangerous when she had secrets of her own to keep. She turned and followed his scent through the trees. That howl had come from near the main gate—and it had been filled with anguish and anger.

Something bad had happened, and she had every intention of finding out what.

Duncan shifted shape and came to a halt three feet from the bloody corpse. The victim was on her back near a melting drift of snow, a look of horror forever etched on what remained of her face. Her throat had been torn out, chunks of flesh were missing from her shoulders and exposed breasts. Her skirt was rucked up, and her panties torn, visible evidence of the violation he could almost smell.

"Moons, René, what in hell have you done?" As much as he tried to keep his voice even, a hint of revulsion still crept through.

René glanced up sharply. His face was a mottled red, the vein in his neck visibly throbbing. "Do you think I'm such a savage I'd do this? By the moon's light—" He thrust a hand through his dark hair. "I like it rough, true, but not like this. Never like this."

"Then why the hell are you here?" He squatted on his heels, studying the bloody rents on the woman's pale skin. The width between the bottom and top jaws was enormous, indicating her attacker was a bigger wolf than normal. Bigger than René, at any rate.

"I was looking for her. We were supposed to dance after midnight. She didn't appear, so I came searching."

"You saw or smelled no other wolf close by?" Blood still oozed from the wounds, its smell sharp, metallic. She hadn't been dead that long. His brother couldn't have missed the killer by more that a few minutes.

So why were there no footprints for them to follow? Why was there no scent on the air beyond that of this female and his brother?

René shook his head. "I heard nothing, saw nothing— other than you and some pretty little hunter over near the pavilion." A mirthless smile touched his mouth. "Thought you had no intention of participating in the dance this time."

He hadn't. The only reason he was here in the mansion at all was at the request of their sire, who'd wanted someone he could trust to investigate these killings. Someone within the family, who knew the system but had no true loyalties to the police or justice. Duncan had certainly seen the inside of more than his fair share of jail cells in his youth, so he guessed it was fair to presume he knew how the justice system worked.

He shrugged. "She made an offer too good to refuse."

And at the very least, her presence by his side would maintain his wild reputation and stop suspicions being raised in the wrong quarters.

René snorted softly. "Certainly looked like it, too."

Silver flashed in the short grass to the left of the victim's head. He shifted slightly, gaze narrowing. It was a hair, short and bristly.

"What color wolf was the victim?"

He felt rather than saw his brother's frown. "From the red pack—why?"

"Then her attacker is silver—unless you were in hunter form when you came here."

"No. But you were."

"I shifted before I reached the body. I doubt this is from my coat."

"It was one of our own?" Shock cracked his brother's deep voice.

"This hair would suggest so."

"It could be a plant."

"Could be." Though he very much doubted it. The rangers already knew it was a silver wolf behind these attacks. Planting one hair didn't make any sense—even though a similar clue had been left at each of the other crime scenes.

René cleared his throat. "Do you know this is the fourth attack in as many weeks?"

"Yeah, I'd heard as much." He rose and studied the trees around them. There were three trails from the gate, but all of them led to Ripple Creek. Had the killer continued on to town, or had he simply turned back around and rejoined the dance? There were plenty of fountains inside the grounds where a bloody wolf might wash—though if he were one of their own, slipping unseen into the mansion was a simple matter. Every Sinclair in the pack knew the locations of the secret passages—and there was one near every gate.

"We'd better get the rangers out here."

René grunted. "Damn horrible way to end the night's dance."

Duncan raised an eyebrow. "That's the first time any-thing has stopped you enjoying the moon fever."

"Yeah, but this is the first time I've seen one of my chosen mates dead." He shrugged. "But then, I haven't the tasty morsel waiting for me that you have."

A tasty morsel whose delights he could *not* enjoy again for a while yet. He had every intention of being here when the rangers arrived. "Go call the cops. I'll go tend to my morsel."

René stepped around the body and clapped a hand on Duncan's shoulder. "Don't take long. I want you to back up my story, or the rangers are likely to throw my tail in jail. They're desperate for a quick arrest on this one."

"Even rangers can't convict without evidence." Though he'd known one or two in his time who were certainly will-ing to concoct it.

He returned through the gates and headed for the pavil-ion. Jasmine stirred the air, and he stopped abruptly, his gaze roaming the trees. She'd been here.

Listening. Watching.

Why?

He remembered the fear in her eyes, the uncertainty. Remembered thinking she was not the usual type of woman found at these moon dances.

Why had she been around the west side of the mansion? It was far away from the dance, and generally considered out of bounds for all but those belonging to the Sinclair pack.

Something clenched deep in his gut. Disappointment, perhaps. Certainly anger.

He was being played.

Someone obviously suspected why he was here. What

better way was there to keep an eye on him than to offer something even his jaded tastes could not resist? Neva was alluring, sensual, a wolf in the full peak of her sexual prowess, and yet oddly, almost innocently, unaware of that fact.

Anger surged through him. He'd taken the bait without thought. Moons, what a fool.

Still, it was a game that worked both ways, now that he was aware of it. Over the next couple of days, he could push their union to the extreme and wait for her to reach the breaking point. She *would* break, of that he was sure. Their one brief mating had confirmed that while she wasn't innocent, she was certainly inexperienced. Sooner or later she'd go running back to whoever was behind this, desperate to end the charade. And once she did, he'd have a suspect to follow.

He took a deep, calming breath, then continued on through the trees.

She was waiting near the pavilion steps, but her welcoming smile faded as he approached. He swallowed his anger, knowing he had to be careful. The Sinclairs might be strong telepaths, but the golden pack far outstripped even them. He couldn't give her the slightest hint he knew her game—not yet. Not until he'd made her desperate enough to run back to the man behind all this rather than away from them both.

And he had to admit, he was rather looking forward to the task. René was right—she was an extremely tasty morsel. He wondered what she was being paid to seduce him. It had better be a lot, because she was certainly going to earn her money over the next couple of days.

"Problems?" Her voice faltered, and fear touched her gaze as she backed away a step.

Perhaps he wasn't controlling his anger as well as he thought. "Afraid so."

He caught her arm, stopping her retreat, pulling her close. Her body molded against his, her flesh trembling, flushed with heat. The musky scent of her desire spun around him, fueling the ache in his loins to greater heights.

They'd certainly chosen their bait well—even knowing what she was, he still wanted her more than he'd wanted any wolf in his life.

He cupped a hand to her cheek, holding her gaze as his lips claimed hers. There was nothing gentle in this kiss. It was filled with the ferocity that burned through his body— a hungry, angry possession that took everything she was willing to give and more.

Her eyes widened, and her fear deepened, until it was something he could almost taste. Yet at the same time, the scent of her arousal intensified. She wanted him, even if she did fear him—or feared what he intended to do.

He touched her, caressed her, made her burn with need. When he thrust deep, she moaned in pleasure, but this was a mating that had nothing to do with that emotion, and everything to do with anger and betrayal. It was hard and fast, a union in which he took but did not give.

When he'd finished, he stepped back. She stared at him, her chest heaving, her lips swollen and red, body still flushed and quivering with unfulfilled desires. But it was the anger, the reproach, in her wonderful eyes that cut the deepest.

"Wait for me here," he said curtly and walked away.

Neva clenched her fists and stared at his retreating back. It took all her willpower not to pick up the fallen tree branch near her feet and throw it at his stiff, uncaring spine.

In the space of ten minutes, he'd gone from a warm and generous lover to a detached, unfeeling rutting machine. A man who cared for nothing but his own needs.

And she wasn't sure why.

Nor could she read his thoughts or taste his emotions to find out why. It was if a wall stood between them, a wall so high and wide she half-suspected even *he* had lost touch with his feelings. He was the first wolf she'd ever met whose mind she couldn't read, whose everyday emotions could snap so suddenly beyond even her skills, and it was more than a little scary. She had a bad feeling she needed to know what was going on in that man's mind.

She rubbed her arms, but it did little to ease the chill racing across her skin. To think only a few moments ago she'd been worried about hungering for his touch so badly that she'd want to remain in this den of darkness. What a fool's thought *that* had turned out to be.

She wasn't about to wait here for more of the same. She may have agreed to be his for the remainder of the moon phase, but enough was enough for one night. With the discovery of the fourth victim, this place would soon be crawling with rangers. It was better she leave now, before anyone recognized her. The last thing she wanted was one of them reporting her presence to her parents. *That* would cause a scene of atomic proportions.

And they certainly wouldn't understand her reasons for coming here. They were old school and believed the dance should be saved until you'd found that one mate.

But as much as she wanted to go home *right* now, she couldn't. Not until she'd taken a closer look at that body— before the rangers took away whatever clues there might be

to find. It was doubtful they'd let her go unescorted into
Savannah's office a second time.

She donned her skirts then resolutely turned and made
her way back to the gate.

The stench of death almost overpowered her. She took a
deep breath, trying to control her stomach's chaotic churning. Her twin faced this type of thing regularly. Surely *she*
could do this once.

She bit her lip and moved closer, stepping in old footsteps
so her own wouldn't show. This death was the image of the
photos she'd studied in Savannah's files—right down to the
bite marks on the woman's shoulder and breasts. But it was
the damage to their faces that Savannah had ringed and questioned. Why such destruction? None of the women had been
extreme beauties—just pleasant. Ordinary. None of them
were similar in any way—they all had different colored hair,
eyes, and facial structures. All belonged to different packs.
Yet the man behind this went to great pains to smash in their
faces almost beyond recognition. It certainly suggested there
was some sort of connection—but if Savannah's notes were
anything to go by, the rangers had no idea what. And if the
Sinclairs knew, they certainly weren't telling anyone.

Her gaze slipped down, stopping at the rucked up dress
and torn panties. Her stomach turned, and she fought the
sudden urge to run from such a brutal representation of
invasion. Lord, it was all too easy to imagine the horror, the
fear . . . She swallowed heavily. The visual evidence might
indicate rape, but the coroner's report on the last three victims certainly didn't suggest forced sex. All victims had
had numerous partners during the night, but there was nothing to indicate rape during death. Which Savannah had
again questioned. Why was the killer depicting rape if he

wasn't actually violating them? It was a puzzle to which there were no answers—as yet.

She raised her nose, tasting the air. Beneath the scent of death lay a myriad of other aromas. Pine and balsam were heavily entwined with the rich bouquet of snowbound loam. Beyond that, a lingering caress of warm spices and freshly cut wood stirred her pulse. Duncan's scent. His brother, who'd been here longer, was a warm touch of muskiness. Beneath that, blood, sharp and metallic. And something else—a scent she couldn't pin down but one that seemed vaguely familiar.

She frowned and walked across to the nearest path. No footprints here, either. Nothing to indicate anyone had traveled past here recently. Only that nebulous scent. She studied the path for several moments, weighing her need for answers with her need to escape, then sighed. Closing her eyes, she reached for the wildness. It came in a rush of power that blurred her senses and numbed the pain as it reshaped and changed her body.

Then it was gone, and she padded through the trees on four legs rather than two. The scent led her halfway down the mountain before it disappeared. She sniffed air and ground, trying to find it again, then noted a flash of silver caught in the branch of a small aspen just off the path. Hair from a silver coat. Paw prints flirted with a slight drift of snow beyond that then disappeared again. The scent no longer lingered. She nosed about a bit more, but knew it was now a worthless quest.

She glanced over her shoulder, contemplating going back for her clothes. But there were voices up at the top now. Maybe the rangers were here. Maybe Duncan and his brother had returned. Either way, she had to get going. The scent of jasmine would linger, and that could lead to trouble if she wasn't careful. Besides, nothing she'd left in the mansion could be traced back to her. Jasmine was a strong scent, which is exactly why she'd chosen it. Not even the strongest of noses would be able to track her true scent through the clothes she'd left up there.

She moved back to the trail and continued down until she hit the stream, then followed that upwind. The water was icy against her paws, but unless she did this, they would trace her too easily back home.

As she continued padding through the water, she reached out, briefly touching her sister's thoughts. No response, no change. She sighed. At least some good had come out of the night. She'd achieved her aim—she had breached the inner circle of the mansion and attached herself successfully to Duncan. Nor did she have to worry about hungering for his touch. For whatever reason, he'd become as unfeeling and as unresponsive as she could ever want.

So why did she feel such a deep sense of loss?

Moon madness, surely. She ducked into a small waterfall, washing the scent of jasmine from her coat, then continued on home.

Two hours later, Duncan made his way through the mansion. The arrival of the rangers had killed the dance, and there were very few people occupying the shadows in the hall. But they would be back tomorrow night. They always were.

He took the stairs two at a time and tried to ignore his vague sense of disgust. He'd taken part in more than his fair share of dances—was still taking part in them, in fact— so he had no right to judge others.

Or were his own actions behind that vague, unsettling emotion?

He frowned. Damn it, she'd come here with the sole purpose of seducing him—he was certain of that, if nothing else. He owed her no right to pleasure. And if anything, her willingness to take whatever he dished out without comment proved her guilt. His actions were not in the spirit of the dance, and she had every right to be furious.

But she hadn't said anything. Why? Because she was being paid to stay by his side. Because she would do whatever it took to remain there.

While he had no regrets about his actions, the reproach in her green eyes haunted him. He'd never been like René. He didn't like roughhouse tactics, found no thrill in fear. Yet tonight he'd tasted both and *had* enjoyed it.

And it was something he would have to continue. He couldn't play the gentle, caring lover with this woman— not if he wanted to stop these murders sooner rather than later. He had to push her, and keep pushing her, until she could take no more.

He stopped at the door at the end of the hall and rapped his knuckles on the wood. A gruff voice bid him to enter. He walked inside and slammed the door shut.

Zeke stood near the window, tall, broad and straight of spine, despite seeing more than a century pass him by.

He turned as Duncan entered, one steel-grey eyebrow raised in query. "I would gather from your entrance that the meeting with the rangers did not go well?"

Duncan walked over to the bar and poured himself a stiff drink. "Quite the opposite. René's not a suspect, and they found skin and blood under the woman's fingernails, which they believe might belong to the killer."

"It was Mariata who was killed, wasn't it?"

He nodded and downed his drink in one swift gulp. The liquid burned its way down his gullet and sat like a weight in his gut.

"Mariata liked pain—and liked inflicting it. I wouldn't be surprised if they find the flesh of more than one wolf under her nails."

Duncan cast a sharp glance his father's way. "You danced with her? Tonight?"

Zeke sighed and turned around. Scratches marred his shoulder blades. "I may be old but the fever still burns through my veins. She and I are old partners."

Just what he needed to hear right now—especially with the rangers insisting on checking all family members for wounds. He poured himself another drink. "Did you dance with any of the other victims?"

"No."

"And my brothers?"

"The first was one of Tye's regular mates, the third one of Kane's."

Tye the oldest of the four of them, Kane the youngest. René was born between him and Tye. He took another drink and felt the anger begin to slip away. He knew alcohol offered no real solutions, but right now it drowned the vague sense of self-loathing. Of that, he was glad.

"Someone's targeting the lovers of you and your get."

"So it would seem."

"Any idea why?" He hesitated. "You haven't pissed off any females or their families of late, have you?"

His father's smile was wistful. "My wild days are behind me, I'm afraid. I'm more staid than many of my mates would wish."

But not *too* staid, if those marks were anything to go by. "Have you told many people I'm here to investigate the murders?"

Zeke shook his head. "None. News spreads fast in a tribe this size, and I didn't want to risk warning the killer— if indeed it is someone from our immediate pack."

"Then you'd better get these rooms swept for bugs, because someone knows."

"I did—yesterday." Zeke hesitated, dark eyes touched with concern. "Why would you think that?"

"Because I've been set up with a mate, and I think she's intending to keep a very close eye on me."

Zeke moved to the bar and poured himself a drink. "So what are you going to do?"

He shrugged. "Nothing."

"I could take her off your hands. Keep her locked away and occupied."

The thought of his father going anywhere near Neva made his veins boil. She was his to deal with, and *no one* was going to touch her except him.

"I'll take care of her." Despite his best effort to remain calm, the hint of steel was evident in his voice.

Zeke raised an eyebrow. "Be wary of the bait, Son. It might just turn around and snag you."

"I know what I'm doing."

Zeke leaned a shoulder against the wall and regarded him with amusement. "So, what are you going to do with her—besides the obvious?"

"I'm going to force her to stay here for the next five days." He took another drink of whisky. "Then I'll push her, and keep pushing her, until she runs back to whoever it was who set her on me."

"The sort of wolf who's willing to profit from the dance is not one who would easily break."

"This one's new to the game. She'll break." And hopefully soon. He had no taste for the game he was about to play.

"And in the meantime?"

He raised his hand, refusing his father's offer to top-off his drink. "I'll start talking to people. See what I can dig up." If this was some sort of revenge killing aimed at his brothers, then someone, somewhere, *had* to know why. As his father had said, a tribe this size held no real secrets. "Did anything unusual happen before the first murder?"

"Not that I can remember. Of course, it's hard to keep a finger on every pulse."

Duncan snorted softly. The day his father didn't know exactly what was going on would be the day death claimed him. And the fact he truly had no idea *why* these murders were happening only made them all the more mystifying. "You've talked to my brothers?"

"As have you. I dare say the responses we got were the same."

They were—he'd surreptitiously listened in. René's shields were not as strong as they should be. "Will you be able to get a copy of the autopsy report? We'll see if Mariata's varies any from the previous three."

Zeke nodded. "You do realize you may also be in their sights?"

"If that were the case, why put a watch on me? The mere fact that they have suggests they consider me some danger."

Zeke snorted softly. "Even the most insane wolf alive would consider you a danger."

He raised an eyebrow, a smile touching his lips. "And here I was thinking I've calmed down since my wild days."

"You have," his father said. "But it makes no difference, because what you do now you do with a clear head."

He thought of Neva, of the reproach in her beautiful eyes. "I do what I have to do," he said, with a trace of bitterness.

"I know. And that's precisely *why* you're considered so dangerous by just about everyone who knows you."

Duncan finished the last of his whisky. It did little to erase the sour taste in his mouth. "When do you think you'll be able to get your hands on that autopsy report?"

Zeke shrugged. "Tomorrow afternoon at the earliest. I don't want to push my source too hard, or he'll start getting a little jumpy."

"Then I'll be back here tomorrow afternoon."

He strode from the room and made his way through the shadow-filled house. But when he reached the pavilion, he wasn't surprised to discover Neva had fled.

Three

Neva rose with the dawn and took a long, hot, scented bath, hoping to erase any scent of Duncan that might linger on her skin.

But she couldn't so easily erase the throbbing in her body, the needy ache that flicked fire through her veins. She wouldn't be surprised if his ears were burning right now, because she'd cursed him long and loud during the night as she'd tossed and turned, trying to find sleep.

And yet she knew relief would not come tonight. Not if their second mating was any indication of his intentions.

She sighed. That was exactly what she'd wanted—a quick, passionless rutting, easily forgotten once this phase of the moon was over. She could hardly complain now that she'd gotten her wish. And she probably wouldn't be, if he hadn't first given her a glimpse how truly extraordinary their mating could be.

She closed her eyes and pushed him from her thoughts. His pack belonged to the night, and that's where all thought of him should remain. She would not let him wreck her days as well.

Besides, she had far more important people to worry about.

She reached out, carefully touching her sister's thoughts. Though there was no response, the sensation of death hovering all too close had fled. And pictures were beginning to unroll through the darkness of her sister's mind, like fractured images of a violent movie viewed through a broken projector. Relief surged, and tears blurred Neva's vision. Savannah was going to live. And she was beginning to remember what had happened. Maybe consciousness wasn't that far off after all.

Neva hoped so. She didn't like this endless silence. Didn't know if she'd want to go on without having Sav's warm, cheerful presence in her mind.

She dressed, swept her hair into a ponytail, then clattered down the stairs to grab a quick breakfast of toast and coffee. Then she snagged her leather jacket from the arm of the chair and made her way outside.

The day had dawned crisp and clear, but the smell of rain was in the air. The weather could change so quickly up here in the mountains, especially in the early days of spring, and it had caught many a tourist by surprise. Not that Ripple Creek was anywhere near as popular with humans as nearby Aspen—but then, most of the wolf packs who lived here didn't want it to be.

Her pack was the exception. Her father even headed the "bring Ripple Creek into the twenty-first century" committee.

A smile touched her lips, but just as quickly faded. She'd have to watch her step around her parents today, or the shit really would hit the fan.

She thrust her hands into her coat pockets and made her way toward the diner. Her parents lived above it—as had she, until her mother's incessant nagging that she find a mate and settle down had grown beyond the joke it had originally started out to be.

Sav certainly didn't cop half the flack she got—but then, Sav had what her mother considered a worthwhile career. She, on the other hand, was simply another waitress in the diner. Which was a job she actually enjoyed doing and had no intentions of leaving.

A bell chimed softly as she pushed open the door. The rich aroma of omelettes and coffee filled the air, stirring her hunger even though she'd already eaten.

"Morning, Cub," her father called from the kitchen.

She snagged an apron from under the counter, tying it around her waist as she pushed through the double swing-doors into the kitchen.

"Morning, old one." She dropped a kiss on his leathery cheek.

He swatted her with his spatula, green eyes twinkling good humoredly. "Enough of the old, thank you very much."

She grinned and pulled herself up on the nearest bench. "Where's Mother?"

"Still at the hospital."

"No word from the doctors on Savannah's progress?"

His mask of cheerfulness slipped a little. He sighed and thrust a hand through his thinning blonde hair. "They said her vital signs were a lot stronger. It's just a matter of waiting now."

Waiting was the one thing *she* wouldn't be doing. "Her thoughts are stronger, Dad. I don't think waking is that far off."

He lightly squeezed her arm. "Thanks. I'll tell Mother that."

"Need anything done in here before I start setting tables?"

"I did it all last night. Couldn't sleep. You want an omelette?"

When she nodded, he slapped one onto a nearby plate

and began making another. She shifted her leg and grabbed a knife and fork from the cutlery drawer underneath the bench, then dug in.

They ate in silence. When they'd both finished, she collected the dishes, throwing them into the dishwasher before pouring them both a coffee.

"Your mother wants to know if you'll come for dinner tonight," he said.

She stared at him for a second, her heart feeling like it was about to race out of her chest. "Is this a request or a demand?"

He grimaced. "You know your mother."

A demand. By the moon's light, what on earth was she going to do now? "I—" She hesitated, but knew it was better to tell a half truth than a straight out lie. "I was planning to go out later tonight, but I can come over if dinner is early enough."

He nodded and raised his eyebrow. Curious, but not overly so. "Anywhere in particular?"

She shrugged nonchalantly. "They're reshowing *Charade* at the Playbox. Thought I might catch that." She'd actually caught it two nights ago, but he didn't know that.

Her dad snorted. "How many times will that make it?"

She grinned. "Only fourteen."

He shook his head. "You're never going to catch a mate if you keep spending your time down at that old movie theater lusting after ancient actors."

"Well, until I meet a man with Cary Grant's looks, charm and style, that's exactly what I intend to keep doing."

"We're never going to get grandkiddies, that's for sure," he muttered. He slapped her leg, amusement dancing in his eyes. "Go set the tables before I get inclined to lecture on the virtues of finding a good man."

Grin widening, she slipped off the bench, planted another kiss on his cheek, and headed off to work.

The morning rush came and went. Arianne, a fellow waitress and long-time friend, swept in at eleven, all color and energy and smiles.

"Such a wonderful day," she all but trilled, shucking off her coat and grabbing an apron.

"Got lucky last night, did we?" Neva commented dryly.

Ari grinned. "No, but I'm intending to tonight. Hooked myself a fine specimen last night."

"And you didn't dance? Good grief, girl, are you sick?"

"Nope. He was with another mate at the time, and it's not polite to steal, you know."

"Since when has that stopped you?"

Amusement twinkled in Ari's dark green eyes. "Since his mate was double my size."

Neva snorted softly. "Good enough reason, I suppose."

"Generally. You filled the salt shakers yet?"

Neva shook her head, and the two of them got to work. Lunch was busier than normal, thanks to the rising influx of fly-fishermen wanting to take advantage of the early season warmth. At one, when there was a brief slowdown in customer traffic, Neva grabbed a soda and leaned wearily against the counter. Lack of sleep was beginning to tell. Thank God it was Monday, and the diner was closed tonight.

Then she remembered what she had to do, and a shiver ran down her spine.

Ari joined her near the fridge, leaning her forehead against the cool glass. "Man, I'm hot."

She raised an eyebrow. "Can't wait for tonight, huh?"

Mischief danced in Ari's eyes. "Well, now that you mentioned it." She hesitated as the doorbell chimed.

"Maybe we should put the 'Closed' sign up. Otherwise, I don't think we're going to get out of here today."

Neva smiled as she glanced toward the door—and felt her smile freeze on her face. It wasn't just *any* old customer who'd entered. It was Duncan Sinclair.

Ari's soft gasp of admiration seemed a hundred miles away. Neva could only stare at him, her mind whirling with a thousand different thoughts and fears.

What on earth was he doing here? Was it just chance that brought him here or something more?

He adjusted a small brown-wrapped box tucked beneath his arm and took off his dark glasses, his gaze skating across the crowded room. No, she thought, knees weak, heart straining with fear. It wasn't chance, but something more sinister.

"Now there's a honey I wouldn't mind wrapping my legs around," Ari whispered. "Moons, what a delicious bod."

He certainly had that, Neva thought with a chill. She'd thought him dangerously handsome last night, but now, when he was wearing dark jeans that hugged his legs with such thigh-defining tightness, and a black sweater that fitted his lean body and seemed to show every ripple of muscle, the impression of a dark angel was doubled. Tripled.

His gaze collided with hers, and something trembled deep inside. Whether it was fear or anticipation, she wasn't sure.

Which of the free tables are yours? His mind voice was brusque, unemotional. A tight beam only the two of them could hear—thankfully, given her dad was next door in the kitchen.

Booth second from the end. She kept her tones as clipped as his.

"God," Ari continued. "Hope he chooses one of my booths."

"Thought you had a date tonight?" she said, hoping Ari was too intent drooling over Duncan to notice the slight tremor in her voice.

"Are you crazy? That honey gives me the slightest indication of interest, and I'm a puddle at his feet."

Neva watched him stride to the booth and had to admit, if only to herself, that if he'd shown the slightest bit of interest in *her*, she would have puddled right alongside Ari.

But he wouldn't. She knew that without a doubt. Whatever his reasons for coming here, it had nothing to do with interest or pleasure—at least not for her, anyway.

Why the hell *was* he here? She'd promised the nights, not the days. What was he up to? And why did she feel with such sick certainty that his appearance here boded her no good?

He slipped into the booth she'd indicated, and Ari sighed. "Typical. The best looking man I've ever seen walks in here, and he sits at one of your tables." She hesitated, visibly brightening. "Can we swap?"

She would have liked to, but there was something in his ebony gaze that suggested retribution if she tried. "Sorry. No can do."

"That's right, be greedy. Keep the hunk all to yourself."

She raised an eyebrow. "And you wouldn't?"

"Beside the point." Ari waved a dismissing hand and slapped a menu into her hands. "Go get him, tiger."

Neva took a quick drink of soda, then made her way around the counter and walked toward him. He watched every step, his dark gaze as impassive as his thoughts. By the time she'd reached the halfway point, her stomach was tumbling worse than a clothes dryer, and she was seriously regretting her quick drink of soda.

"Care for a menu, sir?" she asked, forcing a cheerful smile to her lips.

I think we both know what I came here for. He took the menu from her trembling hands and casually opened it.

It felt like he'd clubbed her in the stomach. She stared at him for a second, knuckles white as she gripped her notepad for dear life. *What the hell are you talking about?* Aloud, she said, "The specials today are spicy chicken burgers with chips and salad, or minestrone soup with a small platter of homemade breads."

I told you to wait for me last night.

So? You also said you'd take the time to pleasure me more fully, and that didn't exactly happen now, did it?

Though there was not the slightest flicker in his shuttered eyes, she knew her barb had hit home. His anger boiled around her, a distant touch of thunder only she could hear.

You agreed to mate with me. You had no right to leave. He studied the menu for a moment, then ordered the chicken burger and fries.

And you have no right to come here chasing me. "Would you like a coffee with that, sir?"

I have every right. "Black, thanks."

She wrote it down, mouth dry. *What do you mean?*

It's one of the more obscure rules of the dance. If a female who has agreed to a mating does not fulfil her promises, then the male has every right to pursue her and make her. He hesitated, his gaze snaring hers with deadly intent. *No matter where she might be.*

Oh *God*. She took a deep breath and released it slowly. Surely he wouldn't. Not here in the diner. Even he couldn't be that wild. That uncaring. But as she returned his gaze, a tremor of fear began deep inside. She may have studied this man, but she didn't know him. Didn't have a clue as to just what he was capable of doing.

I agreed to the nights. I intend to uphold that bargain.

Not last night you didn't.

We mated. If you could call what happened between them the second time mating.

You ran. I was far from finished, believe me.

The trembling was beginning to work its way down her legs. Her knees felt fluid. She so desperately wanted to tell him *she* was finished, that she'd had enough of his stupid dance and magnificent but uncaring body. But she'd couldn't. She was snared by the very net she'd thrown, and she had no choice in this now.

But she had a horrible suspicion she'd better find Savannah's attacker fast, before *this* man destroyed her.

Tell me what you want. Aloud, she added, "Anything else with that, sir?"

His smile was slow and sexy and sizzled heat across every nerve ending. "Oh yes," he said softly. "But we'll discuss that a little later." *When the diner isn't as full.*

She flipped closed her notebook and all but ran back to the counter. Where she stood, back to him, taking deep breaths as she tried to control the shaking. She couldn't go into the kitchen like this. Her dad would know something was wrong and be out here in an instant searching for the troublemaker.

Ari came around the counter. "He has that sort of effect on me, too," she said, voice sympathetic, "And I haven't been anywhere near him."

"I'll be fine once I catch by breath," she said. Which certainly wasn't a lie.

"So what does he smell like?"

"Like a warm whisky on a cold night," she said without thinking.

Ari chuckled softly. "You have got the hots for him *real* bad, don't you? Shame your old man is next door. You could've dragged our sexy stranger into the storeroom and had a quick dance with him."

That was certainly a possibility anyway, if the heated promise in his eyes was anything to go by.

"Of course, you'd have to dust yourself off with bicarb afterward," Ari continued blithely.

Neva blinked and looked at her. "What?"

"Bicarb absorbs smells, does it not?"

"Yeah—so?"

"So, you don't want your straightlaced parents knowing you've actually gone out and enjoyed yourself, do you?" She winked saucily. "Works a treat, believe me. Been doing it for years."

Neva laughed softly and pushed away from the counter. "You're incorrigible."

"But a hell of a lot more satisfied than you'll ever be if you don't start pulling your act into the twenty-first century." She waved a hand toward the kitchen. "Your dad may be the head of the Future's Committee, but *both* your parents are still acting like they were brought up in the fifteenth century."

"Okay for you to say," she said dryly. "You don't have to live with their fifteenth century ideals."

"Neither do you. You moved out two years ago, remember?"

Moving out was easy. Ignoring the twenty-six years spent under their roof, absorbing their influences and ideals, was not. She wasn't even sure she *wanted* to ignore them.

"I'm trying, Ari, believe me."

"Not hard enough if you let that delicious stranger slip through your fingers."

She forced a smile and walked into the kitchen, handing her dad Duncan's order. When it was ready eight minutes later, she grabbed the plate and his coffee, took a deep breath, and walked over.

"Here you go, sir," she said, placing his plate in front of him.

"Thank you." He let his hand slide across hers as he reached for his cutlery.

It felt like flame caressing her skin, and she jumped. The coffee cup she still held tumbled sideways, splashing heated brown liquid all over the table and him.

"Oh God, I'm sorry," she said, horrified. "Are you all right? Are you burned?"

His raised eyebrow suggested he didn't believe the sincerity of her words. "No. Just clean up the table, and me, and it'll be fine."

She pulled the towel from the side of her apron and mopped up the worst of the spill. Ari tossed her another towel, and she finished it. Luckily, the burger had somehow avoided being drenched. She didn't fancy going back into the kitchen right now. "What about the parcel?" She flicked her cloth in the direction of the brown wrapped box.

"It's fine," he said softly. "But you did still miss a bit."

She frowned. "No, I haven—" Her voice faded as he shifted, revealing the dots of coffee on his sweater and groin.

Surely you don't expect me— The thought froze as she met his gaze. He would. And he did.

She took another deep breath, then quickly dabbed the stains from his sweater and jeans. And couldn't help noticing—or feeling—the huge bulge of his excitement.

An odd slither of feminine satisfaction ran through her. At least he couldn't deny his interest in her when the evidence of it was so clearly visible.

"Will there be anything else, sir?" she said, voice a little more breathy than she would have liked.

His smile smoked her insides. "Not right now."

She nodded and retreated to the other side of the diner.

"Impressive move," Ari whispered in admiration. "I'll have to remember that one."

Her smile felt tight. Ari wasn't likely to believe it had been an accident any more than Duncan had.

The time dragged by. He finished his meal and sipped his coffee, which she kept topped-off. Everything she did, everywhere she went, she could feel his gaze on her—a heated caress that promised far more than it would probably deliver.

By three, with the crowd thinning out, she was close to nervous exhaustion. Her dad came out of the kitchen, folding down the collar of the jacket he now wore over his uniform. "I'm heading over to pick Mother up at the hospital. You coming?"

She shook her head. She didn't need to go into that sterile place to see her twin. She could see her anytime she liked by simply opening her thoughts. And she would know a lot sooner than any damn doctor when Sav had woken.

"Your mother thinks you should."

"I hate hospitals, you know that." They were too full of

pain, too full of misery and hurt, and it overwhelmed even the strongest of her shields. "Savannah will understand, believe me."

"Your mother won't."

"Mom doesn't run my life any more." Though she certainly tried. Neva had images of being sixty and still crossing swords with her disapproving parent. "I'll finish up here and close once the last of our customers leave."

He nodded. "Don't forget dinner."

As if she dared.

"Now's your chance," Ari whispered the minute Levon walked out the door. "Go chat with that delicious man."

There were three customers still in the diner, and Ari herself. If Neva was going to confront Duncan's demands, she'd rather do it when they were alone. "I don't know."

"Oh for moon's sake, he's been watching you all afternoon. What have you got to lose?"

Nothing but my sanity, she thought. And what remained of her self-esteem. But she took her apron off, grabbed the coffee pot and a cup for herself, and walked across to his booth.

"Sit," he said, voice soft but holding no inflection.

She slid into his booth and poured herself a coffee. She didn't refill his, simply shoved the coffee pot his way. A tight smile touched his full lips.

"No longer the charming host, I see."

"I'm on a break. What do you want?" Her voice held an edge.

"You," he all but drawled. "Why else would I be here?"

Something in the tone of his voice sent a tingle of anticipation crawling across her skin. Which was ridiculous when the only pleasure he seemed to care about was his own.

"Well, we do make the best burgers in town."

Amusement touched his obsidian gaze, a warmth so fleeting she wondered if she'd imagined it. "But they're not as tasty as the morsel I tried from here last night."

Her cheeks flamed in memory, and she dragged her gaze from his. It was far safer to stare at her coffee than into his soulless eyes. "Tell me what you want," she repeated.

He crossed his arms and leaned forward. "Look at me," he demanded.

Almost against her will, her gaze rose to his. How could a man with a face so beautiful be so totally devoid of anything resembling humanity?

"My pack is having a fancy dress dance tonight, separate from the main one. You will accompany me, and you will wear the outfit I have in this box."

She stared at him, her stomach churning. "I won't be shared. I don't care what your sordid dance rules say, you *can't* demand that of me."

Amusement touched his lips, but again held little warmth. "Have no fear there, little wolf. You are mine, and only mine, for the remainder of the week."

Relief slithered through her—though it was hardly much comfort knowing she had to submit to his uncaring touch for the next five days. Even if that was what she had planned.

She looked at the box, hating to think what sort of outfit he'd chosen for her. Probably a hooker, if his recent treatment was anything to go by. "What if the outfit doesn't fit?"

"You'll try it on. If it doesn't fit, I'll exchange it."

"I'll take it into the back room and try it on now, if you'd like." She started to rise, but he clamped a hand on her arm, stopping her. His fingers burned against the chill of her skin, searing heat deep.

"No. Later, when your friend and customers have left."

She sat back down, her gaze locked by his. And knew, with sickening certainty, that he intended to take what he'd missed out on last night. Right here in this diner, where her dad would return within the hour.

"Don't." Her voice held a note of pleading, but she didn't care. "Please, not here."

He raised an eyebrow. "Do you deny it is my right?"

Damn it, I promised you the nights, not the days. You can't make me do this.

Oh, but I can. His mind voice was silky.

Her throat was drier than the Sahara. She licked her lips, wishing she could pick up her coffee and throw it in his face. But she couldn't, simply because her hands were shaking so much most of it would be spilled over the table long before she tossed it at him. "What do you mean?"

He reached across the table, capturing her hand, turning it palm side up. His thumb stroked her wrist, a gentle, almost possessive caress that sent shivers of desire skating across her skin. God, she hated that he could do this to her—and so damn easily.

"When you participate in certain sports, you should always make sure you understand the rules before you start to play."

"Meaning?"

"Remember what I asked, and how you replied, before our first mating?"

The first, and probably only, time of magic between them—and one she wasn't likely to forget, especially over the next few days. "Yeah. So?"

"So, those words were actually an ancient spell of binding. They allow me to enforce my will on you."

A cold chill ran down her spine. "You're kidding."

He raised an eyebrow. "Am I? Shall we test the theory right now?"

"No." Her voice was little more than a breathy whisper of horror. "Not here."

His smile was mirthless. "Reach up with your left hand and undo the top button of your uniform."

Energy slithered across her skin, through her skin, became a noose that slipped around her mind and pulled tight. She fought the compulsion with every ounce of strength she had, but her hand still rose, her fingers trembling as they touched the button.

"Damn you to hell," she muttered, tears touching her eyes. She couldn't let him get away with it, no matter what he did to her afterward. She wasn't defenseless, and it was about time he realized that.

She channelled her fear, her humiliation, into a thin lance of energy and flung it back at him.

It hit him with enough force to throw him back in the seat. His gaze went wide, eyes filled for the briefest of moments by the echo of everything she was feeling. Then his shields slammed home, and the lance died.

"What the hell was that?"

"A taste of what you'll get if you try to use the binding on me," she said. "You'll pay for my submissiveness, let me tell you."

He studied her for a moment, then smiled. It held very little warmth. "Thank you for warning me. I'll be sure I stop you from using your gifts before I issue any orders from now on."

She wanted to smack him. She really did. She clenched her fists, but rose and walked away instead. This was her doing, her mess. What sort of fool was she to believe she could enter into any sort of sexual game with a man like Duncan Sinclair and come away unscathed?

"So?" Ari whispered. "How did it go?"

She forced a warm smile. "I'll tell you tomorrow. For now, consider yourself rushed out the door."

"Now *that* sounds promising." Ari dropped a kiss on Neva's cheek, then picked up her bag and coat. "I want details. Lots of details. And remember the bicarb."

Once she'd left, Neva headed into the kitchen, checking to ensure that everything was turned off, then walked around the building, locking the doors and windows. The diner's front door was the last one she locked.

"Don't," he said softly when she reached for the blind.

She froze for a moment, then grabbed the base of the blind and yanked it down anyway. A second later, it rolled back up, clattering noisily against the frame.

"Telekinesis," he said gravely, "can be a handy gift in situations like this."

She took a deep breath, but it did little to ease the trembling deep inside. Only trouble was, she knew it wasn't all fear. The full moon was closer tonight, and the wildness was raging to be free. She clenched her fists and turned around.

Without the lights on, the diner was filled with dusky shadows. Evening came early here in the mountains, and of that she was glad. At least it meant if anyone did walk by, there'd be less chance of them seeing what was happening inside the diner.

Her gaze clashed with his and, for the briefest moment,

amusement flashed in the dark depths of his eyes. Then it was gone, locked behind the shutters.

"Come over here," he said, voice as seductive as the kiss of silk against skin.

She forced her reluctant feet forward. He'd shifted from the booth to a table, turning his chair sideways and stretching his long legs out in front of him. The small parcel was still sitting on the booth's seat.

"Undress."

He could have been asking her to clear the table for all the emotion he showed. She stared at him, but she knew she had no real choice. Sure, she could make him pay, but his shields were almost as strong as hers. Now that she'd so stupidly warned him, they'd undoubtedly remain up and would take most of the sting of an empathic attack. Her gift was a weapon best used when a victim's mind was wide open and unaware.

And she'd much rather be embarrassed of her own free will than be forced into it. And in the end, no matter how she fought him, he *would* force her.

She slipped off her shoes and slowly began undoing the buttons on the front of her dress. Hunger slipped warm and bright between them, caressing her mind with its heat. She threw her dress on the other seat, followed quickly by her panties and bra.

His gaze all but devoured her, and pinpricks of desire skidded across her skin. Her nipples puckered, as if in anticipation of his touch, and the longing he'd left unquenched last night stirred anew.

"What now?" she said, crossing her arms.

He leaned forward, gripped her elbows, and pulled her forward. "Straddle me."

She did. He was as hard as she was achy, and she couldn't help the fleeting wish that he were as naked as she.

He raised a hand, skimming his knuckles down her neck and between her breasts. Goose bumps scurried across her skin, and her heart hammered so loudly its beat seemed to echo through the silence.

His hand slipped around her waist then rested against her back, pressing heat into her spine as he gently pushed her forward. His tongue skimmed her skin, trailing fire and sending a delicious shiver of anticipation through her body. He outlined a breast with that liquid touch, circling it, gradually working his way inward. He teased the outer edges of that dark circle, but never touched the aching, sensitive center.

Sweat skittered across her skin, and every muscle quivered. Ached. His whisper-soft touch moved to her other breast. By the time he'd finished circling its center, she thought she was going to die with frustration.

He moved on, tasting her collarbone, her neck. Kissed her ear, her cheek, before finally claiming her mouth. It was a long, slow possession that left her gasping for breath.

His kiss eventually made its way down her neck. When his mouth closed around one aching nipple, she groaned at the sweet delight of it. He sucked hard, sending glorious waves of pleasure lapping across her skin, then claimed her other nipple, repeating the process, leaving her moaning in enjoyment.

"What are you doing for dinner?" he whispered, his breath searing her skin as he kissed her throat.

She blinked at the unexpected question. "Eating with my parents." The slither of unease surfaced again. "Why?"

"Don't you think they should meet the man you're spending the next five days with?"

She stared at him, her throat so dry it ached. "What do you mean?"

"I mean that I want you by my side, and in my bed, night and day."

Horror slid through her. She tried to push away, tried to stand, but his hand held her securely in place. "You can't. I won't." And yet, deep down, she had to acknowledge this was the chance she'd been looking for. It would offer her the freedom, night *and* day, she needed to roam the mansion, talk to the people within the pack—and hunt down the killer.

But the cost would be her parent's respect. Was that too high a price to pay?

She remembered the torn and bloodied remains of the woman who'd been killed last night. Remembered the way her sister had looked, swathed in bandages, so small and frail and pale against the antiseptic brightness of the hospital. Relived the horror of the moment she'd shared with her twin when the wolf had attacked her.

Was the cost too high? She couldn't honestly say.

"You have no right to demand this."

He raised an eyebrow, a gesture that was both eloquent and arrogant. "No right, but certainly the will."

"You must know my parents are old school." Desperation touched her voice, but right then, she didn't care. "They don't believe in the dance or mating for pleasure. Something like this will kill them."

He still caressed her, sending tremors of longing rolling through her. It was as if she were a well-tuned instrument designed only for his touch. As much as she wanted to, she couldn't kill her desire.

"Would you rather I wait until dark, walk into that dinner

of yours, and demand you uphold your promise to mate
with me right there and then?"

Her stomach clenched tight, and for a moment she
thought she was going to throw up. "You wouldn't." But
even as she said it, she knew he would. He was the wildest
of the wild, and seemed overly eager to live up to his reputation—no matter what that might do to her.

And she had no one to blame but herself.

She licked her lips, searched desperately for an argument that might work. "I have to work here during the day.".

"You've never taken a vacation? Hasn't anyone ever
filled in for you?"

"That's beside the point."

"No, it's not. I want you, and I shall have you. I will play
the charming suitor if you wish, but you will leave with me
after dinner, and you will stay with me the next five days."

She stared at him helplessly. Part of her *did* want this—
and not just because of her promise to Savannah. His touch
affected her like no other, and she hungered for all he had to
give. She was a wolf after all, with a wolf's desires and
urges—however repressed she might wish them to be.

"Why?"

"Because I find myself craving to spend more time with
you."

He shrugged nonchalantly, and his casualness hurt her,
though she had no idea why. What else did she really expect
from the man? This coldness was the very reason she'd
chosen him. "After that second excuse for a mating last
night? I find that hard to believe."

He shrugged again. "I've an extremely high sex drive.
Sometimes it will not wait to pleasure my partner."

"Some might call that selfishness."

"Some do. What's your answer?"

She bit her lip, studying him in indecision, even though, in the end, she had no real choice. No matter what she did now, she was going to lose.

Lord, how she wished she'd never started down this crazy path. Wished she'd simply sat back and let the rangers do their job. But she hadn't, and it was too late for regrets now.

"Only if you play the part of a suitor. At least give my parents the illusion you really do care for me."

He brushed a kiss across her lips. "How much of a suitor do you want me to be?"

His touch moved down to her moistness and probed gently. She bit her lip and fought the desire to press into his caress.

"A newfound friend or a lover?"

"Friend," she said, voice little more than a throaty whisper. And hated herself for wanting him so.

"Done." He placed both his hands on her waist and set her onto her feet. "You'd better be getting dressed then, because your parents will be probably be back soon."

She stared at him, aching, trembling, and totally unable to believe he'd done it to her again.

"You're a bastard, you know that?"

"Been called a lot worse than that in my life." The shutters were well down in his eyes, his face impassive. If it wasn't for the rather obvious bulge in his pants, she would have thought him totally unaffected by their little petting session.

Moons, how she wished she could read this man— look beyond the wall he'd raised so effectively and see, or feel, what he was really thinking.

"I'll wait for you out back, if you'd like. Don't forget to bring your costume along when you come out."

He walked away, stride long and oh-so-casual. Once again she had to resist the urge to throw something at his stiff, arrogant back.

But she couldn't help thinking that bringing him to dinner would at least get her mother off her back for a while. He was certainly wolf enough to satisfy even her mother's high ideals when it came to a suitable mate—even if he wasn't man enough to satisfy *her*.

Four

Duncan thrust open the door and stalked across the yard, breathing deep the sweet night air. It had taken a supreme effort to get up and walk away from the warmth and hunger in Neva's eyes. He would have liked nothing more than to give in to the desire that burned them both, but he couldn't. Not if he wanted to crack her defenses and discover whom she worked for.

The quickest way to do that was to keep her off balance. To play the caring lover one moment, the hard, uncaring bastard the next—something many of his past lovers would probably say wasn't much of a stretch.

He stopped at the wire fence designating the end of the property and stared almost blindly into the forest of trees beyond.

At least he'd be able to sate his lust over the next few days. The thought sent a surge of heat through his veins. As much as he'd told himself earlier it was only to keep an eye on her, he could not now deny his reasons were purely selfish. She might be working for whoever was behind these killings, but he wanted her. Wanted to see her warm smile, wanted to hear the rich music of her laugh. Wanted to make sweet love to her until she screamed his name to the moon.

Foolish, perhaps, but a desire he could not deny. Not when he'd spent all afternoon watching her. The way she'd interacted with the diner's customers and her friend had only increased his fascination with her. She was nothing like any of the women he'd known up until now, projecting such an alluring mix of heated sexuality and sweet innocence.

So what did she want so badly that she was willing to destroy her self-esteem and her reputation? He knew how strict families from the golden pack could be. Knew their beliefs about the dance and mates. And while she'd obviously flirted with the dance in the years since puberty, she certainly wasn't a regular participant—her innocence, her shyness with the sexual act, told him that.

Was she doing it for money, or something else? Maybe that was another direction in which he could push—discover more about her wants and needs, and he might just uncover a thread or two about their killer.

The door swung open behind him. He schooled his features into blankness and turned around to face her. She no longer wore the diner's uniform but faded denims and a soft white sweater that rolled around her neck and emphasized the fullness of her breasts. The ache in his groin increased tenfold, and he had to wonder how he was going to get through the next few hours of having her so close and not being able to give in to the need to touch her.

She stopped several feet away, face impassive but contempt obvious in her eyes. She threw the small box at his chest. He caught it instinctively.

"I won't wear that disgusting outfit anywhere."

He raised an eyebrow. "You were wearing a whole lot less last night, were you not?"

Heat crept through her cheeks. "Yes. But the night was dark, and most of the others were wearing nothing at all."

"So?"

"So, chaps and a whip are not my idea of a costume, and I refuse to wear them."

"I can make you."

She crossed her arms and regarded him stonily. "You can try."

He glanced down to hide his slight smile. So there were limits beyond which even she would not step for her employer, and of that he was fiercely glad.

"Then what will you wear?"

Her relief flitted briefly. "Has this dance a theme, or is it just a costume party?"

"The theme is fantasies." And he was certainly having some erotic fantasies right now. With and without the cashmere sweater that hugged the taut peaks of her breasts so tantalizingly.

She regarded him for a second, then shook her head. "What is the fascination you Sinclairs have with all things sexual? There's more to life than just mating, you know."

"Is there?" he drawled. "It's a shame I've never met anyone who's tempted me to discover that."

His implied insult had her cheeks flaming again. "Is there any particular reason you're being such an arrogant bastard, or does it just come naturally?"

"You know the reputation of the Sinclairs. You judge."

She snorted softly, then looked over her shoulder as lights swept across the darkness and the sound of a car engine drew close. "That's my parents," she said, meeting his gaze again. "Remember your promise."

"If you remember yours."

She swallowed, the pulse at her neck running faster than a startled deer. "Friends," she warned, stepping forward and twining her fingers through his. "Not lovers."

Though he nodded, he had no intention of following her rules. By the end of the night, there would be no doubt in her parents' minds as to why he was whisking her away for four days. Nor would they have any doubt of her willingness.

One more crack in her shields. One more push closer to that edge.

On the surface, dinner was a friendly, casual affair. Neva's parents played the charming hosts and Duncan played the suave, likeable guest. But underneath, tension slithered. In her mother's case, it was simply annoyance that she'd been given no warning, no time to prepare a proper welcome for the man she already considered a prospective son-in-law. Her father was harder to read— like Neva, he had his shields fully up, so no one could see what he was thinking. But his emotions leaked regardless, and it was obvious he was well aware of Duncan's reputation. His distaste and anger were an emotive swirl that singed her senses.

She didn't eat much. Couldn't, given the churning in her stomach. Yet its cause wasn't only nerves, but Duncan's very closeness. Her mom had insisted they sit together, and every time he moved, his arm brushed hers, sending lances of longing coursing through her. His actions last night and again in the diner had worked her into a feverish state, and her body responded to his every touch with needy, excited anticipation.

And she was positive it was deliberate. She felt like a cat stuck on a hot tin roof—heat burned every pore, but there was nothing she could do to cure or retreat from the situation.

"Why don't you and Duncan head into the living room," her mother suggested, rising from the table once the meal was finished. "We'll bring in the coffee after we clean up."

Neva nodded and without looking at Duncan rose and led the way into the other room. Once out of the immediate earshot of her parents, she swung around and faced him.

"Stop it," she said fiercely, clenching her fists and glaring up at him.

"Stop what?" He continued to advance on her.

She swallowed and backed away from the almost liquid desire so evident in his dark eyes.

"Stop playing this game. We're friends, nothing more, remember?"

A cold smile teased his lips. He kept advancing. She continued to back away.

"We're not friends, but we *are* definitely lovers. What is so wrong with letting your parents see that?"

Her back hit the wall, and he stopped. She stared up at him, hating him and yet wanting him.

"We're not lovers. I doubt you even know the meaning of the damn word. We danced, that's all."

He slid his hand under her sweater, his fingers so cool compared to her fevered skin. She tried to sidestep, but he pressed his hard body against hers, singeing her senses with his masculine odor, burning her mind with the flames of his hunger. His gaze all but devoured her as he leaned closer still.

"Don't." Her voice held very little force.

"Don't what?" His warm breath stroked her lips and sent a tingle of anticipation down her spine. "You want me to kiss you, Neva. Say it."

"No."

His cold smile became almost teasing. If it wasn't for the hardness in his eyes, it might have tugged at her heart. But he was still playing games, still playing her, for whatever sick reason.

He leaned closer still, and his lips brushed hers as he spoke. "One day you will, you know."

A tremor ran through her. Moon forbid, he was right. She *did* want his kiss. Want him. Footsteps echoed down the hall. Her mother, coming closer. She thrust a hand between them and tried to push him away. It was about as effective as a fly pushing a boulder.

"Not until I get my kiss."

"Damn you to—"

The rest of her words were lost as his mouth took possession of hers. Had it been a harsh, demanding kiss, she might have been able to fight him. But it wasn't. It was a tender and gentle caress that promised things he would never deliver.

The footsteps stopped, then her mother cleared her throat. Heat flamed Neva's cheeks and she thrust both her hands between them. But he would not be moved or hurried.

She could only thank the moon it was her mother. Her father would probably have demanded a wedding right there and then—and given Duncan's eccentric, unpredictable behavior since they'd met, she wouldn't have put it past him to agree. If he was intent on ruining her life, it would certainly be the ultimate act of bastardy.

He dropped a second kiss on her nose then stepped away, his fingers twining through hers. "Sorry, Mrs. Grant. Didn't mean to get carried away."

Her mother tittered like a teenager. "Please, call me

Nancy. And it's all right. I'm not so old that I can't remember what young love is like."

Young love. Neva almost choked on the words. If she and Duncan shared anything it was an undeniably strong sexual attraction. Once the moon had passed its zenith, that would fade, leaving them nothing but dislike.

He pulled her down onto the sofa beside him and wrapped an arm around her shoulders. His long, strong fingers brushed the top of her breast and sent slithers of anticipation across her skin.

Don't you dare, she warned heatedly.

Dare what? This? His thumb pushed across one aching nipple, and she jumped as if stung. *Or this?* He brushed sweet kisses down her neck. *Or—*

Enough! She pulled away, her cheeks so hot she was sure they were glowing. Thankfully, her mother had been too busy pouring coffee to see what he was doing.

You are not a teenager, Neva. Stop worrying about what your parents are thinking and start enjoying yourself a little.

Ari had said the same thing this afternoon—but neither of them had to live with the fallout of such actions. *I have to return to this life once the moon phase is over. You could at least be considerate enough to leave me something to return home to.* She lifted her gaze to his. *Or is my total destruction truly your aim over these next four days?*

Her words shook him. Though there was no slip in the mask that shuttered his face and eyes, she sensed the quick thrust of surprise. And beneath it, just a slither of loathing.

It was that emotion, more than anything, that alarmed her. What had she ever done to this man that some small part of him loathed her? And how could he still want her so badly if he *did* loathe her?

"So, what are your plans?" her mom said, handing them both a cup of coffee before sitting down. "And why haven't we met you before now?"

"I work with the Eagle County search and rescue team. It's hard to get back here with any sort of regularity." He shrugged.

She wondered if he were telling the truth. She hoped he was, because her dad would undoubtedly check. But then, this was all going to go to hell eventually anyway, so it didn't really matter.

And she certainly couldn't picture him as the type willing to sacrifice his life rescuing others.

"Doesn't Mike Maher work search and rescue in that district?" Her dad walked into the room and leaned a shoulder against the wall, regarding Duncan with angry eyes.

"Mike Maher retired eighteen months ago. Dave Richards is in charge now. I'm his second."

It was hard to tell if her dad bought the story or not, as his expression and the tight blanket of anger that surrounded him hadn't changed. "So how did you two meet?"

Playbox, she told him quickly.

He glanced at her, an odd smile touching his lips. "We met at the Playbox. I was there watching *To Catch a Thief* three months ago and literally ran into her. She wasn't too pleased about getting a lap full of popcorn, let me tell you."

Her mother laughed, and Neva relaxed just a little. At least someone had bought the lie.

"And here I was," her mom said, "telling her only last week she'd never meet a nice man if she kept spending all that time watching old—"

"So, what is it you've come here for?" Her dad ignored her mother's reproachful look and continued to glare at Duncan.

Duncan hesitated and glanced at Neva. Just for a moment, indecision touched his eyes. Then the shutters flashed back up, and her stomach began to churn painfully.

"There's an awards dinner next Saturday I have to attend. I've asked Neva to come back with me tonight and attend the dinner with me on Saturday."

Her dad didn't move, didn't blink. "And just where would she be staying?"

"With me."

She closed her eyes. The shit had just hit the fan.

Her mom laughed nervously. "In her own room, of course."

"No," Duncan breathed softly.

You couldn't even leave me that glimmer of respect, could you? She looked at him bitterly. *Just what in hell have I done to you to deserve this sort of treatment?*

You're a smart woman. You figure it out. His thoughts were as angry as hers. *I'm sure it won't be that hard.*

She stared at him. What on earth was he talking about? They'd never met before last night and, realistically, she was the only one who had the right to be angry. He was the one who had taken without giving. Who was still taking.

You could have said we were staying in separate rooms. It wouldn't have hurt.

I could have said we were going to the mansion and the dance tonight, too. Don't push, Neva.

Don't push? What a laugh. Pushing was *all* he was doing. She closed her eyes, took a deep breath, then turned to face the storm brewing on the other side of the room. It was a storm that would probably have happened eventually, but one she hadn't been prepared to face tonight. Certainly not with this man by her side.

"I absolutely forbid it," her mother said, voice flat.

"You can't forbid anything anymore," Neva replied. "I grew up a long time ago, Mother. Accept that fact and stop trying to control my life." Her words held a touch of bitterness that surprised them both.

Duncan squeezed her hand as if in encouragement. She wanted to rip her fingers free of his and smack him in the mouth, but she didn't, simply because she needed this charade to continue if she was to have any hope of her parents ever speaking to her again. Lord, if they found out her true destination was the dance at the mansion . . .

"And what of your sister?" her dad asked softly.

She raised her gaze to his. "She'll understand." But she wouldn't. Not this. But at least she'd be close enough to see Savannah, or talk to her telepathically when she *did* wake. "You're in charge of the Future's Committee, Dad. Like it or not, this is part of that future. It's not a sin to enjoy yourself before marriage." And as Ari was prone to saying, who bought a car without test driving it?

Not that she was buying *anything* but four days of misery and frustration.

Her dad didn't say anything, just walked out of the room. And that hurt deeper than anything she could have ever imagined. She blinked back the sting of tears and glanced at her mom.

"Please understand—"

"The only thing I understand," her mother cut in sharply, "is that you've decided to turn your back on everything we've taught you over the years." She thrust to her feet, a thin, disapproving figure. "I think you'd both better leave until your father and I calm down a little."

Neva stared at her for a moment, wondering if it were possible to hate anyone as much as she did Duncan right at that moment. Then she rose, gathered her handbag and that stupid parcel, and left.

The night air hit like a slap across the face. She took a deep breath, but the shuddering had begun and wouldn't stop.

She leaned her back against the wall of the diner, closed her eyes, hugged her arms across her body, and silently cried. For the loss of her parents' respect. For her own stupidity in ever thinking she could calmly waltz into the Sinclair mansion and come away unscathed.

For the fact that she still wanted Duncan more than she'd wanted any other man in her life, no matter how much she hated him.

The moon certainly had a lot to answer for.

He stopped in front of her, a warm but forbidding presence. She didn't look at him, didn't say anything to him. Nothing she said seemed to make one bit of difference to whatever his agenda was anyway, so why bother?

"Neva—" he began eventually, voice soft but still emotionless.

Just for a moment she had the distinct impression he was controlling himself very tightly, and it was an impression that made no sense at all. Maybe her psychic senses were as rattled as the rest of her.

"Don't," she said, voice harsh. "You've made it very clear you have no respect for me, and no respect for the way I'm trying to live my life."

"It's a little hard for me to show any respect when you

show so little damn respect for yourself," he all but exploded.

His fury charged the air between them. She scrubbed the tears away with the sleeve of her sweater, then opened her eyes. He stood three feet away, a barely visible shadow against the blanket of night. A man with the face of an angel and the heart of a stone devil.

Though his stance appeared casual, the hands he had thrust into his pockets appeared clenched. It was the only visible sign of the angry tension she could almost taste.

"I have my reasons for attending the dance last night—"

"Of that I have *no* doubt."

She clenched her fists. "How dare you judge me, when your own actions over the last twenty-four hours are *no* more worthy of respect than mine."

"I have my reasons," he echoed, voice bitter.

"And what makes you think those reasons are any more noble than mine?"

"So why *did* you join the dance last night? If your reasons are so damn honorable, you have nothing to fear in telling me, have you?"

She was tempted, so very tempted, to tell him. But if he was treating her like this now, what would he do when he discovered she'd deliberately set out to seduce him, that she'd only intended to use him to gain entry into the mansion?

"You're destroying my life," she said softly. "And all I've done to you is agree to share a dance for the length of this moon cycle. Does that equation seem equal to you?"

She didn't wait for his answer, just pushed away from the wall and walked off.

Duncan took a deep breath and released it slowly. He let

her walk away, a slender, angry, and very hurt shadow. It felt as if someone had reached into his chest and squeezed his heart tight. He could barely breathe under the crushing weight of her pain.

Of course, she was right. What he was doing to her wasn't entirely fair. Did the crime of keeping an eye on him befit the punishment of destroying her life? Hardly.

And what if she didn't know the reasons behind the watch? What if she'd been spun some tale that made her believe she was doing the right thing? Given his wild past, any lie would be more than half-believable to those who didn't know him.

He took another deep, calming breath and thrust the uncertainty away. He needed to find this killer. Fast. Needed to get away from the mansion and its environs, get back to the real world of his new life. A life he'd spent the past ten years building.

Problem was, he had no real clues as to the killer's identity, and four women had already lost their lives. If destroying Neva emotionally was the fastest way to find and stop this killer, then he had no real choice in the matter. Neva could rebuild her life. The women whose blood had been shed under the moon certainly couldn't.

These next four days were certainly going to be bittersweet. He might have her physically, but by the time he'd finished with her, she would truly hate him. And he had a suspicion he might well regret that.

Which would just be another item on an already too long list, he thought bitterly.

Neva threw the parcel into the trash can, then stormed into her house and went straight to the cabinet that held the few bottles of alcohol she had. She poured herself a large glass of whisky and drank it in one long gulp.

The liquid burned all the way down, settling like a weight in her agitated stomach. And though it gave her a head rush, it certainly didn't make her feel any better about herself or the situation she'd so stupidly put herself into.

Got what I deserved for sticking my tail in places it had no right to be, she thought bitterly. And yet, at the same time, she very much suspected she'd have reacted the same way even if she *had* known what would happen. Savannah was her twin. She couldn't just sit around and do nothing. Besides, she had no doubt Savannah would have reacted the exact same way—though she probably *would* have picked a better method of entry into the mansion than the moon dance. It was just the quickest and easiest way . . . or so Neva had thought.

She sighed and rubbed her temples. What was done was done. Maybe once all this was over, she could try to talk to her parents. Explain. Or maybe Savannah would. She'd undoubtedly disappointed them. She understood that, but deep down, she was still the child they'd raised.

She walked into the kitchen and reached for the telephone, dialing Ari's cell phone.

"Y'ello," her friend said almost immediately.

"Sorry to interfere with your date," she said. "But I have a favor to ask."

"Hey, no probs. Honey buns has gone to the bar to get us a drink. What's the favor?"

Ari's exuberant tone made Neva smile. At least she was enjoying herself tonight. "Do you think you could call that friend of yours and see if she's still interested in working at the diner? I need a fill-in for the next few days."

"Wow, that coffee spilling trick really did work, didn't it?"

If only. "Yeah, it worked."

"Cool." She hesitated. "You told the folks yet?"

"Oh yeah." Tears stung her eyes, and she blinked them away. The deed had been done, and there was nothing she could do, or say, to take back the hurt. She could only hope they'd see past this sometime in the future. "The 'Sounds of Silence' is the only tune I'll be hearing from them for a while."

Ari snorted. "They'll get over it. And you've played the dutiful daughter long enough. Go screw that beautiful man's brains out and enjoy yourself for a change."

"That's the plan." And somewhere deep down, some small part of her half-wished it was. But in one way or another, she had a feeling the frustration of the last twelve hours would continue.

"So, where is he taking you?" Ari asked. "Somewhere wild and wicked, I hope."

If she told Ari just how wild and wicked, her friend would faint. Ari enjoyed the dance as much as the next wolf, but even she refused to go as far as those at the mansion.

"He has some awards dinner on Saturday." It was better to continue the lie already told, especially since Ari would more than likely give her dad a piece of her mind at the diner tomorrow. Her friend certainly didn't believe in holding back feelings or thoughts, and she'd clashed with Neva's dad more than once over the years. "I'm staying with him until then."

"An awards dinner? Sounds boring."

"But *he's* not." And wasn't that the truth.

"Woohoo!" Ari's excited bellow echoed down the line. Neva winced and pulled the phone away from her ear as Ari continued, "The deed has been done. Was he good?"

"A master." At manipulating. At ruining her relationship with her parents for no justifiable reason. At leaving her so totally frustrated she thought she'd burst.

At giving her a glimpse of the stars, then snatching it away again.

And the fact that her mind placed the most emphasis on those last two only proved how rattled she was.

"Then I expect to see you in a week with the biggest smile on your face. *And* I want details."

"Only if you buy the coffee. I may not have a job when I get back."

"They can't fire you. Who else would they find to work the sort of hours you do for crap pay?"

She had a point. "I'll talk to you next week."

"Take care of yourself, sweetie," Ari trilled and disconnected.

Neva placed the phone back on the receiver and stood staring out at the dark expanse of her back garden. Duncan hadn't followed her into the house yet, and while she had no doubt he would soon appear, she was extremely glad for the breathing space.

She closed her eyes and reached for the warmth of her sister's mind, as she had in the past when in trouble. But there was no response, other than a slight stirring in the cloud of memories. Consciousness was drawing closer, but it could be several days yet before it happened.

She bit her lip and resolutely turned away from the window and made her way upstairs to her bedroom. She packed a bag with enough clothes to last four days then studied her wardrobe for something to wear to his stupid costume party tonight. She flicked through her dresses and eventually pulled out the elegant black dress she'd bought two years ago when Ari and she had gone on a somewhat drunken shopping spree in Denver.

It was form fitting, plunging past her breasts in the front, and to the base of her spine at the back. The skirt was full and swirled around her toes, but the four panels were split right up to the top of her thighs, so that when she walked she flashed a lot of leg. The hem of the skirt was beaded, the tiny drops of color forming gentle flames that shimmered like the real thing with every movement.

Match it with that stupid mask she'd worn last night, and she might just pass as a she-devil. Which was only fitting, given her partner.

She found a matching pair of high heels, then picked everything up and took the lot downstairs. Duncan still hadn't appeared and hope flickered briefly. Maybe he'd given up his whole sordid game—whatever it was. Maybe he was so overcome by remorse that he'd decided to just walk away.

Maybe tomorrow the Earth would stop spinning.

She rubbed her forehead. A large glass of whisky on top of an agitated but basically empty stomach had not been one of her better ideas. She stretched out on the sofa and closed her eyes. The temporary darkness felt like heaven to her aching head.

She wouldn't sleep, just close her eyes and rest a little.

Duncan glanced at his watch as he walked up the path to Neva's front door. It was nearly eight. He'd spent almost an hour on the phone, covering his one lie should Neva's parents call to check. Once Dave, his boss and good friend, had known the reasons behind Duncan's lie, he'd had no hesitation in playing along. He'd even offered use of his contacts in the sheriff's department. And Duncan had no doubt he'd need them before this week was out.

He took the steps two at a time and knocked lightly on the front door. There was no answer, though he knew she was home. The warm scent of citrus swirled around him, a warmer, more alluring scent than jasmine, and one that suited her better. Heat surged through his body, though after this afternoon's efforts, it certainly didn't take much to get him aroused.

He twisted the handle and the door opened. Light shone softly in the kitchen, and a travel case waited near the door, along with a pair of shoes and a long black dress.

"Neva?"

He walked into the living room and found her on the sofa, fast asleep. He squatted beside her and gently brushed the dark gold strands of hair from her face. She stirred slightly, murmuring something he couldn't quite catch.

Her delicate features had a drawn look to them, and the smudges beneath her eyes were as dark as bruises. She'd obviously gotten as little sleep as he last night.

He trailed his fingers down her cheek to the full lips he ached to kiss, then on, past the long line of her neck to the round fullness of her breasts. The cashmere sweater was soft under his fingertips, her nipples hard.

He rose. His family's costume dance didn't start until midnight, so they didn't have to leave just yet. He walked out of the living room and headed up the stairs.

Her bedroom was like her—soft, feminine and golden. The bed was big, crowded with brightly colored cushions and cheerful bears. He swept them aside and pulled back the comforter and sheet. Then he headed back down the stairs.

She hadn't moved. He took a deep breath, then concentrated his kinetic energy and carefully lifted her from the sofa. Holding her several inches off the cushions, he gently pulled off her shoes, then her jeans and panties. The sweater he left. He had too many fantasies about caressing her in that sweater to take it off right now.

She muttered something as the cold air caressed her skin and turned around, pulling at his kinetic hold. Pain tore at the edges of his mind, and a bead of sweat trickled to his chin. He'd lifted people before with telekinesis, people far heavier than she was. But each of those times he hadn't wanted to keep his touch whisper soft. Gentleness wasn't easy.

He tucked his hands under her body, then released his kinetic hold and hugged her close. She snuggled into his chest, her skin so cool compared to his, then sighed softly. It was then he smelled the alcohol on her breath.

Given how little she'd eaten this evening, it was probably that, more than anything, that had made her fall asleep. And would certainly explain why she hadn't woken spitting fire when he'd stripped her.

He carried her up the stairs and placed her in her bed. For a moment, he simply stood there, his gaze lingering hungrily on the fullness of her breasts under the cashmere sweater before moving on, past the flat plane of her stomach to the golden triangle of soft curls, remembering the way her long legs had wrapped around his waist as he thrust so very deep. He almost came just thinking about it.

He quickly stripped and climbed in beside her. She wouldn't be happy to find him there. This was her sanctuary, the one place no woman wanted to find a man unless he was invited.

But he had no intention of leaving or letting her leave, until he'd finished what he'd started this afternoon in the diner.

He wrapped an arm around her waist, pulled her close and waited for her to wake.

The dream was one of pleasure.

Neva lay wrapped in the darkness, part of her covered, part of her exposed and so ready for invasion. And she was invaded. By hands. By tongue. By body. She writhed and moaned, her skin on fire, every muscle screaming for release. The stroking continued. Outside. Inside. It took her higher and higher, until the need was so strong she couldn't even breathe. Then she came with such powerful force she screamed to the moon. It was a sound echoed by her dream lover.

She woke.

To discover it was no dream.

To discover the gentle invasion had not yet stopped.

"That was but a beginning," Duncan whispered in her ear. His tongue gently explored her lobe, and she shuddered under the assault.

She opened her eyes and realized she was home. In bed. *Her* bed.

Anger surged. He had to no right to be here. "What the hell are you doing?"

He shifted his weight off her, then moved his hand down her stomach and gently pressed past her damp curls. She shifted, trying to escape his touch, yet unable to deny the sweet pleasure of it.

"What does it feel like I'm doing?" His voice was lazy, amused.

Her gaze flew to his. His dark eyes were filled with enough heat to start a forest fire. And that was certainly the impact it had on her. "Seducing me in my own bed."

"That's exactly right."

"You have no right." She hesitated, eyes widening as his mouth drew close.

"I have every right," he murmured, breath warm across her lips. "And every intention."

His kiss was a honeyed affirmation of his words. A gentle possession she could not escape. Didn't really want to escape. The moon was high, and given this afternoon's and last night's frustrations, she so very desperately needed his touch. Needed him. Though she would never have admitted as much.

His mouth moved on, trailing fiery kisses down her neck to her breasts. She still wore her sweater, but he didn't seem to care. His teeth encased one aching nipple, biting lightly. She squirmed, trying to deny pleasure as he sucked and nipped one aching nub, then the other. As the gentle assault continued, she gave in to the urge to touch him, and she ran her hands down the muscled plain of his stomach to stroke the still hard length of him. He shuddered, thrusting into her touch. An oddly primitive sense of power ran through her. Whatever else he might think or feel about her, he couldn't deny his need for her right now.

A small comfort that was better than nothing, she supposed.

She continued to explore as he explored—by taste, by touch. Heat rose, shimmering between them, warming the night. Warming them.

His touch pushed her into a place where only sensation existed. The air was hot and thick and almost impossible to breathe. Every inch of her quivered under the relentless assault of his fingers and tongue. Then the convulsions began, the power of them curling through her body like a tidal wave.

It was a wave that became even more glorious as he thrust inside her again. She groaned and wrapped her legs around him, forcing him deeper still, until it felt as if the rigid heat of him was claiming every inch of her.

Her climax hit, stealing her breath, stealing her sanity, sweeping her into a world that was sheer, unadulterated bliss. A heartbeat later he went rigid against her, the power of his release tearing a groan from his throat. He held her for one last thrust, then his lips sought hers, his kiss a lingering taste of passion.

In that one moment, all the fears that had plagued her the first time they'd made love returned in a rush. Because this time he hadn't only let her glimpse the stars, he'd well and truly taken her past them.

Worse still, there was something in the way he touched her that she'd never felt before, and it scared her. Because no matter how powerful the dance, it would never mean anything to a man like Duncan Sinclair. He was a lone wolf, a man who lived for momentary pleasure, who searched for nothing beyond it. He'd certainly proven time and again over the last twenty-four hours that he cared nothing for *her*.

And the mere fact that she was even thinking something like that, after the abominable way he'd treated her, showed just how dangerous the next four days were going to be.

He rolled off her onto his back, one arm flung across his

forehead as he stared up at the ceiling. He might have been alone for all the notice he seemed to take of her. The night air caressed her rapidly cooling skin, but it had little to do with the shiver that ran down her spine.

"You'd better be getting dressed," he said. "We have to be back to the mansion by twelve."

His voice was flat, unemotional. She certainly wouldn't have thought they'd shared a mind-blowing dance only moments before.

"Right," she said, keeping her voice as flat as his. "I'll just go take a shower."

"Don't."

She stared at him. He didn't look at her, didn't acknowledge her, just continued to gaze at the ceiling. And it was beginning to grate. "Why not?"

"Because I want everyone to smell my scent on you. I want them to know you're mine, and mine alone."

Relief slithered through her. At least he was keeping one promise. "I can't see how having a shower will affect that."

"It's the dance and the moon rides high. They must know I have claimed you tonight, or there will be challenges."

Her stomach began to churn. What in the hell type of dance was he taking her to? "What do you mean?"

He shrugged. "What I said. Tonight is my pack's get-together. Some bring mates. Others bring dancers to be shared. If you don't have my scent on you, you'll be considered the latter rather than the former."

The implications of that swirled through her and settled like a weight in her stomach. "So it's an orgy?"

He finally glanced at her. Amusement sparked briefly in his eyes before it was lost to the shutters. "The whole moon dance is an orgy."

She supposed it was—at least where the Sinclairs were concerned. "Can I at least clean up a little?"

"If you hurry." He hesitated, and a mirthless smile touched his full lips. "Wouldn't want to miss any of the fun, now, would we?"

Her stomach began to churn, and she wondered yet again just what she'd gotten herself into.

Wondered how in hell she was going to get through the rest of *this* night, let alone the next four.

Five

Duncan stopped at the top of the stairs and let his gaze roam across the lust-filled darkness. This ballroom was far smaller than the main one, but no one here really cared. Tonight was a night for the main pack to come together and rejoice in the freedom of the moon. And if ever there was a time to discover discontent, it was tonight, when the heat of the moon and the whispering magic entwined through the music to make blood boil and tongues loosen.

Neva edged closer to him. Her hand was tense in his, and he could smell her fear as clearly as he could taste the seductive aroma of her femininity.

And while he could certainly understand her desire not to be here, right now he had no choice. Not only was it a perfect night to catch nearly the whole pack in the one place, it also provided yet another opportunity to push her that little bit farther.

He spied his father and two of his brothers near the buffet table. He swept his gaze around the room again and saw René enjoying the delights of a statuesque blonde he vaguely recognized. He smiled grimly. His brother certainly wasn't bothering to mourn the loss of a mate. But then, why would he? In the heated rush of the moon, she'd been just another face. Just another body to sate his lust on. René might have momentarily mourned her loss but, in the end, he didn't truly care. There were plenty of willing replacements to be found here in the Sinclair mansion.

A fact Duncan knew entirely too well. And one he was no longer satisfied with.

Only trouble was, he wasn't sure if there was anything else out there. Not for him, anyway.

He led the way down the steps and into the crowd. The heavy beat of the music throbbed though his veins, and the air was heavy with the rich aroma of sex.

He glanced at Neva. Though the mask covered half her face, he could see the glow of color in her cheeks. She kept her gaze firmly fixed ahead, but the smell of her arousal stung the air. She might be of the golden tribe, but she was still a wolf, and she could no more ignore the scents and sounds of those around her than he could.

His gaze slipped from her face to her body. She looked absolutely stunning in the barely-there black dress, and every step she took revealed tantalizing flashes of warm, golden skin. Her hair was a river flowing down her back, swaying like golden silk with every movement, drawing the eye to the perfection of her rear. He wasn't the only one who hungered for her—it was a feeling that followed them as they made their way through the crowded room, a sensation she would feel more acutely than he could.

And while he knew his proprietary hold on her ensured no one would approach her, she didn't. Left alone, the fear so evident in her pretty eyes would rise, and maybe, just maybe, she'd run to whoever had employed her to watch him.

He reached the far wall and found space enough to press her back into the shadows.

Heat climbed into her cheeks. "What now? You ravage me in front of your packmates to show what a big man you are?"

If he'd had the time, most definitely. He ran his hand

down the long line of her neck, noting the wild flutter of her pulse under his fingertips. It wasn't fear, just as the widening of her pupils wasn't fear. Underneath the strictness of her upbringing, there was a wild wolf desperate to be free. And if what they'd shared so far was any indication of what was to come, he certainly wouldn't mind being her mate when that wildness finally asserted itself.

He leaned close, letting his lips brush hers as he said, "Is that what you want me to do?"

Her breath caught, then caressed his mouth with quick warmth. He let his hand drift down to her breasts and gently rubbed one firm nub through the silk of her dress. She shivered, her lips parting, her breathing rapid.

He pressed himself closer, so that it seemed every inch of their bodies were molded together. He could feel her trembling, feel the heat radiating off her skin. The musky scent of her desire spun around him, the wild beat of her heart resonating through every fiber of his being.

"Tell me what you want," he murmured and brushed another kiss across her lips.

"Food," she all but gasped. "Not sex."

He grinned and pushed away. "Then food you shall have."

Surprise flitted through her eyes. Good—because the more he kept her off balance, the more likely it was that she'd make a mistake.

"Wait for me here. I have to go talk to my father, then I'll bring you back something to eat."

"Why can't I come with you?"

"Because I have pack business to discuss, and you're not of my pack. Wait here." He turned and walked away from her.

Neva crossed her arms and watched his muscular back disappear into the crowd. The urge to run after him was fierce, but she fought it. As much as she didn't want to be left alone in this place, it at least provided an opportunity to do some investigating. She swept her gaze across the room. There was a feel to the air she didn't like, a feeling that went beyond wanting, beyond lust. Was almost angry.

Not the entire room, just some sections of it, and it was a feeling she couldn't pinpoint to one person or group. Not yet, anyway.

The ballroom was smaller than the one she'd seen last night, but just as dark. There was no dance floor, just couples moving through the shadows—some talking, some making love, some doing both.

Most of the women wore outlandish costumes, the men leather pants that left little to the imagination. Chaps and a whip seemed almost tame by comparison to some of the attire in the room, but she was damn glad she'd refused to wear them. There'd been enough hunger aimed her way as Duncan led her across the room. Chaps would have only increased that hum of interest tenfold.

A small band of musicians sat in the far corner of the room, and their music was a caress of sound that raced through her veins, a sensual and erotic melody designed for one thing only—seduction.

She shook her head. The Sinclairs were certainly a hedonistic lot, but surely that wasn't a justifiable reason to be killing their mates. Especially when the women involved weren't even of the Sinclair tribe.

She blinked at the thought. Was that a clue? Could the killer be going after only those who *weren't* of the Sinclair pack?

It was certainly a possibility. Maybe the hatred she could feel in this room tonight wasn't aimed so much at the Sinclairs, but at the outsiders among them. Of which she was one.

She rubbed her arms, her gaze seeking Duncan. He stood near the buffet table with three other men. Given the similarities of their features, it wasn't much of a guess to say two were his brothers and the other his father. And it was easy to see where the sons got their looks. Even though his hair had long gone silver, the Sinclair pack leader was a picture of male perfection.

From all reports, the sons had learned their wild ways from their father. While all four had been born by one woman, Zeke Sinclair never committed himself to her, preferring to chase the tails of many during the moon dance.

Her gaze slipped to Duncan. Would he chase other wolves during this moon phase? While sanity suggested it would be good if he did, some small part of her reacted almost hostilely at the thought.

Which was totally, utterly insane. She'd come here for one reason only—to catch a murderer. What Duncan did or said during the next few days didn't really matter in the scheme of things—particularly when he'd made it so clear he was only after one thing from her. At least if he was with other mates, she'd have more time to investigate. Which is exactly what she should be doing right now.

Tearing her gaze away from him, she scanned the room again. She saw a mask that was familiar, and surprise rippled through her. Betise hadn't mentioned that she'd be attending the dance this week, and Neva wasn't sure whether to be happy about seeing her or not. While Betise was a regular customer at the diner, she very rarely spoke to anyone but her and Ari. The chance of Betise mentioning Neva's presence here at the mansion were slim.

Even so, she briefly thought about retreating to the shadows and keeping out of sight. But if anyone would know the secrets of this place, it would be Betise. She'd certainly proven a reliable source of information so far.

The blonde wolf was dressed in what looked like a dozen gauzy veils, and every movement revealed glimpses of flesh. She was talking to the man Neva had seen Duncan with last night. Even as Neva watched, the man made a chopping motion with his hand then walked away. What Neva could see of Betise's expression was savage, to say the least.

If that look was anything to go by, it probably wasn't the best time to be asking Betise about the Sinclairs and that man, but right now, Neva had little choice. She might not get a second chance.

She took a deep breath, then headed back into the crowd. The sensual beat of the music was accompanied by sighs of pleasure and the slap of flesh against flesh. Revulsion stirred, yet the fever rose in her blood, and the deep-down ache Duncan had started only minutes ago became fiercer. *She* might hate this sort of wanton, exhibitionist behavior, but the wildness within hungered to join them. Hungered to become part of this lusty, sweating crowd.

She definitely *wasn't* that different from any of those here tonight, no matter what her parents might have taught her over the years. High ideals meant little in the heat of the moon, it seemed.

She finally broke free of the crowd and saw Betise heading for a side exit. She followed, breathing deeply the crisp night air before she called out to the other wolf.

Betise swung around, and surprise flitted across her hard features as she took off her mask. "Neva. I didn't expect to find you here tonight."

Neva shrugged and stopped several feet away from the other woman. "If I had any choice, I wouldn't be." Though perhaps *sense* would have been a better word to use than *choice*.

Betise frowned. "Why not?"

"Apparently I agreed to some form of ancient binding without even realizing it, and now I'm stuck here for the remainder of this moon phase."

Betise's pale eyebrows rose. "Duncan did a moon binding with you?"

"Yeah. What a bitch, huh?"

"I guess it is if you don't want it." The slight edge in Betise's voice suggested a binding was something she certainly wouldn't have minded.

"Well, I don't, believe me."

Betise smiled. It never reached her silvery green eyes, and the thick sensation of envy briefly stung the air. "Being bonded to Duncan the rest of this phase will be a pretty amazing experience."

Amazing was certainly one word that could be used to describe what they'd shared so far. Harrowing was another. So was life-destroying. And it was all self-inflicted. No one had forced her into this situation. She'd stepped into it with her eyes wide open.

She raised an eyebrow. "I take it you've danced with Duncan?"

"In times past." Betise waved a hand toward the distant fountain. "I need to cool down. You want to walk with me?"

Neva nodded and fell into step beside the older wolf.

"When was this?" She kept her voice carefully neutral, even though she was desperate to know.

The moon and this place were making her insane, for sure.

"Before he left to go to Denver. He and I were an item for the last year he was here." Betise sighed again. "We were planning to perform the moon ceremony. We wanted to start a family."

Something twisted deep inside Neva. The moon ceremony was a life-bonding ritual that was performed the night before the full moon—and one that was only ever performed between soul mates. But if Betise and Duncan were soul mates, why was he with her rather than Betise? "So what happened?"

"I don't know. He disappeared for several weeks, then ended up in jail down in Denver. By the time I got down there, he'd been released and I lost track of him again."

"And you never tried to find him?" If *her* soul mate had disappeared, she would have moved Heaven and Earth to find him again.

Betise's glance was dark. "Of course I did. But by the time I did, a couple of years had passed, and he wanted nothing more to do with me. I still don't know why."

Neva frowned. That made no sense—not if they were soul mates. "You've talked to him recently?"

"No." Betise hesitated and raised a sculptured eyebrow. "But I might try this phase, if you don't mind."

"Go ahead," she said. Even though the insane part of her *did* mind. Very much.

The older wolf stopped next to the three-tiered fountain and scooped up a handful of water. She took a sip then splashed the remainder across her breasts. "How's your sister?" she asked, after a moment.

"Slowly recovering. I think she'll probably wake in the next day or so."

Betise nodded. "Must have been a big wolf who attacked her."

Memories rose—quick snapshots of broad shoulders, long legs, big teeth. Teeth that had torn so very deep. Neva shuddered and forced them away. She didn't want to relive Savannah's assault. Not ever.

"Extremely big," she somehow managed to say.

"I was surprised you decided to come here to the mansion when your sister is so ill in the hospital."

Neva scooped up some cool water, sipping at it slowly as she tried to think of a plausible answer. "The day before she was attacked, Sav and I were discussing the things we wanted to do before we die." She hesitated. "I guess her accident brought home just how close death really is, and how little I've done with my life."

"And a moon dance was on top of your list of things to experience?"

Right alongside sprouting wings and flying to the moon. "Yeah, but one night, not five."

Betise chuckled. "At least you're with Duncan. He's one of the best lovers you'll find here at the mansion."

But only when he wanted to be, Neva thought sourly. She forced a smile. "Sounds like you've had a dance or two with a few of the Sinclairs."

Betise's smile was almost wistful. "You could say that."

"And that gorgeous specimen I saw you dancing with a few minutes ago?"

The older wolf's smile faded, and her face became hard again. "That was René, one of Duncan's older brothers."

"I take it things aren't going well between you?" And why was she dancing with René if Duncan was her soul mate? None of this was making any sense.

"No." Betise's reply was short. Sharp. "He's just as bad as the rest of them. They all make promises in the heat of the moment but never—" She bit off the words and took a deep breath. "Sorry. I don't mean to go on."

Neva wished she would. She had a feeling she'd learn a whole lot more that way. "I totally understand, believe me. Duncan hasn't exactly been a picture of politeness in the day I've known him."

Betise grunted softly. "It's a wonder someone isn't killing Zeke's get, rather than just their lovers."

Bingo, Neva thought. Nothing in any of Savannah's reports had indicated the victims had been anything more than casual dancers. She ducked her gaze away, taking another sip of water as she tried to calm her racing heart. "So it's their mates being targeted?"

Betise hesitated. "So rumor has it."

At least it gave her a lead she could follow. While she couldn't risk talking to Duncan's brothers, she could certainly track down their mates and talk to them. "Did you know any of them?"

Betise shook her head. "Though I may have met them here, the masks make it difficult to say."

Neither of them seemed to have had any trouble recognizing each other, even with the masks on. But Betise had always been a loner at heart and tended to keep to herself. It was probably why her hair salon wasn't doing as well as it should. Most women went to a hairdresser's to relax and chat. Betise wasn't inclined to allow either.

"Aren't you worried that you might be in danger?"

The older wolf's smile was bleak. "No. From what I've heard, the victims were more permanent mates rather than casual dancers."

"Why haven't you gone to the rangers with this information?"

"With little more than a rumor? I doubt it would be appreciated—by the rangers or the Sinclairs."

The Sinclairs might not appreciate it, but the rangers sure would. Right now, they were desperate for the slightest scrap that could lead them toward the killer.

"So make an anonymous phone call."

"Not from the mansion, you can't. The phones are tapped."

Thanks for the warning, Neva thought. "Who by?"

"Zeke ordered it, apparently."

"Why?"

"Who knows? Maybe he just wants to be sure none of his get have murderous intents."

If that had been his plan, it would hardly be common knowledge. It defeated the purpose.

Betise glanced skyward and stepped away from the fountain. "I have another dance to get to. You here day and night?"

"Unfortunately."

Something flashed in Betise's pale eyes. Annoyance. Or envy, perhaps. "Then I'll see you tomorrow night." She spun away and walked toward the row of aspens and red-trunk pines.

Neva took another sip of water then glanced at the ballroom. As much as she didn't want to go back in there, she needed to find out who danced with each of the Sinclair brothers. She couldn't risk asking anyone and raising suspicions, which left her with only one option—watching them. And on a night like this, and in a place like this, that wasn't going to be an easy task.

Duncan glanced at the side exit for the umpteenth time. Neva had left a few minutes ago, and if she didn't return very soon, he was going after her. Though he really doubted that she'd risk meeting her employer right now, he couldn't take the chance she wasn't.

"Any progress?" Zeke asked softly.

Duncan shook his head, switching his gaze from the door to René as his brother began talking to a pretty redhead. "Did you manage to get a copy of the autopsy report?"

"My source doesn't want to risk being seen by anyone he knows, so he's not coming here until after four."

By which time, only a few diehards would be left here at the dance. "Who's that redhead René's with?"

Zeke hesitated. "Rozin, I think her name is. Why? Fancy her yourself, do you?"

Duncan gave his father a wry smile. "Hardly. I've got my hands full with our little spy."

Zeke's dark eyes gleamed with amusement. "Wolves from the golden tribe can be surprisingly wanton once they shuck the restraints."

Neva hadn't yet thrown off her restraints, but the wildness within was certainly beginning to show. "Is Rozin one of René's regulars?"

Zeke frowned. "Not that I know of, though he's certainly been with her a few times this phase. Why?"

He swept his gaze around the room looking for his other brothers. "What about Tye and Kane?"

"Kane's got two regulars left alive, Tye one."

"If the killer is going after the lovers of your get, it might be wise to arrange watchers on those women. The last thing we need right now is another death."

Zeke nodded. "Arranged it this afternoon."

"I hope they're discreet. You know how Tye feels about being watched."

"A fact the first guard I'd placed on his mate discovered a little too quickly. The second is keeping a more sensible distance."

Zeke's voice was dry, and Duncan smiled. "And well out of the range of Tye's fist, I gather."

"Exactly." Zeke paused. "The rangers want to finger-print the five of us."

"So they've finally found a print?"

"Taken it off the last victim's skirt, apparently."

"If she was here the whole night, that print could belong to anyone."

"It was a blood print, and evidently it matches the blood type they've found under the previous victims nails."

"The reports we have said the blood they'd found was A-positive. None of us are."

"The rangers don't know that."

He glanced back at the door. Still no sign of Neva. "It might be best if we cooperate with them on this. Maybe when they realize it's not one of us, they'll start looking for the real killer."

Zeke smiled. "You really think that?"

"No." Because the last time *he'd* cooperated with the police, he'd ended up in jail anyway. "I'll drop by the ranger office tomorrow and make arrangements."

"Do that. And come to my suite about five. We'll see if Mariata's autopsy report varies any from the other three."

Zeke hesitated, his smile widening. "If you dare spend the time away from your pretty spy, that is."

Duncan grinned. "With what I intended to do to her over the next couple of hours, she'll undoubtedly be in a deep and exhausted sleep come five o'clock." He clapped his father on the arm, then headed for the door.

Neva had barely taken three steps when Duncan appeared in the doorway. The moonlight gleamed off his skin and caressed his face, making him appear more like a dark angel than ever. His obsidian eyes were almost otherworldly.

And so hot. So hungry.

Her throat went dry, and she stopped. His gaze swept down her body, and he might as well have been caressing her with his hand, because every inch of her responded with heated delight.

"What happened to the plate of food I requested?" Her voice came out little more than a husky whisper, and his eyes gleamed in response.

"The buffet has been sitting there for a while. I thought something fresher would be better."

"A burger would be good right now." And though she doubted he'd comply, at least the suggestion kept up the illusion that she was here unwillingly. If what he'd said to her at her parents' place was any indication, he was suspicious about her reasons for being with him, and the more she did to waylay those suspicions, the more chance she'd have to snoop.

His slow smile made her stomach flip-flop. "I had something more substantial in mind."

She let her gaze roam down the firm planes of his body

until she came to the very visible evidence of his arousal under his jeans.

"So I can see," she murmured, and even as she said it, she wondered where her mind was. Playing games with this man was *not* a good idea.

Not when his need blanketed the air, making it difficult to even breathe. Not when desire skated across her skin and it felt like her heart was going to race out of her chest. And she knew it wasn't the moon's influence, but the man himself. *She* might hate him, but the wolf within wanted him. Badly.

But she didn't dare give that part of herself complete freedom. Not here, and definitely not with Duncan. Once the murderer was caught and this moon phase was over, she had bridges to mend and a life to get back to. A life *he* had practically destroyed.

"Why don't we take this discussion somewhere a little warmer?" His voice was soft and sexy enough to melt chocolate.

She nodded mutely. He touched a hand to her back, searing heat past her spine. A tremor ran through her. What was it about this man that got to her so badly? Surely it was more than just his experience and skill when it came to the art of lovemaking. Lord, she might be new to the mansion and its environs, but she *wasn't* new to the dance itself. She'd had several mates over the years since puberty, but none of them had ever affected her this deeply. This quickly.

There again, none of them had the reputation that Duncan had, either.

He led her along the path and past several doors. The caress of music from the ballroom gradually died, and the only sound to be heard was the soft crunch of gravel under their shoes. The moon caressed the night with its silver light, and the heat of it raced through her veins, seeming to pool where his fingers pressed so lightly, so tenderly, against her back.

He guided her through an arch, then opened a door and ushered her inside. Though the room was dark, her night sight was wolf keen. They were in what looked like a commercial kitchen, filled with stainless steel appliances and bench tops.

"We're raiding the kitchen?" she asked, amused.

"Can you think of a better place to get fresh food?"

"I guess not."

She pulled herself onto the bench and caught the loaf of bread he tossed her. He turned on a small light near the stove then continued on to the refrigerator, pulling out a platter of cold meats and a platter of fruit. Which was exactly what she'd wanted five minutes ago, but definitely not what she wanted right now. The thought sent a shiver across her skin. Being with this man, in this place, was dangerous. It made her hunger for things that just weren't safe. Or sane.

He placed the two platters on the table, then met her gaze. His dark eyes were shuttered, his face shadowed. If not for the hunger that burned through the night, she might have thought him immune to the moon fever and her.

So why was he even with her? Especially when Betise was at the mansion? It didn't make sense, particularly given the loathing she'd sensed in him earlier.

Or was there more to the story than what Betise had said? Did Duncan celebrate the rising of the moon with casual partners because he had no other choice? Had she turned away from him rather than him her?

She didn't know, and she suspected he wouldn't tell her if she asked.

He pressed her knees open then stepped between her legs and pulled her close. Her breasts were lightly squashed against his chest, and she could feel the wild thumping of his heart. Could feel the heat radiating off his skin, surrounding her in a furnace that was desire.

"Anything else you want?"

His breath caressed her lips, and a tremor ran through her. "A knife to cut the bread would be good."

"And a soda?"

She nodded. She couldn't do anything else because her voice seemed to have fled.

His mouth brushed hers, a tingling, tantalizing promise of what was to come, then he stepped back and returned to the refrigerator. "Ice?"

Again she nodded. Within seconds, he was back with two drinks and a bread knife. He cut several slices of bread, offering one to her as he slid the meat platter closer. She made herself a sandwich and ate it, her skin tingling with awareness as his gaze did a slow tour of her body.

She finished her drink and put the glass down on the bench. The remaining ice clinked softly, a sound that seemed to reverberate in the tense, overheated silence.

Or maybe it was just she who was overheated.

He stepped closer again. She instinctively inched back. A smile touched his sensual lips, and he reached out, gently running his fingers down her neck and across her shoulder, displacing the thin strap of her dress as he continued on down her arm.

She swallowed, but it didn't seem to help the dryness in her throat. Didn't seem to help the dizzy tripping of her pulse. He was far too close. All she could smell was the earthy spice of him, all she could feel were his breath on her skin and the caress of his hand. And all she wanted was to feel him inside.

It was crazy. Totally and utterly crazy. For seemingly no good reason, this man had, at the very least, forever altered her relationship with her parents. And while that might have happened eventually, it was a change she hadn't been pre- pared to deal with just yet. Especially when the man by her side was Duncan—a wolf so totally opposite to everything she wanted in a mate.

But the moon was burning through her veins, and at this particular moment she didn't care who he was or what he'd done. In all the years since puberty she'd never felt anything this strong. And that in itself was a scary thought. But maybe it was nothing more than a combination of the moon and being in the presence of a wolf well versed in the art of seduction.

His fingers slipped back up her arm and across to her other shoulder. The second strap slid down her arm, and her breath caught as her dress shimmied to her waist. His gaze met hers, and in those dark depths she saw a desire so intense it made her squirm.

"You feel hot," he murmured, leaning forward to brush the line of her neck with feather soft kisses.

She closed her eyes, enjoying the sensation. "It's warm in the kitchen."

"Very warm. Perhaps we should try to cool you a little."

The glass clinked again, and she opened her eyes. "Ice is not a good idea."

He raised an eyebrow, a smile teasing his lips. "Really?" He ran his hand up her arm, the cube of ice trapped in his palm. The momentary chill of the ice was quickly lost to the heat of his touch, and the overall sensation was incredibly arousing.

His hand reached her chest and moved down. She tensed, her breath catching in her throat. The cube skimmed one breast, then the other, and she gasped, jerking back from his touch. He chuckled, then his mouth enclosed on one hard nub, and she forgot the chill, forgot everything, and simply enjoyed as he sucked and nipped.

When she was all but squirming with need, he continued on, past her breasts, down toward her stomach. The ice had become little more than droplets of water running past the heat of his fingers, quickly soaked up by the folds of her dress. But the silky material provided no barrier to his hand, and as his fingers slid into her moist heat, she groaned and leaned back, giving him greater access.

"You want me, little wolf. Say it."

"No." It was obvious that she wanted him, but she was never going to admit it. Because if she admitted *that* she'd have to admit just how badly he affected her. And that was one pleasure she refused to give him.

"What harm is there in admitting you have needs like everyone else?"

He continued to slide a finger through her moistness, every stroke providing just the right amount of pressure. Ripples of pleasure radiated across her body.

"Great harm," she somehow managed to croak, "when the man who asks seems intent on destroying my life."

"Freedom always has its price." He leaned forward, nuzzling her ear, nipping lightly at her earlobe, all the while continuing his gentle, insistent stroking, sending her insane with need.

"I didn't come here to find freedom." Did she say the words out loud or merely in her mind?

His tongue skimmed her skin, trailing fire down to her breasts. When he flicked one aching nipple with that rough moistness, she shuddered and thrust toward him, wanting to feel more than just his tongue on her breasts. He chuckled softly and captured them in both his hands, lightly pushing them together. His gaze held hers as he ran his tongue from one aching nub to the other. She shuddered and shifted, not sure how much more sweet torment she could take.

"What did you come here to find, then?" he said softly.

You, she thought. Only he'd turned out to be a whole lot more dangerous than she'd ever imagined. "Not this."

"Then what?" He lightly nipped one nipple, then the other, and sweat prickled across her skin. Her heart was hammering so loudly its cadence seemed to fill the silence, and every muscle in her body was quivering. Aching. For him.

"I was just curious. Nothing more, nothing less. I never meant for this to happen."

"You're lying, little wolf."

And the fact that he sensed it was scary, because it meant he was reading her far better than she was reading him.

"I'm not lying," she said, almost desperately.

He released her breasts, and his fingers slipped into her moistness again. She gasped, arching into his touch.

"You will tell me the truth, you know. And before this night is over."

Mutely, she shook her head. His steady stroking was taking her higher and higher, until the need for him was so strong her whole body was shaking and she could barely even breathe.

The sound of a zipper being pulled down was almost lost in the frantic beating of her heart. Anticipation raced through her.

He pulled her closer, but nowhere near close enough. The quivering tip of him pressed against her moist heat, but went no further. His hands slid to her rear, cupping her lightly. The effort of control had him trembling, and she wondered what, exactly, he thought she was up to.

Perhaps she should tell him why she was here. But if she did, she had no doubt he'd force her from the mansion. These murders fell under the category of pack business, and he'd already made it perfectly clear he had no intention of letting outsiders get involved in such matters—that included not only her, but the police as well.

And if she told him, she'd have basically destroyed her life for no damn reason at all. At least by withholding the truth a little bit longer, she had a chance of discovering something—anything—that might give her a clue as to the murderer's identity.

She'd made her promise. She intended to stick to it. Though in many ways, she had no other choice now.

His hands tightened on her rump, pulling her forward. His hardness slipped inside a little more, and it felt so good she moaned.

"Tell me what you seek, Neva." His words were harsh, his breathing heavy. He was punishing himself as much as he was her.

She shook her head and knew she had to end this before the need for release overwhelmed common sense and loosened her tongue. She wrapped her legs around his waist and pulled herself forward, taking him deep inside.

He groaned and began to move, his strokes quickly

becoming fierce, hungry thrusts that shook her entire body.
The sweet pressure built and built, until it felt as if she
would explode with sheer pleasure.

Then she did.

"Oh moons, *yes*!" Her body bucked wildly against his.
He came with her, his roar echoing across the silence, his
body slamming hers so hard the whole bench seemed to
shake.

He caught her lips, kissing her fiercely as their orgasms
ebbed and sanity returned. She opened her eyes and stared
into his. For the briefest of moments, the shutters were
opened, and in those black depths she saw compassion and
surprise and warmth. It was almost easy to believe they
were lovers who actually cared about each other, then the
shutters slammed home and the cold stranger came back.

But before either of them could say anything, a scream
rent the silence.

It was the scream of a woman in pain.

Six

For a heartbeat, Duncan didn't react, too lost in the warm aftermath of loving Neva to really register what he was hearing.

Until the scream came again. The voice sounded vaguely familiar, yet it brought no immediate images to mind. He stepped back from Neva and wondered who in hell was playing it a little too rough. He hoped it wasn't René. "Stay here," he said, fastening his jeans.

"No." She slipped off the bench and pulled up her dress.

"Neva—"

"No," she repeated, her expression determined as her gaze met his. "I know the voice—I was talking to her just before we came here. I may be able to help."

He frowned. Given her reluctance to let anyone know she was here at the mansion, it was surprising that she'd risk talking to anyone. "Who?"

"Betise."

She gave him a strange look as she said the name, and he wondered why. The voice might have sounded familiar, but the name certainly wasn't. And while he had no desire to drag her into any pack business, she was right about one thing. If there was an hysterical female to deal with, she could be of some assistance. He had no doubt this was nothing more than a wolf playing the dance a little too hard, simply because it broke the well-established pattern set by the murderer. As another scream sounded, he grabbed her hand, and they raced out the door.

The night air was glacial against his lust-heated skin, and the wind had sharpened. Overhead, the moon was lost to the gathering of thick, dark clouds. There would be a storm by morning. Part of him hoped it was one of those early spring monsters Ripple Creek was renowned for. At the very least, it would keep everyone indoors and the rangers away a bit longer, giving him the chance to find and deal with the monster behind the murders.

They raced past the row of aspens and pines and across the well-manicured lawn, heading toward the pavilion where he'd first danced with Neva. He didn't hear anyone else speeding through the night, neither ahead nor behind them—undoubtedly thanks to the wind blowing the sound of the wolf's screams away from the ballrooms. Of that he was glad. Right now, they didn't need an audience, and they certainly didn't need any more rumors circulating around Ripple Creek.

The sound of soft sobbing broke through the night. He couldn't smell the presence of another male, only a female. She was a hint of musk and sourness on the icy wind—an odd, unpleasant aroma, and one that stirred memories. He'd danced with a wolf who'd smelled like that, though it was a long time ago, back in the hellion days of his youth.

The old pavilion came into sight, and he slowed. Neva wrenched her hand from his, but he caught her again before she could run ahead.

"If this *is* another attack by the murderer," he said, before she could speak the rebuke he could see in her expressive eyes, "then racing blindly into the situation might well destroy any clues."

Not that he really thought there'd be any to find. Even

this close, he couldn't sense the presence of another wolf. Only the female, though as they walked closer, it became obvious she'd danced many times over the night. The scent of many males stung her skin, and that in itself *did* match previous attacks.

They found her sitting on the pavilion's floor, huddled next to a seat wrapped in shadows. She was willowy and blonde, reminding him of the wolf he'd seen his brother dancing with when he and Neva had first walked into the ballroom.

She looked up. There were tears in her eyes, and the hard planes of her face were gouged and bloody. The arms she had wrapped around her drawn up knees were littered with bite marks. Marks made by a wolf with huge jaws.

Neva made a strangled sound, then she tore herself free of his grasp and went to the older wolf, kneeling down beside her.

"By the moon's light, Betise, what happened?"

"I was supposed to meet someone here, but he was late." The older wolf's voice was little more than a broken whisper, but one that grated against his nerves. And he couldn't say why—it certainly wasn't all that unpleasant.

"Another wolf came out of the shadows . . . and he . . . he . . ."

If another male had been here, why couldn't he smell him? "Where did he go?" he asked, voice clipped.

The look Neva gave him was dark. "Does it matter right now? Why don't you give Betise some comfort—"

The older wolf placed a hand on Neva's arm, silencing her. "The last I saw of him, he was heading for the main gates."

"Stay here, both of you."

He spun and shifted shape, running swiftly for the main gate. The air was fresh and cold, the wind stronger. He might have thought it possible that the weather had blown away all aroma of the attacker, except for the fact that the tang of balsam still rode the air, as did the flowery scent of several females who'd obviously passed through the gates recently.

Betise had obviously been attacked, but by whom? And if the attacker hadn't retreated this way, where had he gone? Was Betise lying to protect him, or had she been too confused and terrified to truly notice which way her attacker had fled?

He suspected it was the former, though why he felt this, he had no idea. But he'd learned long ago to trust his instincts. Over the years, they'd gotten him out of more trouble than he could remember.

Neva glanced up as he entered the pavilion again, the rich and exotic mint of her eyes making the older wolf's seem almost silver in comparison.

"Do you have a doctor in this place?"

The scorn evident on the word *place* more than emphasized her thoughts about the mansion, which only confirmed his suspicion that she was here to watch *him*, not dance.

"Yes."

He squatted down beside her. The sunshiny, slightly citrus scent of her spun around him, thankfully overwhelming the other wolf's unpleasant, very used smell. He couldn't really remember dancing with her, and it was only the familiarity of her scent that told him he had. Looking at her now, he had to wonder what had attracted him. Beyond her hair, there was nothing even remotely pretty about her, though that probably wouldn't have mattered when he was younger. A lust for alcohol and a willing bit of tail was all he'd been interested in for more years than he cared to remember.

"Can you describe the wolf who attacked you?"

She shuddered. "He was big . . . and silver-coated."

So was the murderer, apparently, but that in itself wasn't much of a link. There were plenty of big silver wolves in the mansion—a whole pack of them, in fact.

"And you didn't recognize him?"

Betise shook her head, but something flickered in her pale eyes, and he knew she was lying. Was she trying to protect her attacker, or did she have other motives. He intended to find out, and maybe he could use Neva's apparent friendship with this wolf to do that.

"Duncan, enough." Neva's voice was sharp. "She needs medical attention."

She did, though he suspected her wounds were not as bad as they looked. "Can you walk?"

Neva's expression got darker. "Of course she can't. Carry her, for moon's sake."

The *last* thing he wanted was this wolf's scent on him again. He frowned and suddenly wished he could remember what had happened between them all those years ago. At the very least, he could then warn René to be wary of her—something he might do anyway.

"Her legs aren't injured from what I can see," he said coldly. "I'll go find the doctor. You help her to the study. She knows where it is."

"Bastard," he heard Neva mutter as he walked away.

He smiled grimly. He was all that and more—and would continue to be that way for as long as this murderer was loose.

He strode past the rows of wind-tossed aspen and pine. As he got closer to the ballroom, the music began to seep through his blood again, and need rose. He ignored it, but he wondered if that was going to be at all possible in the coming nights.

He might have practiced restraint over the last ten years, but coming back to the mansion seemed to have loosened the control he had over his old habits. Part of him ached to celebrate the rising of the moon as he had in the past—to drink himself senseless and lose himself in the pleasure of a female's body, over and over and over. Only right now, it wasn't any female he hungered for but one with dark golden hair and leaf green eyes.

It was a need that was more than a little worrying. If she wasn't in jail by the time this was all over, then she'd certainly hate him more than she already did. It would be the mother of all ironies if, for the first time in his life, he'd actually found a woman he wanted to spend more than one moon dance with, and *she* couldn't even stand the sight of him.

Though undoubtedly fate would probably think it a fitting retribution for his youthful unthinking and uncaring behavior.

He walked into the ballroom, and the heat and the smell of sex hit him like a punch to the gut. He took a deep breath, half thinking of grabbing the nearest free female to mate with, if only to ease the sharpness of the moon-spun pain. He resisted the temptation and swept his gaze across the rutting, sweating crowd. His father and Tye were nowhere to be seen, but René and Kane were both still here. After a second, he saw the doctor heading out another side exit.

He pushed through the crowd. The associated scents and sounds of lovemaking flushed heat across his skin, and though he'd made love to Neva less than ten minutes ago, he wanted her with a fierceness that made it difficult to concentrate.

His father's warning ran through his mind. He would indeed have to watch the bait, or he really could end up getting hooked.

He caught the doctor heading for the stairs leading to the wing housing staff and guestrooms.

"Hey, Duncan," Martin said with a smile. "Long time no see."

"Certainly has been." In his heyday, Martin had been responsible for the delivery of most of the Sinclair cubs, but failing health and the odd, often long, hours of obstetrics had forced him to retire just before Duncan had left ten years ago. These days, he did little more than ensure all male wolves attending the dance received the injection that kept their fertility under control. Wolves might only be fertile during the week running up to the full moon, but given the number of partners many had, Ripple Creek would quickly be overrun with cubs if he didn't.

And while the presence of werewolves might be tolerated in the human world, human tolerance only went so far. Ripple Creek had survived where many other reservations had failed, simply because they kept their numbers under tight control and didn't push the boundaries.

"I need you to do me a favor, Doc," he said.

The old wolf raised a bushy white eyebrow. "What?"

"A female's been attacked in the pavilion. She claims she didn't know her attacker, but I think she's lying. I'd like you to clean her wounds and, in the process, see if you can grab a sample of saliva from them." He hesitated, then added on impulse, "and perhaps sneak a sample of whatever lies under her nails."

"A tall order." Martin hesitated, dark eyes worried. "Is this attack linked to the recent murders?"

"In some ways, it's similar, but we can't be sure."

"And you're not calling the rangers?"

"I can't see the point, but if she wants to, we will." Though he very much doubted she would.

Martin nodded. "What do you want me to do with these samples?"

He hesitated. His boss, Dave, had offered the use of his contacts, and it was possible those contacts included someone in the labs. "Keep them secure until I can arrange for them to be tested."

"I'll just go get my medical kit. Where is she now?"

"I've put her in the study."

"Is she bad? If so, it might be better if she heads into the hospital—"

"Just scratches and a few bite marks on her arm."

The old wolf nodded. "I'll meet you there."

Duncan spun on his heel and headed for the study. Once the doc arrived, he'd have to keep Neva out of the way just so she didn't see Martin taking samples. If Betise *had* been attacked by the killer, then the last thing he wanted was Neva running back reporting to whoever had set her on him.

Both women jumped when he thrust open the study door. Neva stood, her expression hostile. But her gaze slithered down his body, and awareness flashed between them.

An awareness her clenched fists suggested she was fighting. "Where's the doctor?"

"On his way." He glanced at Betise. The older wolf was

lying on the sofa, eyes closed and breathing even, but he could feel the tension in her. Feel the anger. "We've danced, haven't we?"

The smile that tugged her thin lips was bitter. "Yes," she said, not opening her eyes. "We have."

"I don't remember."

Neva gasped softly. *Do you really enjoy being such a callous bastard?*

Neva's thoughts were acrid and filled with anger. Obviously, Neva knew a whole lot more than he remembered. He looked at her and raised an eyebrow. *It's nothing more than the truth.*

He'd had so many women since his first moon dance, how could he possibly be expected to remember his time with every one? That he recalled this wolf's scent was a miracle in itself.

You were with her for a year. Surely that in itself would be a momentous enough event for a womanizer like yourself to recall.

He'd never been with *any* wolf longer than the period of one moon dance. Had never wanted to be, especially in his youth. *If she told you that, she lied.*

A sound not unlike a disbelieving snort ran through his mind. *Or you're lying, for whatever sordid reason you might have.*

I may be many things, but a liar isn't one of them. He hesitated, then added harshly. *Shame you can't say the same thing, isn't it?*

She blushed, but she held his gaze almost defiantly. *I haven't lied to you.*

She was lying now. *Then tell me why you came to the mansion.*

To try the moon dance.

And?

I'm regretting every damn minute of it.

That, at least, was a truth, and one he *did* regret. *It's a shame you've got four more nights to go, little wolf. Rest assured I aim to enjoy every one of them.*

Bastard, she said again.

He smiled grimly and switched his gaze back to Betise. "When, exactly, did we meet?" Not that he really cared. He was just puzzled as to why she'd bother lying.

"You were twenty-two."

Which was a year before he'd left to go to Denver and had ended up in jail while the police sorted out the mess of his accident. While it hadn't been one of his more sober years, he was sure he'd remember having a semipermanent mate. He'd never been like his brothers in that respect— he'd never made half promises to the women he mated. Even back in his hellion days, he'd been honest enough to admit he was after nothing more than a good time, and those he was with always knew that. So why this woman believed *he'd* believe they'd been together more than one moon dance was beyond him. Unless she thought he'd been so drunk he wouldn't even remember.

Even so, what would it gain her?

"And we were together how long?"

She hesitated. "Nearly the whole year."

No way. He couldn't stand this woman's scent. Maybe drunk he wouldn't have cared so much, but even so, they couldn't have been together an entire year without him at least remembering some part of it. He'd never been *that* drunk. And he *could* recall most of the year—just not her part of it, which to him implied she'd never played a major part.

"Sorry, but I have no memory of you or our time together."

Moons, you're such a cold—

Yeah, he cut in, oddly annoyed at Neva's insistence at believing her friend rather than him. *I know what I am. What I don't know yet is what you are.*

The door behind him opened, and Martin stepped inside. "Ah, nasty wounds you have there, young lady."

Betise's smile held the first true hint of warmth Duncan had seen, but it did little to wipe the hardness from her face.

"I hardly think I can be called young any more."

Martin smiled as he placed his medical bag on the table and opened it up. Duncan noted the small, empty vials inside. "Compared to me, you're little more than a pup."

Duncan glanced at Neva. "Why don't you and I move out to the balcony while the doctor looks after Betise?" He made it an order, using the power of the moon bond to force her into obedience.

Her eyes flashed and her fists clenched, but she had no option other than obeying. She spun and all but stomped out the French doors.

He followed her. She didn't go far, stopping to the left of the doorway. She crossed her arms and glared at him. *You'd better keep those shields of yours well up, because the minute you lower them, you'll pay.*

Then he'd better make sure he did something worthy of the pain she planned to inflict. He continued to advance on her. Her face went pale, and she held out a hand, pressing it against his chest. "Don't."

He stopped, took her hand from his chest and lightly kissed her fingers. "Don't what?"

"You know what." Her soft voice was a mix of breath-lessness and scorn. "We can't, not with Betise this close."

"I don't particularly care about Betise. Never have."

Her gaze searched his, then she shook her head. "How can you say that?"

"Easily. I open my mouth, and the words come out."

"You haven't got a heart in that chest of yours, have you?"

"I certainly haven't discovered one yet. Take off your dress."

Anger ran around him. "No." She wrenched her hand from his and crossed her arms.

He raised an eyebrow and reached for the power of the moon again. She swore softly and vehemently, and amuse-ment swam through him. "And I thought the golden tribe were such gentle souls."

"We are, generally. Must be the company I've been keep-ing of late." She threw her dress on the ground then crossed her arms again.

The moon caressed her golden skin, and her nipples were taut with cold and arousal. He was as hard as hell and wanted nothing more than to take her right there and then. But that's exactly what she expected him to do, so it was the one thing he couldn't.

He reached out, gently running a finger across her breasts. She trembled under his touch, swallowing heavily. Hate and desire warred in the emotive swirl that briefly sur-rounded them both.

"How well do you know Betise?"

Surprise flickered briefly in her eyes. "She's a regular customer at the diner. Been going there for years."

"Uncross your arms." He made it an order, and she bit

her lip, her knuckles whitening as she battled the command. It was a battle she had no hope of winning.

"So it's a casual thing, not true friendship?" he added, running his finger to the center of one breast and slowly circling the engorged point. Goose bumps fled across her skin, and the smell of her arousal was rich and sweet on the strengthening wind.

"Yes," she said, voice breathy, eyes angry.

"Why aren't you afraid that she'll report your presence here to your parents?"

She snorted softly. "Betise hates my parents. They're against the moon dance, against everything the mansion stands for."

Which made Neva's decision to come here all the more suspicious. "But what about other friends? Might she not mention it to them?"

She hesitated, and fear flickered through her pretty eyes. "Maybe."

"Then why didn't you avoid her?"

"Maybe I was just so desperate to see a friendly face."

He shifted his touch to her other breast. She trembled, her skin flushed and hot under his fingertips. "And maybe you had some information for her to pass on."

She frowned. "I have no idea what you're talking about."

He sensed no lie in her words. Whatever the reason for Neva being here, Betise wasn't a part of it. He reached for the moon power again then said, *I want you to question her about her attacker, and I want you to report every word back to me, and only me.*

And by using the moon power, he'd ensure she couldn't go running back to her employer with any information Betise might give her.

Her eyes practically spat fire. He smiled and slid his hand down her stomach. "Yeah," he said softly. "I'm a bastard."

He gently delved the golden triangle of curls. Lord, she was so hot, so moist. He probed deeper, sliding through her slickness, until her muscles pulsed around one finger, then two. Her whole body quivered, and the smell of her need stung his senses, testing his strength, his will. He wanted her every bit as badly, but right now the need to push her into revealing what she knew and who employed her to watch him was stronger than the need to dance with her.

Though he wasn't entirely sure it would remain that way.

He kept stroking her, until her skin was flushed with heat and the fine sweat of desire, and the tremors in her body indicated she was close to the edge.

At that moment, he withdrew his touch and stepped away.

Heat climbed into her cheeks, and she clenched her fists. "Why are you doing this to me?"

His smile was tight. In many respects, he was punishing himself as much as her. "Anticipation is half the pleasure."

"Believe me, it's not."

He raised an eyebrow. "Perhaps we should see."

She studied him warily—an aching, golden angel he desperately wanted to lose himself in.

"What do you mean?"

"Go up to my room and climb into bed. You will wait there until I return, and go nowhere else until then."

He made it a command, and she swore again. Her eyes narrowed slightly, and he hastily raised his shields to full.

Even so, the trickle of fury that got through nearly blasted his mind. She wasn't kidding when she'd said he'd have to watch himself. With that sort of power, she'd probably be able to fry his brain.

"That could get awfully damn messy if I have to go pee," she muttered eventually.

"You can go to the bathroom. Nowhere else."

"Isn't *that* so goddamn generous of you?"

"Go," he ordered. "Now."

She picked up her dress and stomped down the stairs. He watched her until she'd fled around the corner, clenching his fists against the desire to go after her. Right now, he had more important matters to tend to. Satisfying his lust could wait.

He went back into the study. Martin glanced up and gave a small nod, and Duncan relaxed a little. He looked at Betise. As he'd guessed, her wounds were not as serious as they'd looked.

"Are you staying for the remainder of the night's dance or going home?"

"Going home." She arched an eyebrow, and her voice became little more than a husky whisper as she added, "Are you offering to escort me?"

He hesitated, but knew in reality he had little choice. Not if she *had* been attacked by the murderer. "Yes."

A smile touched her thin lips, and the smell of her desire stirred the room—but not him. Neva's scent clung to him, and it was her he wanted, not this well-used dancer who claimed to have some sort of past with him.

Her gaze switched to Martin. "Thanks, Doctor."

The old wolf nodded. "You're most welcome. Duncan, I'll talk to you later about that other matter."

He nodded. Betise raised an eyebrow as she climbed off the sofa. "Other matter?"

"Pack business," he said flatly. "Are you changing before you leave?"

Her fingers toyed with the gauzy material of her gown, drawing his gaze down her body. She was very shapely, but these days it took more than just a well endowed body to catch his interest, though Neva had captured him with little more than a wistful thought.

"I can't see the point," she said huskily. "Not when I plan to come back tomorrow night."

"Fine. Let's go." He pressed his fingers to her back, ushering her out the door. Once outside, he dropped his hand and ensured there was plenty of distance between them.

She noticed. "I won't bite," she said softly. "Not unless you want me to."

He didn't even glance at her. There was nothing about this wolf that attracted him, and nothing he wanted from her. Which was odd, given the hunger that boiled through his blood.

"I don't want you." He kept his voice harsh and flat to leave her in no doubt as to his feelings, and he felt rather than saw her gaze slide down his body. It was a touch of heat that left him itchy.

"Your body suggests otherwise," she said.

They walked past the pavilion, heading for the main gate, and he briefly wished Ripple Creek was a little closer. He had no desire to be in this wolf's company any longer than necessary. "My body does little more than react to the power of the moon. Believe me, it's not you I want."

"Neva."

She practically spat the words, and he frowned. "Neva is nothing more than another dancer I'm spending time with this moon cycle, and she certainly has nothing to do with my lack of desire for you."

They passed through the main gates and headed for the trees. He paused, allowing her to go first down the narrow path.

"You *have* changed your tune over the years, haven't you?" she growled. "There was a time when the opposite was true."

"You and I both know we did little more than share one dance," he bit back. "And I'd like to know what you think to gain by stating otherwise."

She glanced back at him, pale eyes gleaming with fury. "We shared more than one dance."

They hadn't. He was more positive of that than ever. But why was she so adamant that they had? "Either way, it doesn't matter. The past is something I have no wish to relive."

She snorted. "You're as bad as your bastard brother."

He smiled grimly. "Which one? I have three."

She hesitated. "René. You all make promises in the heat of moon passion, but when the sanity of the sun returns, you renege."

He very much doubted that René had made any promises. His brother enjoyed his freedom and the dance far too much. Still, at least it was one thing he could check. René didn't drink and would certainly remember what he had—and hadn't—said. "I take it that you've danced with Tye and Kane as well?"

Her voice was bitter as she all but spat, "Who hasn't?"

She had a point. None of them were exactly reluctant

when it came to enjoying the pleasures of the moon dance,
though it was unusual for all four of them to have mated
with the same dancer. Their tastes in women were very
different.

"So you're not exactly sorry that the Sinclairs are in trouble at the moment?"

"Oh, I'm sorry all right—sorry the murderer is taking
out innocent dancers rather than you lying pack of
bastards."

He smiled grimly. Must be his night for being called a
bastard. They walked through the remainder of the trees in
silence, and the lights of Ripple Creek eventually came into
sight. The town was quiet, which didn't surprise him, given
the somewhat puritanical hold the golden tribe had on the
place. Those who truly wanted to celebrate the glory of the
moon did so in private or at the mansion.

Betise lived in a small, somewhat rundown house on the
outskirts of town. He walked her to the front gate then
stopped.

She swung around. "You're not coming in?"

The heat was back in her eyes, the smell of her arousal
thick and heavy on the air. Yet two minutes ago, she'd been
wishing him dead.

"I have no desire for you," he repeated.

She caught his arm and stepped close, wantonly pressing her body against his. "A wolf with experience can give
you far more pleasure than an uptight bit of fluff like
Neva."

Anger surged through him. Neva was more wolf than
this bitch would ever be. He grabbed her shoulders and
none too gently pushed her backwards. "Go inside and
lock your door. And if I hear you've mentioned Neva's

presence at the mansion, I'll ensure you never again attend another moon dance." And for a wolf so hooked on the pleasures of the moon, that was a threat worse than death itself.

Her pale eyes glittered silver in the night, and for an instant, it seemed sanity had fled their depths and all that was left was hate.

"Bastard," she muttered.

"So I keep getting told."

She spun and walked away, but halfway up the path, she hesitated and looked over her shoulder.

"There's something you should know. Three weeks ago, Levon Grant pulled me aside in the diner and began asking questions about who was dancing with whom up at the mansion."

Shock rippled through him. Neva's father had been asking about the mansion? Why? While it was obvious Levon Grant had no liking for the dance, he'd never been one of those who spoke out against it, either. Duncan had been under the impression that while Levon might hate what the dance represented, he also understood that the mansion provided a secure outlet for the moon-spun urges and kept Ripple Creek safe for human and werewolf alike.

But maybe he'd been wrong all along. Maybe Levon had just been waiting for the right opportunity to take matters into his own hands.

But if that were the case, why was Neva at the mansion? Would a wolf so against the mansion's moon dance force his daughter to join them?

Given what he'd seen of the man, he doubted it. And yet, the niggle was there. He couldn't say for certain, and that was worrying. Maybe he was being played more than he realized.

"You'd better watch what you do over the next couple of days, wolf." Betise's cold words seemed to echo his thoughts. "It might just turn out that you're dancing with the murderer's not-so-sweet accomplice."

Seven

Duncan rapped his knuckles against the wooden door leading into his father's suite, then entered without being asked. Zeke wasn't in the main room, but he could hear soft voices in the bedroom. He strode over to the bar and poured himself a large bourbon. A habit he'd have to watch, he realized, even as the liquid burned down his throat. The last thing he wanted was a return to the bad old days.

He leaned against the bar and listened to the murmurs of conversation in the other room. While he couldn't hear many words, one thing was obvious. His father's source was female, not male.

A cold breeze whistled around his ankles, indicating the French doors had been opened. Two seconds later his father entered the room, wearing little more than a black silk robe.

"No wonder you didn't want me appearing before five," Duncan noted dryly. "You knew you'd be busy paying off the messenger."

Zeke smiled and didn't refute the accusation. He poured himself a drink, then slapped a folder on the bar. "There's the report. There don't seem to be any variances from the other attacks."

"Did they find any more coat hair?"

"Other than that one you saw, no. But one hair is all they need to place a suspect at the scene."

"If they had a suspect."

"True." Zeke paused and took a drink. "My source did drop one interesting revelation that's not in the reports."

"What?"

"While the coroner's report couldn't confirm whether sexual penetration had occurred during the attack, the rangers themselves believe none of the women were raped. They believe it's only being made to look like they were."

If that were the case, the murderer was damn good at make believe. "Why would anyone want to do that?"

"You might as well ask me why the murderer is targeting these women," Zeke replied dryly. "When we know why, we'll find our killer."

Duncan glanced down at his drink for a moment.

"What do you know about a wolf named Betise?"

His father's lip curled. "She's a dance addict and has been well-used over the years. I've never danced with her, but I believe René and Kane both have. And you." Zeke hesitated, dark eyes glinting with sudden amusement. "But then, you did have a reputation to live up to."

He grimaced. There was no use regretting his past, and there was certainly nothing he could do to change it. "She was claiming tonight that we were an item for nearly a year."

Zeke snorted. "Even at your drunkest, you had more sense than that."

"That's what I figured." He took a drink then said, "She was attacked tonight."

"By the murderer?"

"I don't know. She claimed it was a big silver wolf, and the bite marks on her arms certainly attest to the fact it *was* a big wolf."

"But you don't believe her?"

"I don't disbelieve her, either. She *was* attacked."

"But?"

"But if it was the murderer, then he's breaking set patterns. It happened in the pavilion not near the gates. She was waiting for another dancer, not leaving the mansion. And there were no signs of bites on her breasts or neck. She had scratches on her face, and there were bites on her arms, but neither were very deep. I doubt they'll even scar."

Zeke's expression was thoughtful. "It is always possible the murderer has changed his pattern. There are no set rules governing that sort of thing, you know."

"I know. But he's been so careful up to this moment, so why would he risk attacking a wolf who was obviously waiting for someone? It just doesn't ring true."

"Maybe he thought he had no other chance."

"Maybe." He picked up the bottle and half filled his glass. "I asked Martin to take some saliva and skin samples from her. I thought I could use Dave's contacts to get them tested."

"I'll get them tested. It'll be quicker and easier."

Duncan nodded. The sooner they knew whether Betise's attack was linked to the murderer, the better. "What do you think about Levon Grant?"

Zeke snorted. "Why would I even bother thinking about him?"

"Betise told me tonight that he'd been questioning her about the mansion and the dancers. From what she said, it happened just before the first attack."

His father frowned. "Levon's many things, but I believe he understands the necessity of the dance."

"Neva's his daughter."

"Then he surely doesn't know she's here, because if he did, he'd be here dragging her away by the scruff of the neck. He's not *that* understanding. "

Which is exactly what Duncan had thought. Yet the itchy feeling that Neva was up to something still remained. And if she *was* here at her father's request, she wasn't going to admit it. He could force the information out of her, of course. But to do so would tell her he was on to her, and if she ran, he doubted it would be back to the person behind her presence here.

He downed the rest of his drink and felt the liquid burn all the way down to his gut. It only fueled the fire already burning in his veins. "Even so, I think it's worth digging around for information on Levon. Maybe his turn-the-other-cheek attitude is little more than a front."

"Maybe." Zeke's expression was doubtful. "What are you going to do about Neva?"

"Keep pushing her. I'm sure she's here for a reason, and I'm just as sure she'll run very soon."

"Might be worth doing a check on her, as well. Maybe she's got a sibling who was slighted by you or your brothers."

"I doubt she'd dance with *me* just to get a little revenge."

"You don't know her well enough to guess what she's capable of."

A truth he knew he would probably regret for the rest of his life. He put his empty glass on the bar. "I'm also going to run a check on the murdered women. See if there was any other link between them other than the mansion."

"I imagine the rangers would have already done that."

Duncan's smile was grim. "They have to stick within the boundaries of the law to find their information. I don't."

"True."

He glanced at the clock. "Time to go do a little more pushing. If I find anything, I'll let you know."

He spun and walked out. His rooms were in the far wing and a long way away from the main halls and the dancers. As much as he'd enjoyed the dance over the years, he enjoyed his solitude more. Always had.

He wound his way through the dark hallways. He couldn't smell anyone in the rooms he passed, but he wasn't surprised. This wing was part of the old section and hadn't yet been fitted with central heating. He doubted it ever would be. As big as the pack was, the mansion was bigger—a rambling network of rooms and halls that had once been filled to the brim with laughing cubs, but never would be again. Not these days. All the packs had to be watchful about birth control. Human law forbade any pack growing beyond a certain size. Werewolves and shape-shifters may have finally been acknowledged in the eyes of the law, but lawmakers the world over still feared the consequences of allowing them to breed unchecked.

As if they could ever compete with human birth rates, he thought sourly.

In the silence of the long halls, the wind seemed to howl, battering at the roof and windows. In the chill sharpness of the air he could smell snow. A Ripple Creek Special was definitely headed their way.

He walked into his suite. The air here was almost icy, thanks in part to the row of French doors lining the outer wall. He closed the drapes then walked over to the fireplace and stoked the fire to life. If it was this cold now, they'd certainly need its warmth by dawn.

When the fire blazed, he headed into the bedroom. Neva was sound asleep in his bed, and he stopped, caught by the sheer beauty of her. Her long hair was a river of gold that swept across her pillow. And in sleep, she looked so angelic, so innocent, it was hard to believe she could be anything else.

But the fact was, she could be. She was here for a reason, and until he discovered that reason, he had no choice but to keep on pushing her.

And it was certainly a task part of him *did* enjoy. Maybe he was more like René than he cared to admit.

He stripped and climbed into bed. She stirred, murmuring something he couldn't quite catch before turning away from him. He spooned behind her, pressing himself against the warmth of her skin and the richness of her scent. Her very closeness had the heat surging through his veins, and he wanted her so badly it was painful. Their lovemaking tonight would be hard and fast. It couldn't be anything else when the fever burned so fiercely through his veins, and it was what he needed to do to keep on pushing her.

He slid a hand down her belly to the triangle of hair between her thighs. She was still so gloriously wet with need, even though a couple of hours had slipped by since he'd touched her. She shifted under his caress, pressing back against him. It was a sleepy invitation he was more than ready to accept. He slid deep inside her, groaning at the sheer glory of it. She felt so good, so hot and firm.

She woke. Though she didn't move, a sound that was part pleasure, part surprise, and part anger whispered from her lips. He wrapped an arm around her waist, holding her still as he continued to thrust inside her. With the urgency of the moon driving him so hard, there was nothing gentle about it now. He claimed every inch of her, delving so deep, her taut muscles quivered against the entire length of him.

The red tide rose, becoming a wall of pleasure he could

not deny. He came, a hot, torrential release whose force tore a shout from his lips and sent his body rigid.

But the moon and he weren't finished yet. Not by a long shot. He withdrew and tugged her around to face him. Her eyes flashed with anger, but before she could say anything, he claimed her lips. He kissed her, caressed her, licked every inch of her, until her scent and her taste were imprinted on every fiber of his being, inside and out. Then he loved her.

And continued to make love to her through the rest of the night and well into dawn.

A constant rattling woke Neva many hours later. She groaned and flung the thick comforter off her face, then squinted in the general direction of the noise. Though the clock on the bedside table said it was nearly eleven, the day beyond the rattling French doors was dark and filled with a swirling whiteness. She blinked, but the image didn't seem to get any clearer.

It was a blizzard, she realized. And while Ripple Creek had a reputation for wild and sudden spring storms, this one looked like a doozey.

But for once, maybe it was a good thing. Maybe it would keep the killer away and the dancers safe for one more night. Surely not even the most ardent dancer would chance weather like this.

She yawned and rolled onto her back. Duncan wasn't in bed with her, and she had no idea when he'd left. But if the lack of warmth on his side of the silk sheets was anything to go by, he'd been gone a while. Maybe even immediately after he'd finished loving her senseless.

Heat flushed her cheeks, and she closed her eyes. She

had no idea what to think about this morning's efforts. He'd been harsh and uncaring one moment, taking what he wanted and giving nothing in return. Then he'd turned it all around and become so generous, so caring and thoughtful, she all but melted for him. He'd pushed her through such a gamut of emotions in a few short hours that she felt burned out, physically *and* emotionally.

She still didn't know how she felt about him, other than the fact he confused her. Totally and utterly. She should hate him—every sane, rational cell in her body knew that. She wasn't sure that she did, and yet she wasn't sure that she liked him, either.

And the fact she was so uncertain frightened her.

As did the jealousy that had risen when she'd smelled Betise on his skin last night. For the briefest of moments she'd wanted to rip out the throat of the older wolf—a territorial emotion she had no right to, and no true desire for. Not when it came to someone like Duncan, a loner who was after nothing more than enjoyment.

And in truth, she shouldn't really have been surprised he'd enjoyed himself with Betise before coming back to her. Not if they were soul mates. The only *truly* surprising thing was the fact that he'd come back to her at all.

She rubbed a hand across her brow. Her head ached, but it was probably nothing more than lack of sleep. She'd had little more than three hours overall, and given what had happened over the last few nights, it was nowhere near enough. Not that she was likely to catch up on any more sleep over her remaining days here. Duncan had certainly made that perfectly clear this morning.

A tremor ran through her, and she wasn't sure if it was excitement or trepidation. Maybe it was both. What she needed right now was someone sane to talk to. Someone like her sister. And while Savannah would probably go ballistic when she realized what Neva was doing, she was the only one who *would* understand. After all, Sav had done some pretty damn crazy things herself in the past.

She reached out with her thoughts. Warmth sparked briefly through the fog of memories in her sister's mind, then faded. Consciousness was close, but not yet close enough. Neva sighed. She was briefly tempted to call Ari, but she knew her friend would probably tell her to forget about feelings and just enjoy the dancing. Though Ari would have a fit if she realized Neva was at the mansion rather than tucked away safe and sound in boring old Eagle.

Sighing again, she thrust aside the comforter and climbed out of bed. The chill hit her immediately, and she shivered, grabbing Duncan's robe off the end of the bed. The black silk whispered sensually across her skin, and the scent of spice and forest enveloped her. Desire rippled through her. Why was she so attuned to his scent and his touch? Or was it simply a matter of her inexperience being totally overwhelmed by a man whose skills at the dance were almost legendary?

Frowning, she thrust the question aside and headed out to the sitting room, wincing slightly at the ache in her muscles. No one had ever told her dancing could be so . . . active. But then, no one had ever told her it could be frustrating one moment and totally amazing the next. And the couple of mates she'd had before Duncan certainly hadn't prepared her to be played by a master.

She stoked the fire with more wood, then padded back through the bedroom and into the bathroom. To discover someone had very recently poured her a bath. Two towels had been placed on a chair at the end of the big old claw-foot bath, along with shampoo and soap. She picked up the bar of soap and sniffed it lightly. The faint scent of citrus teased her nostrils. Her favorite. She wondered how he'd known, given she'd been wearing Jasmine when they'd first met. Then she remembered he'd been in her house. And in her bed.

Heat flushed through her again. Even thinking about the damn man made her want him. The moon, she thought, had a lot to answer for. And yet there seemed more than just the moon fever between them, which, in itself, was crazy thinking because it could never be anything more than what it was now. Because of Betise.

Damn it, she didn't even know if she *liked* the man. And why in hell was she even worrying about it? Once this moon phase was over, she'd never see him again. Which is what she'd wanted—planned—from the very beginning.

Only she wasn't so sure it was what she wanted now.

Crazy. She was definitely going crazy.

She stripped off the robe and climbed into the bath, sighing in pleasure as she eased into the hot water. She soaked in the sweet-smelling tub until the water began to cool, then washed. Climbing out, she grabbed the towels, wrapping one around her hair and using the other to dry herself. Then she padded into the bedroom to grab some fresh clothes from her bag.

She was sitting on the bed brushing her hair when the sensation hit her. Heat flashed white hot across her skin and fear clawed at her, making it next to impossible to breathe. There'd only been one other time in her life when she'd felt something like this—like someone had reached into her chest and attempted to pull out her heart. It had happened when she was eight years old and Savannah had been about to get caught in an avalanche. The link between them had saved Sav's life back then. Maybe it was about to save it again.

She reached for her sister, but the response was still the same, and Neva thrust to her feet. Blizzard or not, she had to get down to the hospital. Now.

She shoved on her shoes and ran to the French doors. She couldn't chance going through the halls and running into Duncan. He'd undoubtedly stop her, and he'd definitely want an explanation—something there was no time for. She'd have to leap from the balcony and hope the snow was deep enough to cushion her.

The wind ripped the doors from her hands, smashing them back against the walls. Snow swirled in, thick, fast and oh-so cold. She shivered and battled the storm to the balcony's edge. The world beyond was a sheet of white. She couldn't see the ground let alone the trees. She climbed over the rail, hanging by her fingertips for several seconds as the wind battered her sideways, then let go.

She hit the ground with a grunt, falling backwards into a thick snowdrift. Wild flurries of white danced around her, quickly coating her body. She rolled onto her hands and knees and called to the wolf within.

It came in a rush of power, and she leapt forward on all fours. But the snow was thick and soft under her pads, forcing her to bound rather than run, and the fear swelled. She was running out of time. And so was Savannah.

She surged through the main gates and down into the trees. The snow here was lighter, allowing her to pick up speed. But the wind tore at her coat, and it felt like the ice in the air was invading every pore. She was so cold it hurt to move. Not even the thick winter coat of a wolf provided much protection against the force of a storm like this.

She couldn't yet see the lights of Ripple Creek, and normally they would have been visible by now. The fierceness of the storm was whiting everything out. She leapt the stream and raced on, her heart slamming against her rib cage and her tongue lolling as she battled for breath.

The minute she came out of the protection of the trees, the wind hurled her sideways. She tumbled downhill, gathering momentum until she smashed into a tree. She yelped, and pain rose in a red tide through her body.

Neva?

The tremulous voice cut through the pain, blanketing her mind, and joy swept through her. *Sav, I'm coming.*

She scrambled to her feet and, ignoring the ache in her ribs, ran on. The smell of wood smoke and humanity stung the freezing air. She was close to Ripple Creek, even if she couldn't yet see it.

There's someone here.

Oh God. *Who?*

Confusion swirled through the link between them. Savannah was holding on to consciousness by the slenderest of margins, and if she slipped away, she'd die, of that Neva was certain.

I don't . . . Her voice faded away.

Savannah!

Here. But her reply was soft. Distant.

Neva raced down Main Street, suddenly glad for the storm. At least she didn't have to worry about traffic. *What do you smell? Tell me.*

Age. Death. Antiseptic.

Sav didn't realize she was in the hospital, obviously. *Look beyond that.*

Sour milk.

Sour milk? What on earth did that mean? *Give me more, Savannah. You're a wolf and a ranger. Use your skills, damn it.*

The link was silent for a long moment. Neva raced left onto South King Street and saw the warm glow of lights through the icy whiteness. She wasn't that far away now.

I remember that smell. It belonged to the wolf who attacked me.

Fear flashed though her, spreading like fire through her body, lending her feet greater speed. *He's in the hospital with you?*

Not in the room. Sav hesitated. *But close.*

Can you see him?

No. Can't see anything. Bandages.

Neva felt like cursing. The severity of the wounds on her sister's face had forced many painstaking hours of microsurgery, and most of Savannah's face and neck had been bandaged.

Listen, then. What do you hear?

Footsteps. Coming closer.

She was never going to get there in time. *Feel for the buzzer, Savannah. Call the nurse.*

It might be the nurse.

Not if she smells the same as the wolf who attacked you. None of the nurses in the hospital smell like sour milk.

Neva changed shape as she raced through the hospital's main entrance. An almost overwhelming tide of emotion hit her—not Savannah's, not hers, just the misery and pain of countless hospital patients, past and present, lingering in the air. She slammed up her shields, but the emotive swirl still seeped past, making her ache. And her parents wondered why she refused to come to the hospital much.

She continued on towards the stairs, knowing she couldn't afford to wait for the elevator. Not when the killer was in the hospital and going after Savannah. Nurses shouted after her, telling her to slow down, telling her visiting hours weren't for another two hours. She ignored them and took the stairs two at a time.

She crashed through the door to the third floor corridor and raced down the hall. There were nurses running ahead of her, and fear surged. Both hers and Savannah's.

Surely the murderer couldn't have gotten to her sister. Sav was still listed as critical, and no one but immediate family was supposed to be allowed in the room. Down the far end of the hall the exit door slowly closed. Was it the killer retreating or someone else?

The nurses are here. He's not. Savannah's mind voice was stronger. *He's left. Don't give chase.*

Like hell she wouldn't. She was not only going to go after him, but she was going to kill the bastard. Going to grab his mind and fry his brain with emotion.

No! Savannah's horror stung her mind.

He has to be stopped, Neva said grimly.

He has to face the weight of the courts, not be killed.

Neva snorted. *Yeah, right. With good behavior he'd be out in ten or less. That's not enough punishment for what he's done.*

I'm a ranger, Neva. I can't condone vigilante behavior, and I certainly can't let you do this.

I made promises to the moon—

I don't care. You can't do this. I won't let you.

Right now, you can't stop me.

If you want to do something, follow his trail. But nothing else. Promise me.

Neva hesitated under the weight of her sister's fury.

Promise not to kill him! Sav all but yelled.

Neva winced and sighed. While she still so desperately wanted to avenge what had been done to Savannah, she also knew her sister was right.

All right. I promise. She slid to a stop outside her sister's room. There were two nurses inside, and Savannah was waving her hand weakly at them and trying to get up.

Are you all right? Neva asked.

Yes.

Then lie down and lie still.

Damn it, you can't do this—

Sister, you have no idea what I can and can't do. Believe me. Up until a few days ago, even *she* hadn't been aware of the extremes she'd go to in order to protect those she loved.

Savannah's sigh was a warm breeze through Neva's mind. *Just make sure you don't get too close.*

Neva's smile was grim. She didn't have to get close to use her empathic abilities. All she had to do was find him. And she'd keep her promises—both of them. The killer would experience the pain he'd inflicted on Savannah and the others, but she wouldn't kill him.

And part of her was extremely glad of that fact.

She continued on and pushed open the exit door. Footsteps rattled down the steps below her, and the smell of sour milk stung the air. She leaned over the railing, briefly catching sight of a lone figure with black hair wearing a white coat—the sort of coat doctors wore. Then the door below opened, and he was gone. She raced down the stairs and flung open the lobby door.

No white-coated male to be seen anywhere. She sniffed the air and followed the scent toward the exit. The doors swished open, and the chill of the storm swept in. She shivered and headed out, even though there was no hope of finding a scent in this sort of weather. She did find the coat in the trash can near the entrance and saw a trail of footsteps leading away. She followed for a little while, but they were quickly obliterated by the storm.

Cursing, shivering, she headed back to the hospital to talk to her sister.

Duncan leaned back in the chair and rubbed his eyes as the words on the computer screen began to blur. He'd only been sitting here for a couple of hours, but he'd had little more than an hour's sleep in the last twenty four, and probably three or four in the last forty-eight. He had to be getting old. Once upon a time he could have gone four or five days on that amount of sleep.

The phone beside the computer rang. He swiveled the chair and rested his feet on the edge of the desk as he picked up the receiver.

"Duncan Sinclair," he said, stifling a yawn.

"Lance here. Got those search results you wanted."

Lance Wilton was a computer geek he'd met while whiling the days away in jail. Lance was a hacker beyond compare, but he'd liked to drink just a little too much and had very few qualms about driving when drunk. He'd ended up almost killing someone and, in the end, had landed in prison for five years.

"That was quick work."

"Hey, you saved my life by getting me this dream of a job. It's the least I can do."

Duncan smiled. Lance's dream job was developing software for Tye's small but profitable company. Being stuck in front of a computer screen for long hours was not a job *he* would have considered a dream, but he'd always been a wolf who preferred work that gave him the freedom to roam.

"Did you come up with any connection among the four victims?"

"Other than the fact they all lived in Ripple Creek and were regular attendees of the dance, no."

"What about Levon Grant? Anything interesting on him?"

"He's squeaky clean. No police record, never even had a parking ticket. School records show he was a middle range student who didn't live up to the potential he showed. He apparently hated sports, but loved debating. Never did drugs or alcohol, but was an outspoken advocate in saving oneself for marriage."

The word boring came to mind, but then, most of the wolves from the golden tribe tended to be. It was only the current generation who were starting to break the leash of control and at least enjoying life—and the dance. Though some, like Neva, were doing so more reluctantly than others.

"What about Nancy Grant?"

"Ah, now there's a totally different proposition."

Duncan raised an eyebrow. Holier-than-thou Nancy had a past? "Why?"

"Nancy was born and raised on the Bitterroot Reservation over in Idaho. She was an A-grade student until she got in with the wrong crowd, and as a sixteen-year-old was part of a pack that raided the Sinclair stronghold over there and burned it to the ground."

Though he'd been too young to remember it happening, he could recall reading about it in later years. Thirteen people had died that night, and many more were injured. "Was she charged?"

"No. Word is her father slipped a lot of cash to the right people, and a blind eye was turned. She was sent to relatives in Ripple Creek, and that's how she met Levon."

"Anything since then?"

"Quiet as a mouse."

Did that mean her involvement with the raid had merely been a one-time prank that had gone horribly wrong? Or did the anger that had led to the raid still simmer deep inside? "Did you find any connection between Nancy and the four murdered women?"

"None. But you'd probably uncover more by talking to her relatives in that respect."

Probably. Only he very much doubted whether her relatives would tell him the time of day right now. Which left him with Neva—and she certainly wasn't going to tell him anything willingly. "Nothing else on either of them?"

"Nothing you wouldn't already know."

He hesitated. "You want to check into the Bitterroot raid a bit more? See if you can get names and perhaps trace what has happened to those who were charged?" It was always possible one or two of the others had recently gathered in Ripple Creek and old prejudices had flared. It was certainly a link worth exploring.

"Sure. I'll get back to you."

"Thanks for your help, Lance."

"No prob."

Duncan hung up, then glanced across at the window as the glass rattled. The Ripple Creek Special had well and truly hit. They'd only get the diehards at the dance tonight, that was for sure.

He looked at the computer screen again, then grimaced and reluctantly continued his search. He'd spent most of his time this morning going though the on-line news. Something must have triggered the start of these murders three weeks ago, and if it was at all newsworthy, it would be mentioned in one of the papers somewhere. A long shot, but one worth trying. He had very little else to try right now—at least until his father got those test results back from the samples Martin had taken from Betise. Talking to his brothers again had provided nothing new in the way of clues.

He worked his way through the remainder of last week's news reports for last week and was just about to give up when he caught sight of a small photo that looked horribly familiar. Something clenched in his gut as he enlarged the image.

Neva. In a ranger's uniform.

Impossible. There was no way on this Earth she was a ranger.

He glanced down at the name under the caption. Savannah Grant. Neva's sister—twin sister, if this photo was anything to go by. And now that he knew, he could see the slight differences. Neva's mouth was slightly lusher, the look in her eyes less analytical, and her hair longer.

He quickly read the accompanying article. Savannah had been attacked and left in critical condition while continuing investigations at the scene of the last murder. Her attacker and the murderer were believed to be one and the same.

Which meant it was more than possible Neva was here to find her sister's attacker, not spy on what he was doing. And if that were the case, they'd been working on the same side all along, despite his conclusions to the contrary.

He swore softly and rubbed a hand across his eyes. What a goddamn mess. He stared at the photo a few seconds longer, then thrust up from the chair. It was time he got some answers, and if she wasn't forthcoming, he'd force them out her. She already loathed him, so it didn't really matter anymore.

He strode down the silent corridors, unable to believe no one had bothered mentioning the fact that Neva had a sister who was a ranger. A sister who was lying critically ill in the hospital. But then, maybe his father and brothers had presumed he knew.

Nor could he believe she'd go to such lengths to track down her sister's attacker. To come to the dance and give herself willingly to pleasure when it went against everything she'd ever believed in was an incredible act of selflessness. And, in many ways, also incredibly stupid. The killer had almost overwhelmed her sister—a trained ranger. What made Neva think she'd fare any better?

But if it *was* the killer who'd attacked Savannah, then that surely crossed Nancy Grant's name off the suspect list—or would, if they'd actually had a list of suspects. She might be against the dance, but there was no way she'd attack her own daughter. Not from what he'd seen of her, anyway.

Which led him to another question—why did Neva believe the killer was here at the mansion? What information had her sister given her?

The wind whistled icily around his ankles as he entered

the old section, and he frowned. It felt like there was a door open somewhere. These halls were normally cold, but not *this* cold. Or windy.

He opened the door to his suite only to be greeted by a snow storm. He cursed loudly and made his way into the bedroom, where the storm seemed to be originating. Neva wasn't there. And the French doors were wide open. He swore again and walked out onto the snowbound balcony. She'd gone, and if the depth of snow inside the bedroom was any indicator, she'd left at least an hour ago. He swept his gaze across the swirling whiteness and knew something bad must have happened for her to leave in a storm like this. And that something undoubtedly involved her twin. If she was willing to risk her reputation and her relationship with her parents to find the man who'd attacked her sister, this storm certainly wouldn't provide much of a challenge.

He spun and walked back into the bedroom, closing the French doors behind him. He swept a disparaging glance around the mess, then picked up the phone and called his father.

"I'm going to Ripple Creek," he said the minute Zeke answered. "I may or may not be back tonight, depending on what the storm does."

"Why?" His father didn't sound surprised, but then, he'd raised four sons who all walked the wild side of life. Maybe nothing they did surprised him any longer.

"Neva's gone."

"Well, you were expecting her to run. Looks like you've achieved your aim."

"I don't think she's running from me. Did you know Neva had a sister?"

"Of course. She's a ranger."

"The ranger who was attacked the day after the last murder."

Zeke swore softly. "I knew a ranger had been attacked, but it never occurred to me to find out who."

And he obviously hadn't read the newspaper, or he would have seen the photo and article. "It puts a somewhat different spin on her possible reasons for being here."

"Maybe." Doubt edged his father's voice. "Though part of me doubts *anyone* from the golden tribe would go to such lengths merely to avenge an attack. They tend to be pacifists."

Nancy Grant wasn't. And Neva certainly appeared to have inherited some of that fire. "Lance came through with some interesting information." He quickly filled his father in on everything Lance had said.

"Detrek's the head of the Sinclair pack over in Bitterroot, and an old friend of mine. I'll give him a call and see what he remembers of the night."

"Good. I'm not sure how or why the two could possibly be connected, but it's certainly something worth checking."

"Especially given we've got very little to go on so far." Zeke hesitated. "I'm posting security at all entrances tonight. I know the storm will deter some dancers, but I'm not risking another death. The guards will stay until after the full moon."

"Good idea." Anything that made life difficult for the murderer was worth trying. "Give me a call on my cell phone if you get the results back from the samples we took off Betise."

"Will do. Just be careful out in that storm."

"I will." He hung up, then stripped the sodden comforter and sheets off the bed and shoved them down the laundry chute. He relit the fire to help dry the rest of the room, then grabbed his jacket and headed out to find Neva.

Neva wrapped her hand around Savannah's warm fingers. She'd been allowed to stay with her sister a little longer, though it had been against the doctor's recommendation and only at Sav's insistence.

"The rangers have been called," she said softly. "Once they get here, make sure you arrange for twenty-four hour protection."

"Don't start trying to tell me how to do my job." Sav's voice was little more than a harsh whisper, but Neva had never heard a sweeter sound. "And why are your hands like ice?"

"Came through a snow storm to get here, and I got both wet and cold when I chased the killer back outside."

"You should go home and change before you catch a chill."

"Right now, catching a chill is the least of my worries."

Sav's curiosity swam around her. "Where in hell were you, anyway? It felt farther away than either the diner or your place."

She hesitated, but there was really no putting off the truth. Sav would have to know sooner or later, and right now, Neva needed help from someone who knew what they were doing. Someone who could possibly see the clues she was missing. She took a deep breath, then said, "I've been continuing your investigations."

With Sav's face bandaged, Neva couldn't see her reaction. But she could feel it. And right now, her sister was annoyed . . . and more than a little apprehensive.

"What do you mean?"

"I mean I raided your office and read the files." She hesitated again, then added, "And I've been up at the mansion."

The sense of apprehension increased. "Doing what?"

Celebrating the moon with an incredible man I can't quite hate. She cleared her throat and hoped like hell her sister didn't catch the thought. She still had her shields up, but with the two of them, that often didn't mean much. "Your files suggested the Sinclairs were high on your list of suspects. So, I've been talking to them."

"*We* can't get them to talk to us. How would you be able to?"

She didn't suspect, Neva thought. Or didn't imagine. But before she could answer, a babble of voices rose from outside the corridor. Angry voices, male and female. One was altogether too familiar—as was the scent that touched the air. Neva closed her eyes and silently swore. The last thing she needed right now was for Duncan to make an appearance.

Footsteps echoed—a sharp tattoo that spoke of anger. A nurse came into the room, face flushed and blue eyes irate.

"Sorry Miss Grant," she said, her gaze seeking Neva's. "But there's a man outside who claims to be your mate, and he demands to be let in the room."

Savannah's shock stung the air. Neva took a deep breath and slowly released it. So much for keeping her tryst with Duncan a closely guarded secret. And given who her father was, the whole damn town would know tomorrow. "Let him in."

The nurse spun and marched back out. Savannah's grip on Neva's hand grew fierce.

"By the moon's light, Neva, what in hell have you done?"

Eight

What hadn't she done? Especially in the last forty-eight hours? Heat flushed Neva's cheeks, and she was suddenly glad her sister's face was still bandaged.

"I told you. I was up at the mansion."

"But to join the moon dance?" Sav's voice was incredulous. "Even *I'm* not that foolhardy."

"I told you I was going to find the bastard and make him pay for what he did."

Sav took a deep breath and slowly released it. "Who did you use to gain entry?"

"Duncan. He's the only one you didn't have under suspicion."

"And the wildest. He even spent a few days in jail."

"For drunk-driving related offenses."

"He's a repeat offender. A fool."

Neva had no doubt Duncan would probably now be the first to admit it. And then wondered why in hell she was tempted to rise to his defense. Duncan certainly didn't seem to care what anyone thought about him, so why should she?

Sav was silent for a moment, and the sharp rap of approaching boot heels seemed to echo as loudly as Neva's heart. And she wasn't sure if it was trepidation or merely the excitement of being close to him once again.

"I can understand why you did it," Sav said quietly. "Because I know if anyone ever hurt you, I'd do whatever it took to bring them in. But moons, you'd better hope Mom and Dad don't find out."

Neva smiled grimly. "They know about Duncan. They just don't know I'm up at the mansion."

"Oh God—" Sav cut the rest of her words off as Duncan entered the room.

Neva met his gaze. His dark eyes were still shuttered, his face impassive. It was impossible to even guess what he was thinking right now. He stepped toward them, and suddenly the room didn't seem big enough. Nor did it contain enough air.

"Did you have to tell the nurse you were my mate?" she snapped, annoyed by both his presence here at the hospital and her continuing reaction to him. The moon wasn't even *out* at the moment, so why was she still feeling a buzz of excitement?

He raised an eyebrow. "It's the truth, is it not?"

His rich voice was neutral and gave no clue as to his thoughts. "Only as far as this moon phase goes."

He shrugged. "Why didn't you tell me about your sister?"

She wondered how he'd found out. Betise, perhaps? "Would you have allowed me entry into the mansion if I had?"

"No."

"Then that's your answer."

He studied her for a moment, then switched his gaze his Savannah. "Are you going to introduce us?"

She did. Savannah didn't offer him her hand, just turned her bandaged face in his direction. Imprinting his smell, Neva knew. Feeling his thoughts. She wondered if Sav would have more luck than she had.

No. Sav's mind voice sounded tired. *But I like the smell of him.*

So did Neva. His smell and his taste and his touch. She just didn't know if she liked the *man*.

"Why are you here, Sinclair?" Savannah asked, voice getting hoarser. "The dance is tonight. You have no right to the days as well."

"In this case, I do."

Moons, Neva, you didn't agree to a bonding, did you?

Afraid so. Seemed logical at the time.

And now?

I'm discovering I'm a little wilder in nature than I ever thought.

The warmth of Savannah's smile ran around her.

That's something we all discover, sooner or later.

"Would you two mind keeping the conversation to conventional methods?" Duncan said. "Because there are several things we need to discuss."

"Like what?" Neva and Savannah said in unison.

A small smile touched his sensual lips and just as quickly fled. "Like why you believe the killer is one of the Sinclairs and not one of the dancers who join us."

"Considering how little help you Sinclairs have been to our investigations," Savannah bit back, "do you really think it's surprising we suspect one of you?"

"On what evidence? The fact that it's a big silver wolf?" Duncan snorted softly. "I can name half a dozen silvers in all the packs that match that description."

"But those same wolves don't have the . . . shall we say zealous? . . . reputation that the Sinclair pack have when it comes to the dance."

"In all the years the Sinclairs have run the moon dance, there's never been a death. Until now. It's not one of us."

"And, of course, I can trust the word of a felon," Savannah snapped.

He didn't react in any way. Not physically, nor

emotionally. Maybe he'd been expecting such a reaction from Savannah, who was, after all, an officer of the law. "If you won't trust the word of a felon, then it's not much use me offering what I know, is it?" He glanced at Neva, obsidian eyes slightly narrowed. "You and I need to talk. I'll wait outside for you."

He walked from the room. Savannah puffed out a breath. "If that man looks half as sexy as he sounds, wow."

Wow seemed nowhere near adequate when it came to describing Duncan. He was a man with a wild past, a man with the face of an angel and a body designed to corrupt the virtuous. A man who could be both incredibly generous and utterly selfish when it came to lovemaking. But above all else, he was a man who held the world at a careful distance. She very much doubted if anyone actually knew the real Duncan Sinclair. Certainly not anyone here in Ripple Creek, anyway.

And maybe not even the man himself.

"You should talk to him about this case. I've got a feeling you're both on the same side on this one."

"I know. But we'll do it on my terms, not his." Savannah's voice was little more than a raw whisper.

Neva switched to telepathy. *Bit hard to do it on your terms—or even your turf—when you're stuck here in the hospital.*

I'll be out in a couple of days.

Your stitches won't even be out in a couple of days.

I don't care about the stitches. I care about catching this killer.

And you have deputies who are more than capable. Use them. Stop trying to do everything by yourself.

This from the wolf who decided to sidestep the official investigation and undertake her own.

Sav's mind voice was dry, and Neva grinned. *I think it's a case of do as I say, not do as I do.*

The nurse stuck her head around the corner. "Time's up," she said. "The doctor wants Savannah to rest a little before your parents get here."

Neva nodded and rose. *I'll keep in contact.*

Make sure you do. And I want to know everything that man says, especially if it's anything related to the case.

Neva hesitated. *You know he can use the bonding to forbid me to mention anything?*

He can't forbid what's a natural part of you—he can't forbid the telepathy we share. Savannah hesitated, and her thoughts become a touch grim. *Believe me, I know.*

Neva raised an eyebrow. *I sense a story I haven't been told.*

Savannah waved a hand. *Old history.*

But not forgotten hurt, from the sound of it.

Let's just say I know a little about being used and leave it at that.

Would you leave it at that?

Sav's smile was a flutter of warmth through her mind.

I guess not. I'll tell you when I'm feeling stronger.

Neva hesitated, then said, *I've found out a few interesting snippets of information I have to tell you. But later.*

Tonight. Savannah's thoughts were becoming sleepy.

Neva leaned forward and placed a kiss on her sister's nose, then she released her hand and walked out. Duncan leaned against the wall, arms crossed and face impassive. With his damp black hair, the black leather jacket straining across the width of his shoulders, and dark jeans clinging to his lean but powerful legs, he looked sinister and yet so sinfully delicious that desire curled through her. He looked every inch the dark angel—a man who skirted the lines between good and bad, and who didn't seem to give a damn what anyone thought.

And she realized then it didn't even matter what *she* thought of him, because no matter how good it sometimes seemed between them, in the end it was only physical. It never could and never would be anything more than that. All he wanted out of a mate was a few days of pleasure. He didn't believe in love or life mates and certainly wasn't the type to settle down. She wanted all those things. Always had.

She stopped and crossed her arms. "Do you wish to go back to the mansion to talk?"

He shook his head. "The storm is getting more severe. Your place would be better."

She didn't want this man in her house. Didn't want his scent on the air or memories of him to linger once this moon phase was over and he was gone. Nor did she really want to risk her parents dropping by. Right now, she wasn't ready to face them—or the questions they'd undoubtedly have. She glanced out the window, studying the blanketing whiteness for a moment. A motel room really wasn't a good option, though, especially in a town this size. If her parents were determined to find her, they would. All they'd have to do is follow the trail of gossip.

"Let's go," she said, not bothering to look back at him as she moved toward the exit.

He didn't say anything as they walked down the stairs, but as they headed toward the exit, he took off his coat and offered it to her. She glanced at it, then him, and wished she knew what was going on behind the shutters.

"I'm all right, thanks."

"You're so damn cold your lips are practically blue, and goose bumps have become a permanent feature on your skin," he snapped. "Take the damn coat."

She glanced down at the coat he held out, then shifted shape and raced out into the storm. Maybe she was being stupid, but right then she didn't want to be bound to Duncan any more than she already was, even when it came to something as simple as accepting the offer of a coat. She might be obliged to mate with him for the entirety of this moon dance, but she wasn't about to lean on him, not in *any* way. She'd chosen him to be a means to an end, nothing more, though whether he'd let her continue her investigations now that he knew who she was, she didn't know. But undoubtedly soon would.

Her teeth were chattering by the time she reached her house, and the goose bumps he'd mentioned were practically boulders. She flicked on the lights and the heating, then moved into the kitchen to fill up the coffee pot.

"I'm going for a shower," she said, flicking the switch. "Alone."

She turned to face him, and all thought of showering immediately fled at the desire so evident in his dark eyes. Her heart began a double-time dance, and she knew with certainly this time it had nothing to do with fear. Freezing cold or not, she wanted this man with a fierceness that was almost scary. As was the fact that she'd never felt anything like this before. But then, she'd never been with a wolf as wild as Duncan before. Her previous mates had been sensible choices—the sort of wolves her parents would have approved of.

She stood her ground, and he stopped, leaving only inches between them. The heat of him melted the ice from her skin, and the wave of his anger and passion burned at her mind. She might have her shields at full strength, but right now she was feeling this man's emotions all too clearly.

"Tell me one thing." His voice was soft. Emotionless. But his dark gaze held hers with an intensity that curled her toes. "Is Savannah the reason you're at the mansion?"

She nodded, wishing he'd touch her. Hoping he didn't. Crazy, that's what she was.

"You joined the dance for no other reason than to hunt down her attacker?"

Again she nodded. With the emotive soup of passion and need and hunger swirling around her, through her, she could do little else.

"And no one else knew of your decision?"

She couldn't help a derisive snort. "Not until you announced to the whole damn hospital ward that I was your mate this moon phase."

Something flickered in his eyes. What, she wasn't sure, though she doubted it was regret. This man didn't seem to regret anything he did.

He ran the back of his fingers down her cheek, his gentle touch sending a shiver of longing through every fiber of her being. Then he dropped his hand and stepped back.

"Go have your shower."

She stared at him for a moment, wondering what sort of game he was playing now. Or was it merely an extension of the same one? His behavior over the last day certainly suggested he enjoyed stirring her to the point of climax then pulling back, and while she was nowhere near that point at the moment, his closeness had her so hot it wouldn't take much to reach it.

"Go," he said when she didn't move. "I'll rustle up something to eat."

She went, though in truth, it was really the last thing she wanted to do. By the time she'd showered and changed, the aroma of deep fried chicken wafted through the air. Her stomach rumbled a reminder that she hadn't eaten breakfast, and she hurriedly dried and brushed her hair before padding barefoot down the stairs.

Stopping in the doorway, she watched him dish up two plates of chicken and vegetables. He'd taken off his coat and rolled up his sleeves, and he looked so completely at home in her kitchen that something stirred in her heart. He glanced up, his dark gaze catching hers and seeming to delve deep into her soul. The intensity that flared between them went beyond the natural heat of moon-spun lust. It was deeper, stronger. But just how deep or strong was something she had no intention of finding out. Such exploration would only lead to a disaster with this man.

"That smells good," she said, breaking the moment and refusing to contemplate what that moment actually was.

He picked up the two plates and brought them over to the table. "Living on my own for so long has taught me to cook. Eat up, while it's still hot."

It was hard to imagine Duncan being on his own for *any* length of time. And he'd hardly have the reputation he had if he was. She sat down on the opposite side of the table from him, picked up the knife and fork, and quickly discovered the meal tasted as good as it looked. They ate in silence, and when they'd both finished, he took the plates over to the sink and poured them both a mug of coffee.

"So," he said, sitting down once again. "You want to

explain why you and your sister are so adamant the killer is hiding in the Sinclair mansion?"

"You want to explain why you think he isn't?"

His smile was grim. "I know my family. They're many things, but they're not killers."

She raised an eyebrow. "Even you?"

He met her gaze squarely, and though his face was expressionless, his exasperation and anger stirred around her. "Even me."

She leaned back in her chair and contemplated him over the rim of her coffee cup. "Then why did you go to jail?"

"You mean you haven't already gotten all the details from your sister?"

"She's only just woken, so I haven't had time." Besides, she wanted to know just how willing he was to be honest with her now that he knew what she wanted—and why she was at the mansion. "But I do know it was drunk driving related. Did you kill someone?"

"No. And I didn't spend a lot of time in jail—just enough for the police to find the evidence that backed my story. "

"Not a lot of time could be one month or one year, depending on your point of view," she said dryly.

He didn't react, though the anger touching the air increased. In some regards, that surprised her. After all, he didn't seem to care what anyone else thought, so why did it matter what she thought?

"In this case, it was only a couple of days while the police checked my story, and only because I couldn't make bail. A man who suspected I was having an affair with his wife cut the brake lines, and I couldn't stop the car. Luckily for us both, the driver of the car I crashed into wasn't seriously hurt."

"But you *were* drunk at the time."

"Like most wolves, I have a high tolerance for alcohol. I was nowhere near drunk, but I *was* right on the legal limit."

Until the lawmakers decided how to legally deal with the different makeup of humans, werewolves and shapeshifters, all of them had to cope with the laws as they were. And it didn't matter diddly-squat if the legal limit was barely tipsy for a wolf. It was the law, and they had to live with it. "So you got a fine and did community service?"

"Yes."

"So why is it that Savannah thinks you're a felon?"

"Because it's not the first time I've landed in jail for being drunk, though the other times, I wasn't driving."

"So you were a fool thrice over?"

"Yes."

"And were you having an affair with the husband's wife?"

"They were separated."

"So the answer is yes, you were."

He shrugged and didn't answer, his dark gaze as impassive as his thoughts. If not for the mix of exasperation, anger and hunger that burned between them, she would have thought him totally disinterested in both her reaction and *her*.

"Have you seen her since you got out of jail?"

"A fool I might be, but an idiot I'm not. I got the hell out of Denver the minute I legally could."

"And you've been with search and rescue since?"

"Basically."

"And sober?"

"Definitely. I have no intention of ever going back to jail. Being locked up for a couple of days was long enough for me to realize that being locked up for a long time would kill me." He regarded her for a moment, then said, "Satisfied I'm willing to tell the truth?"

It would be easy enough to check the authenticity of everything he'd said, though she really didn't doubt he was telling the truth. "Can I ask one more question?"

He raised an eyebrow. "What?"

"Why did you leave Ripple Creek, and why did you come back?"

"Why I left is none of your damn business, and you've already guessed why I'm back."

She sipped her coffee and mentally made a note to ask Savannah to do some digging into his background—if she hadn't already. "So you *are* here to investigate the murders for your pack?"

"Yes."

He crossed his arms and leaned forward on the table. Hunger slipped between them, caressing her skin with its heat, stirring her mind with its fervor. The deep-down ache increased, and she squirmed, trying to ignore the sensation. She might as well try to ignore the rising of the moon.

"Now," he continued softly. "Are you willing to offer the same sort of honesty?"

She hesitated. "Yes."

"Then tell me why the rangers suspect it is one of the Sinclairs behind the killings."

She took a deep breath and slowly released it. Savannah wasn't going to be happy with her for doing this, but instinct suggested she had to trust him. And right now, instinct was the only thing she *did* trust. She certainly wasn't about to trust common sense, which was currently suggesting she leap this table and dance herself senseless with this beautiful but uncaring man.

"They haven't got anything concrete, and certainly nothing that would be admissible in a court of law."

His dark eyes watched her intently. Hungrily. "But?"

"They found scent trails near two of the three victims that led back into the mansion, and they've identified them as belonging to Kane and Tye."

"Considering they were the ones who found the bodies, that's logical. They undoubtedly found René's scent near the fourth victim, as well as mine."

And probably hers, though it had been well covered by the scent of jasmine. She'd have to remember to tell her sister who was responsible for that particular scent, otherwise the rangers might waste precious time chasing a dead end.

"They also found several hairs on the first and third victims."

He nodded. "From a silver coat."

"No. These were human."

"Really? It wasn't mentioned in the reports I read."

She gave him a long look. "I wouldn't be telling me something like that. Not unless you want it reported back to my sister."

He reached across the table, capturing her hand, turning it palm up. His thumb stroked her wrist, a gentle, almost possessive caress that sent shivers of desire skating across her already overheated skin. "You won't tell on me, will you?"

It wasn't a question, but an order. And the power that slipped between them ensured she'd obey. She tried wrenching her hand from his, but he held her tight.

"You could have just asked. You didn't have to use the moon bond."

"Didn't I?" The smile that touched his sensual lips was laconic. "Considering the lengths you've gone to track down your sister's attacker, I think I'll continue to play it safe."

"So, you're asking me to trust you, but you're not willing to offer the same?" Annoyance bit through her tone, and he smiled.

"If it came down to a choice, you'd take your sister's side every time."

He was still stroking her wrist, and it was beginning to do weird things to her breathing. "Naturally. She's family, and I love her."

"Exactly. While I—" he hesitated, his gaze seeming to deepen. "Mean absolutely nothing to you."

"As little as I do to you." But as her gaze got lost in the obsidian depths of his eyes, she had to wonder if either of them was telling the entire truth.

"And these hairs they found—are they matching or different?"

Right then, she didn't particularly care. His fingers had slipped up her arm and were caressing the inside of her elbow. It felt so damn good desire trembled through her. "Matching," she somehow managed to say.

"Black hair?"

His fingers slipped further up her arm, and the back of his hand brushed against her breast. Her nipples ached to feel his touch, pressing almost painfully against the restrictions of her bra. She swallowed, and said, "I presume so. I only read the prelim reports."

"No chance of getting back into your sister's office and reading the rest?"

His touch retreated back down to her wrist, and she almost groaned in disappointment. "About as much chance as we have of this storm stopping by nightfall."

"Then ask your sister."

"My sister is still listed as critical. She won't be looking at anything for a while yet." Which wasn't exactly the truth. Knowing Savannah, by tomorrow morning she'd be demanding full reports on everything that had happened since she'd been attacked.

"And that's the only evidence the rangers have that's it a Sinclair?"

She raised an eyebrow. "You tell me. You seem to have had better access to the files than I did."

His sudden smile was warm and sexy and all too fleeting. "It's not much evidence to believe that it's one of us, is it?"

"Well, no, but who else could it be?"

He leaned back in his chair, the shutters well and truly in place. It made her uneasy, though why she had no idea. It wasn't as if she'd been able to read too much emotion in his expression anyway.

"Someone who disagrees with the dance, perhaps?" he drawled softly.

The uneasy feeling increased. She eyed him for a moment, then said, "Half the golden pack doesn't like the idea of the dance, me included. Are you trying to imply we have some sort of conspiracy going on?"

"Is it any more implausible than one of the Sinclairs being the murderer?"

"Well, yeah. My pack are strong telepaths. A secret *that* big would not stay secret for long."

He raised a dark eyebrow. "The fact that you're all strong telepaths means you all have strong shields, doesn't it?"

When she reluctantly nodded, he continued, "So why is it implausible?"

"Because my pack aren't murderers."

"And the Sinclairs are?"

She wished he'd get to the point—if he had one. "Well, you Sinclairs do have a rather wild reputation you're not afraid to live up to."

"There's a difference between being wild and being a murderer."

"From what I've heard, a lot of the Sinclair pack walk the edge."

"Walking the edge doesn't make us murderers."

"No." She hesitated, then put her coffee cup on the table and crossed her arms. "So, who do you suspect?"

He studied her for a moment, face impassive, dark eyes hard. The air around her practically buzzed with tension—both his and hers.

"Your mother was born on the Bitterroot Reservation over in Idaho, wasn't she?"

It felt like he'd punched her. Her breath left in a whoosh of air, and for several seconds, she couldn't even breathe. Couldn't do anything more than look at him in horror.

"Did you know," he continued mercilessly, "that as a sixteen-year-old she took part in a raid of the Sinclair stronghold over there and burned it to the ground?"

"*No.*"

"Yes." His voice was monotone. Relentless. "Thirteen people died that night, and many more were injured. Your mother was never charged because her old man paid off the right people."

She slapped her palms on the table and thrust upright. "Get out."

His smile was grim. "She's done it once, Neva. She could easily do it again."

"I said, get out." Her voice shook with the force of the fury rolling through her.

"A good investigator considers all options."

"My mother is not an option. Now get the hell out of my house."

He didn't move. Didn't even blink. Might have been made of stone, and she was certain his heart was.

"Then perhaps you should consider your father," he said, his rich voice as cold as the storm outside. "Did you know he'd been questioning Betise about who was dancing with whom up at the mansion?"

She'd been questioning Betise—and the older wolf had certainly never mentioned her father doing the same. And she would have, if only because Betise hated Neva's father. It was actually doubtful whether she'd give him the time of day. "I said get out. I meant it."

"Your days and nights are mine, little wolf. I'm not going anywhere."

"You're a . . ." Words failed her. Somehow, bastard just didn't seem strong enough.

His smile contained little warmth. "So you keep saying."

She hit him. Not physically, but emotionally. Hit him with all the anger and humiliation and pain that had built up over the past couple of days. Although his shields were up, the force of her emotive blow still leeched all color from his face and thrust him backwards, off the chair and onto the floor.

"It's not a nice feeling, is it?" His voice was little more than a hoarse whisper, and beads of sweat dribbled down his face. "Having your family as suspects?"

She met his soulless gaze and wondered why in hell this

man got to her so badly. Not just physically, but emotionally. Damn it, if any of the rangers had mentioned her mother's past, would they be now writhing on the floor? Definitely not. She'd be asking them to show her the evidence to prove it. Or running back to her mother to confirm what had really gone on.

But right now, that was something she could not do.

She let the power slip away and slumped back on the chair, covering her face with her hands. After a few seconds, he climbed slowly to his feet. She could feel the heat of his gaze on her, but she refused to look up.

"I'll be back at dusk," he said softly. "And I will claim what I am owed."

His words made her tremble, but it was a reaction that had nothing to do with fear.

And that, she thought, as his footsteps retreated to the door, was a major problem. He could push her buttons as easily as he breathed. He didn't even have to touch her. All he had to do was look at her.

Cold air swirled around her as the back door opened and closed. Shivering a little, she dropped her hands, surprised to find that he really had left. Given the heat that had been flaring between them, she'd expected the conversation to end in bed.

Had half wanted it to.

She rose and walked over to the coffee pot. How could she want a man she hated?

Easy. She didn't really hate him. Never had.

She closed her eyes at the thought but knew it was a truth she finally had to acknowledge. Despite everything he'd done, she *didn't* hate him. In fact she rather liked him, at least when he wasn't being such an arrogant fool.

But what good did such an admission do? It wasn't as if anything could develop between them. It was one moon dance, nothing more. She'd known that going in, and he'd certainly emphasized it more than a few times since.

But that deep down crazy part of her wanted more.

She sighed softly and wondered what the hell she was going to do. Because the one thing she'd feared the most after their very first mating was beginning to happen.

She didn't want to let him go at the end of this moon cycle. Didn't want to walk away. Didn't want *him* to walk away. Just wanted to explore the possibilities that might lie beyond the heat that flared between them.

Which was stupid thinking. Especially when his soul mate didn't live all that far away.

She bit her lip and glanced at the clock. Betise owned a small hair saloon on Main Street. With this storm, it was doubtful whether she'd have any customers.

The perfect time to catch up with her and ask some more questions.

Nine

Duncan shivered and pulled up his jacket collar. As he headed across town to Neeson Jones' place, the force of the wind was pushing him along the street so hard that he was almost running. The old wolf had only recently retired as editor-in-chief of the *Ripple Creek Gazette,* and if there was anyone in this town who'd know all the secrets and hatreds, it would be him.

Though right now, battling this storm and talking to the old wolf were really the last thing he wanted to do. He'd much rather be curling up with Neva in her big old bed, loving her and holding her until the storm had fled. But given what he'd done over the last day or so, it was very doubtful that she'd dance with him willingly. Not during the day, anyway. And he certainly wasn't going to force her. He wasn't *that* callous.

He briefly closed his eyes, remembering her shocked expression, seeing again the hurt and anger shining in her pretty eyes, and swore softly. Part of him had needed to push, had needed to confirm what he already knew in his heart—that she had no part in whatever was going on. But mostly, he just felt like the bastard she kept calling him.

And that he regretted. Very much.

But he'd set his path, and it was too late to change it now. He just had to be thankful the moon was still rising. If nothing else, he at least had the nights to enjoy.

He sped past houses he couldn't really see, their shapes lost to the white blur of the storm. Neeson lived up on

Seventh Street, not far from the building that housed his beloved paper. Duncan wondered why he'd finally decided to retire. Ten years ago, he'd been adamant he'd die on the job.

He swung onto Seventh Street, and the wind hit him broadside, sending him staggering several steps before he caught his balance. The dance was in trouble tonight. It was doubtful if even the most dedicated follower would be willing to battle this storm for the sake of pleasure.

He ran across Neeson's lawn and rang the doorbell. Inside the house, bells chimed an annoying melody that seemed to go on and on. After several minutes he heard shuffling steps approaching.

"Who is it?"

"Duncan Sinclair. I need to talk to you."

The door opened, revealing the stout, silver-haired figure Duncan remembered. But as his gaze met the old man's, he saw the reason for Neeson's retirement. His blue eyes were all but white. The cataracts were so bad he had to be nearly blind.

And the white cane he held confirmed it.

"Come in, come in," Neeson said, opening the door wider. "You want a drink to warm the ice from your bones?"

"Coffee would be good."

Neeson snorted softly as he slammed the door shut. "I can remember a time when you would have sneered at the mere mention of coffee."

"A few days in jail can alter a wolf's thinking," Duncan said wryly.

The old wolf tapped his way down the hall, but once he got to the kitchen, he put the cane down and moved with more assurance. Obviously, he spent most of his time here and didn't have many visitors—or at least many who used the front door.

"So," Neeson said, picking up the coffee pot and feeling for the mugs. "You didn't come here to talk about old times, as we haven't had many. What do you want?"

"I'm trying to hunt down this killer for my pack." He saw no reason to lie to the old man. Neeson might be blind and he might be retired, but he probably still knew more about what was going on in this town than anyone else. And his next words confirmed this.

"Thought you might be, considering you swore ten years ago never to set foot in this . . . what did you call it? 'Blighted town'?"

Duncan smiled. "I don't believe I was that polite."

"I wouldn't have been, either. Darcy set up quite a campaign. Had more than half the town convinced you were the father of his daughter's kid."

"And the other half ready to come after me with shotguns." He kept his voice dry, though in truth, anger still lingered even now. "You think he'd be peeved enough at the outcome to plan a little revenge?"

"No. Darcy wouldn't have the brains to come up with something like this and pull it off. If he intended to come after any of the Sinclairs, he would have done it the old fashioned way. With a gun."

Duncan murmured a thanks as Neeson slid a chipped mug across the table, then said, "What about Nancy Grant?"

Neeson's rheumy gaze studied him for a moment. "You've obviously been digging."

He shrugged, even though he knew the old wolf couldn't see the movement. "I have to start somewhere."

"Nancy Grant isn't what I'd call a start."

"Why not?"

"Because she was sixteen when the Bitterroot fire happened, and she was fueled up on alcohol and drugs. She's been on the straight and narrow since."

"No rumblings whatsoever about the dance?"

"Nothing more than any of the golden tribe."

"What about Levon?"

"Doubtful. Besides, both he and Nancy are golden wolves. The killer is silver."

"The evidence points that way, but it could be planted."

"The rangers don't think so."

True. But then, the rangers were convinced it was someone in the Sinclair pack, despite having no real evidence to prove it. "I'm told Levon was recently asking about the dance and who was partnering who."

"Then the person who told you is a liar."

If Betise was lying, he'd have to find out why—and what she hoped to gain by doing so. "What makes you say that?"

"Because Levon knows the dance is essential. He might hate it—he might not want any of his immediate pack involved with it—but he's never said a word publicly against it, and he'd never try to stop it. Did an interview with him about five years ago. You should read it if you want to get a handle on the man. Very interesting."

He might dig it out, but only because it might give him more insight into Neva. "Have there been any rumblings about the dance in recent months? Has anyone been trying to close it down?"

"There's always rumblings about closing it down. Always will be. But it never is, because everyone fears what might happen if they did."

Duncan swallowed some coffee, then asked, "So, nothing more than the usual grumbling?"

Neeson hesitated. "There has been more than the normal amount of anger directed toward the Sinclairs this last month. Someone is stirring up trouble, but I haven't been able to discover who."

Join the club, Duncan thought. "Where have you been hearing this?"

"Everywhere." Neeson hesitated and smiled. "People seem to equate blindness with deafness. Some of the things I hear amaze even me."

"And what's the opinion on the street about the murders?"

"That it's one of the Sinclairs. That your games have finally crossed the line."

"And your opinion?"

"It's too pat, and it just doesn't feel right." His sudden smile was a touch wistful. "Just the sort of juicy story I loved when I was at the *Gazette*."

"Who's running it now?"

"Some fancy pants from Denver. He's as useless as a neutered dog."

Duncan smiled. "If you hear any more interesting rumors, would you mind letting me know?"

"As long as you come back when this is all over and give me a blow-by-blow account of how you found the killer."

At least someone outside his family thought he'd find the killer. "Planning to submit a story to the *Gazette*?"

Neeson snorted. "And give that asshole a great scoop? No way in hell. I just like knowing outcomes, that's all."

He nodded. It was *that* desire, more than anything, that

had made Neeson a great reporter and an even better chief. "It's a deal."

"Good." Neeson rose and escorted Duncan to the front door. "Where you off to now?"

"I think I'd better talk to my lying source of information."

"Good idea." He opened the door, and Duncan hurriedly left before the icy touch of the wind stole too much heat from the old man's house. Then he shifted shape and ran through the storm, heading towards Betise's house.

Neva thrust through the hair salon's door and slammed it shut behind her. The heat hit her immediately, making her gasp, and she quickly shed some layers.

"Don't tell me," Betise said dryly as she came from the rear section of the salon. "You felt an urgent need to finally cut your hair."

Neva grinned as she took off her ski mask and shook loose her hair. "You and I both know that's not going to happen, so quit asking."

"You sure? You'd look fantastic with a shorter cut styled to suit your features. And it would bring out your eyes more."

"My eyes are just fine the way they are." She shook the snow from the mask and her coats, then draped them over the nearest chair.

Betise crossed her arms and leaned a hip against the counter. "So what can I do for you, then?"

Though the friendliness had not fled from her voice, there was a touch of wariness in her green eyes. And guilt in an emotive trickle leaking past her shields.

Probably because she'd been caught in a lie, Neva

thought grimly. "Why did you tell Duncan my father was asking you about the dance?"

Betise sighed. "I'm sorry, but Duncan was wasting time asking me all sorts of questions."

Hostility rose in a wave, and Neva briefly looked away. She had no right to feel proprietary when it came to Duncan, and if anyone should be angry at sharing, it was Betise.

"But why say something like that?" she said, once she was sure her voice was under control.

"Because he's been away for so long and is the only one in town likely to believe such a silly statement."

That was certainly true. The animosity between her parents and Betise was no secret. Though why her father was so against Betise and not the other regular dancers who came into their diner was something Neva had never been able to understand—or get an answer to.

But maybe it was time she tried again. She should question her mom, at any rate. They'd know she was here— the hospital staff would surely have mentioned it—and she'd much rather confront them than have them seeking her out. Given the way her luck had been running of late, they'd probably walk in and find her and Duncan in the middle of a heated dance. That was something she *didn't* need right now—not if she wanted to start mending bridges.

"I gather he's been harassing you about your parents," Betise continued, sympathy in her voice.

"All but accused my parents of being behind these murders." Neva sat in one of the chairs and stretched her legs towards the heater vent to warm her feet. "My mother may not have the past of a saint, but she's not behind these killings."

"Anyone with half a brain would know that," Betise agreed and pushed away from the counter. "Would you like a soda? Or a coffee?"

Neva hesitated. "Just a half cup, to warm my insides before I venture out again. I have to head up to the hospital to see Savannah."

"She's awake?" Betise moved behind the small screens.

"Yes. And itching to get back to the investigation."

"Good for her." There was the sound of liquid being poured, then Betise asked, "She remember what happened?"

"Right now I don't think she even wants to think about the attack. She just wants to get better and find the killer." Neva hesitated. "Do you mind if I ask a personal question?"

Betise came back out carrying two white mugs. Though her expression was still friendly, the wariness evident in the air became strong enough to almost taste. "Sure."

Neva accepted the full mug with a nod of thanks. "If you and Duncan are soul mates, why are you still apart?"

Betise didn't answer for several seconds, then grimaced and looked away. "Because I was the only one convinced that we were."

Neva blinked. Of all the answers she'd expected, that wasn't one of them. How could you not know your own soul mate? It was a state that transcended the heart, transcended the mind, became a linking of spirit. It was something you just knew and couldn't escape. Or so her father had always claimed. Never having met her soul mate, Neva couldn't say for certainty what it was like. "He didn't believe you were?"

She shook her head. "Duncan's not one to be pinned down, even by a soul mate. So he claimed he felt nothing."

"You knew he'd lie?"

Betise's smile was touched with sadness. "Yes. When a bonding is that deep, you can't help knowing everything the other is feeling. It's instinct."

Neva frowned. Something didn't gel. While she'd sensed no lie in Betise's statement, she hadn't sensed a lie in Duncan's, either, when he'd claimed Betise and he had shared only the one dance and nothing else. So which of them was stretching the truth? And why?

She sipped the coffee and shuddered at its strong, almost bitter taste. It had obviously been sitting in the pot for a while. "Is that why he left?"

Betise hesitated. "Partly, I guess."

"There was another reason?"

"He had a reputation with the ladies. It got him into trouble more than once."

If his behavior then was far wilder than it was now, Neva could understand why. He wasn't exactly the caring, sharing type. "So why haven't you tried to pursue him now that he's back?"

Betise snorted softly. "You heard him deny our relationship. What point is there?"

Plenty, if they were soul mates. For one, it meant Betise could never settle down with another. But maybe that didn't worry her—not as long as she had the moon dance.

She sipped her coffee and decided she'd better get to the point. "I'm going to report your attack to my sister."

"Don't. We're not really sure it's linked, and I don't want the rangers fussing over me."

Neva raised her eyebrows. "But if it *is* linked, you might hold some clue that could catch this fiend."

"It's doubtful. I didn't really see much, and to be honest, the rangers annoy me more than your father."

Neva smiled. "Then tell me, and I'll pass it on to my sister. That way, if there *is* nothing interesting, you don't have the hassle of talking to the rangers."

Betise hesitated, then nodded. "Ask away."

"What did he smell like?"

"Why would that matter? It's not admissible in a court of law."

"Well, no, but it could lead the rangers to our killer."

"I was under the impression they didn't find any scents at the murder scene."

"According to the papers, no. But they did find one at the hospital."

Betise raised an eyebrow. "Hospital?"

Neva couldn't see any point in holding back the information, especially since the head nurse was dating the current editor of the *Gazette*. It was a pretty sure bet it would be the lead story tomorrow morning. "We think the killer may have tried to get to Savannah."

"So you *were* there."

"Yeah. I sensed Savannah was waking and came down."

A smile touched the older wolf's pale lips. "I wondered why Duncan had let you out of his bed. Normally, he'd keep his mates occupied day and night."

Heat touched Neva's cheeks. "Yeah, well, he actually didn't know I slipped away."

Betise considered her for a moment, then said, "My attacker smelled like old sweats."

Not a smell anyone was likely to forget in a hurry, and not the scent she'd chased in the hospital. It was a strong smell that would not dissipate easily, and while the wind had been strong last night, it had been almost nonexistent in at least two of the other attacks. Surely the rangers would have picked up such an unusual aroma. "What did he look like?"

Betise shrugged. "As I said, big. Silver. I was too busy defending myself to take much notice."

"No identifying marks? Scars?"

"None that I saw."

"Eye color?"

"Yellow."

Which was the standard eye color of a true wolf, not any of the packs that lived in Ripple Creek. Were they dealing with an outsider? Perhaps a wolf that had drifted in from one of the other reservations?

"Was his coat silver or gray?"

"It wasn't an old wolf. He was young. Virile."

"So he tried to . . . you know?"

Betise looked away, her face suddenly pale. "Thank the moon you and Duncan were so close. You scared him off."

They'd scared him off but couldn't smell him. Not even on Betise. Odd. Unless she was lying. Or unless, for some strange reason, she knew her attacker and was protecting him.

Which is exactly what Duncan had thought, even if he hadn't come right out and said it.

She put her half-finished coffee to one side and stood. "You're right. I don't think it's the same person."

Betise glanced at her quickly. "Why?"

"Because the rangers aren't sure the murdered women are being raped."

"Really? They implied in the papers that they were."

"And you can believe everything you see in print," Neva said dryly. She picked up her coats and mask and quickly put them on. "I'll still report your attack to Savannah, though I really think you should report it yourself."

Betise's smile was wry. "Given where I was and what I was doing, the rangers aren't going to take it all that seriously."

"*Any* attack is serious. The man who attacked you might just try his luck with someone else." And right now they certainly didn't need another lunatic running around.

"I very much doubt it."

It was a statement that basically confirmed the theory that Betise knew her attacker. "Thanks for the coffee and the info."

"You sure you don't want that hair of yours styled?"

Neva just smiled and opened the door. The wind hit her, almost blowing her back inside. Shivering, she closed the door but remained under the cover of the entrance for a moment, reaching out with her thoughts. There was little response from Savannah—her sister was asleep. No use going to the hospital just yet then.

She glanced up the street. On a normal day, the diner was within easy walking distance. In the midst of a storm, it might as well be in the next county. Or was that cowardice speaking? As much as she knew she had to speak to her parents, she wasn't sure she was ready to do it just yet. But then, would she ever be? She certainly hadn't confronted them before now, and maybe, if Duncan hadn't have forced the issue, she never would have. Moving into her own home had been her only attempt to break the leash, and even then, her parents still had too much control over her life. As Ari had often commented.

But the attack on Savannah, and being with Duncan these last few days, had forced her to see there was more to life—more to *her*—than blindly following the path her parents had set.

And while she had no intention of becoming a frequent visitor at the mansion once this dance was over, she *was* tempted to explore her wilder side. Not so much sexually, not even emotionally. She just wanted to step beyond the boundaries of her life so far and explore possibilities. Discover what else there might be out there for her. True, she was happy enough working at the diner, but it was a job that would always be there. There was a world beyond Ripple Creek to explore. Savannah had taken off years ago on a quest to find herself. Maybe it was way past time *she* did, too.

Only trouble was, that deep down crazy part of her wanted to explore it with Duncan at her side.

She shoved her hands into her pockets and ventured out into the storm. The strength of the wind had, if anything, increased in the last half hour. It was as if nature itself was intent on pushing her back towards the diner rather than home.

She let it blow her along the empty street. The cold began to seep into her bones, despite the multiple layers of clothes, and her limbs felt leaden. What she needed was a good eight hours of solid sleep. Whether she'd get it before the full moon finally rose was another question.

Main Street swung right, and the buildings momentarily cut the full force of the wind. She tripped, caught herself before she could fall, then glanced behind her to see what had snagged her foot. There was nothing to see—not even the cracks in the pavement. She shook her head and continued on. Above the howl of the wind came the sound of an engine. She glanced over her shoulder, glimpsing an old blue truck moving slowly along the street. At least she wasn't the only fool out. Though she *was* the only fool walking.

She tripped again and cursed softly, smacking her hand against a shop window as she tried to steady herself. Her goddamn feet seemed intent on tripping over each other, no matter how hard she tried to lift them. This wasn't good, and it meant she was more tired than she'd thought.

She studied the snowbound street ahead—or what she could see of it. Her house was closer than the diner. Maybe she'd better head home and take a nap. The way she felt, she'd fall asleep long before she got to the diner, and in this storm that would be deadly.

The wind hit her again as she came out of the protection of the buildings to cross the road. She staggered sideways like a drunkard, battling to keep upright against the force of the storm and the sudden weakness in her limbs. Fear slithered through her. It was almost as if the utter cold of the day was leeching all her energy.

She sighed in relief as the next row of shops gave her a brief respite from the wind, but she knew worse was to come. Her street was the next one, and to get home, she'd have to walk against the force of the storm.

She stopped at the last shop, leaning a hand against the glass to support herself as she took several deep breaths. Her eyes drooped closed, and she forced them open again, blinking rapidly. The slither of fear became stronger. She could so easily fall asleep right here and now. All she had to do was close her eyes.

She had to get home. Fast.

The wind slapped against her the minute she stepped out into it, forcing her back several steps. She gritted her teeth, leaned forward and walked on, but it felt as if she were walking through glue. Icy cold glue, at that. Every single step was an energy-draining effort. Her breath tore at her throat, and the iciness of the air seemed to shred her lungs.

She counted the houses as she passed each one, needing to keep her mind off the effort to walk. Off the need to simply lie down and sleep. Eight houses to go . . . seven . . . a street corner loomed into view. Once she'd crossed it, she was almost there. The thought seemed to rush fresh energy into her limbs, and she stepped out onto the road.

Above the howl of the storm came the roar of an engine. Too late, she became aware of the sullen gleam of head-lights rushing down on her.

She yelped and tried to leap away, but the truck clipped her hip and sent her sprawling. She smacked against the ground, saw stars, and for several seconds couldn't seem to breathe.

Then oblivion rushed in, accompanied by the harsh sound of laughter.

Ten

Duncan rapped his knuckles against the old wooden door. There was movement inside, so he knew someone was home. After a few moments, he heard the scuff of heels against wooden flooring approaching the door.

"Yes?"

The voice was harsh, elderly. Not Betise, then. "Duncan Sinclair," he said. "I'd like to speak to Betise, if possible."

The door opened. Cool air rushed past him, accompanied by an unpleasant smell that was both the woman and the house. He resisted the urge to step back into the fresh air of the storm, and studied the woman in front of him. She wasn't as elderly as he'd thought, probably in her mid-fifties, and was a tall, angular stick of a woman with harsh yellow hair and grey-green eyes.

She looked him up and down, and an almost disdainful smile touched her thin lips. "You'd be a Sinclair, then?"

"Yes. Duncan Sinclair, as I said." He paused. "And you are?"

"Iyona. Betise's mother. What do you want with her?"

"I just need to ask her a question."

Iyona snorted. "Yeah right. The day the Sinclairs just want to talk is the day the moon will stop rising." She sniffed and stepped aside. "I guess you'd better come in, then. I just got a call from her. She's shutting down her shop and coming home. Shouldn't be too long."

Good, because he certainly didn't want to be stuck long in this unripe smelling house. He stepped inside, the sharp rap of his boot heels against the old floorboards echoing in the empty hallway.

Iyona slammed the door shut then shuffled past. "You'd better wait in the living room. I'm cooking sweetbreads, and the smell can get overwhelming if you're not used to it."

That was an understatement if ever he'd heard one. He walked into the room the old woman had indicated and looked around. Like the hall, there was very little in the way of furniture. A couple of sofas, a TV, a stack of newspapers and magazines piled high on an old pine coffee table. The floor was carpeted, the pattern long since faded to grime. An analogy that could very well be applied to those living in the house.

He tossed the papers scattered on the sofa to one side and sat down. The room, like the hallway, was cold. He couldn't hear the breeze of forced air heating, and there wasn't a fire lit in the old hearth. Maybe Iyona didn't feel the cold.

He tapped his fingers against the sofa arm for several minutes, then glanced toward the kitchen. There was no sound of movement. No soft intake of breath. "Have you been in Ripple Creek long?" he asked, wondering if she was still there or had gone somewhere else.

Water flushed and a moment later, Iyona appeared, shuffling toward the sink to wash her hands. "Came back about a month ago."

"Where were you before then?" Not that he was really interested. He was just trying to make conversation to get his mind off the awful smell.

"Here and there." Iyona shrugged. "Shame about the murders happening up your way."

"The rangers will catch whoever is behind them." If *he* didn't get the bastard first.

She glanced at him, amusement glinting in her silvery eyes. "Seems to me the rangers haven't a clue."

Her tone was as amused as her look, and he raised an eyebrow. "You don't seem all that sorry about it."

"The murders?" Iyona snorted softly. "I personally think it should be you Sinclairs being taken out, not the fools who choose to dance with you."

Betise had said much the same thing. Maybe it was a speech she'd learned from her mother very early in life. But if that was the way she felt, why had she wasted more than half her life attending dances? "You have a problem with my family?"

Her look was scathing. "Yeah. All you Sinclairs are nothing but a pack of lying bastards."

Again, that was something he'd heard Betise say more than once. But then, Neva had called him a bastard more than a few times these last couple of days, and with good reason. He frowned as he thought of her, and he had to control the sudden urge to get up and go find her. He'd promised not to go back until dusk. If he wanted to undo the mess he'd made of everything and start making amends, he couldn't break that vow.

And the mere fact that he even *wanted* to make amends surprised the hell out of him. She was his for the rest of this moon phase. He could rightfully lose himself to the pleasure of her body until the full moon finally rose and forced them all into wolf shape. But he wanted more than just that. He wanted to *know* her. Wanted her to smile at him the way she'd smiled at her friend in the diner.

He wished he'd met her under more normal circumstances, and beyond the time of the rising moon. Maybe then he wouldn't have destroyed any chance he had with her.

At that moment pain flashed, rising from his hip and spreading upwards like a flame, until his whole body was encased in agony. Then as quickly as it came the sensation faded, leaving only fear and a cold churning in his gut.

He fought the sudden urge to leave this stinking house. It was crazy. Neva was safe at home. Besides, she had a weapon more formidable than teeth and claws, and could undoubtedly defend herself against most attacks.

He rose and began pacing the small room. "What has my family ever done to you?"

Iyona snorted. "Your lot wrecked my life."

"You've never danced at the mansion." Though he wasn't sure why he was so certain. Iyona was old enough to have been dancing long before he'd ever started.

"There's more than one pack of Sinclairs isn't there?" she bit back. "You must have bred like damned rabbits in the early years."

Her words sent alarms off somewhere in the back of his mind. He stared at her for a moment, then asked, "I gather from that statement that you spent some time over at the Bitterroot reservation?"

The smile that touched her lips sent a chill down his spine. "No. But I wish I had been. I would have enjoyed watching your lot burn."

He sensed no lie, and yet he suspected she was doing just that. "If you feel that strongly, why invite a Sinclair into your house?"

She snorted again. "Because this is my daughter's house, and she seems to have a passion for your lot."

And yet, she'd wished them dead not all that long ago. Or was that merely an aftereffect of exchanging heated words with René? He was definitely going to have to speak to his brother when he got back to the mansion, if only to uncover what sort of game Betise was playing. Especially given the fantasy she had of being a long time lover of *his*.

Outside the house, a door slammed shut, then a shadow whisked past the windows. Two seconds later the back door opened, and Betise appeared. Her smile became a look of surprise and quick excitement when her gaze met his.

"Duncan," she said, voice warm. "What a nice—"

"I'm here to ask a question," he said quickly. "Nothing more."

Annoyance and perhaps a flash of anger flitted through her grey-green eyes. She stripped off her coat and gloves and tossed them on the back of the chair. "Let me guess. You discovered my lie. Surprise, surprise."

"Then why bother lying in the first place?"

She shrugged and sat down. "You seemed so damn enamored with the virginal Neva, and I guess it just pissed me off."

Her tone had much the same effect on him as nails down a blackboard. He shoved his hands in his pockets, half wishing he'd never come here. "What does it matter to you if I'm enamored with her? You and I shared one dance, nothing more."

Something flashed in her eyes. Something more than anger. Something almost crazy. She yanked off her boots and tossed them into the corner. "I knew you'd race back and question her. Wish I could have seen her expression."

He wished he *hadn't*. Wished he'd resisted the urge to voice his doubts. Wished he'd simply trusted her. "I thought you and Neva were friends."

She glanced at her mother, and the two shared a strange sort of smile. "Acquaintances more than friends," Betise said. "We chat at the diner and the hair salon, but it's nothing deeper."

And of that, he was extremely glad. He'd hate to think that Neva hung around with someone as unsavory as Betise. "So what did you hope to gain by lying?"

She raised an eyebrow, amusement touching her thin lips. "What do you think?"

"If I had any idea, I wouldn't be asking."

She stared at him for a moment, eyes so bright they were almost otherworldly. "You really don't, do you?"

He glanced at Iyona, saw the same, almost maniacal look in her eyes, and frowned. Something was going on here, something he didn't understand.

"Told you," Iyona said, voice shrill. "They're all no good."

"Seems that way, doesn't it?" Betise's voice was flat, dead, and something in his gut clenched. The house might be cold, but these two could have frozen hell itself.

"Look," he said, meeting Betise's gaze. "You and I shared one dance, nothing more. I have no idea what game you're playing, but if you don't stop your lies, I'll have you banned from the dance."

Iyona snorted. "That's a typical Sinclair response." Her voice was so full of venom he could almost smell it.

He glanced at her. With her thin arms crossed, angular hips resting against the bench and eyes narrowed, she really did remind him of a snake. Neeson might not have any idea who was behind the animosity being directed at his pack, but *he* certainly did. And he had a suspicion he'd better find out why.

He pulled his gaze away from her, concentrating on Betise. "I'm warning you now, stay away from my brothers."

"Who made you pack leader?" she spat. "You can hardly control your own damn actions, let alone your brothers.'"

Which might have been true enough in times past, he supposed, but not nowadays. Control was the one thing he never lost—except, perhaps, when it came to Neva.

The itchy feeling that something was wrong with her not only remained but was growing stronger. He had to go. *Had to.*

"I'm speaking for my father," he said curtly. "Watch your step, or you'll never take another inside the mansion."

"René owes me. I want him to fulfil his promises, nothing more."

"René makes no more promises than I do."

"Not even to the virginal Neva?"

"Not even." Yet the words tasted sour on his lips. If ever he could have made promises with someone, it might have been Neva. "But while we're on the subject of Neva, quit telling her tales about you and me. There *is* no you and me. There never has been."

Her eyes glittered, but he wasn't sure if it was tears or merely the light catching the silver in her eyes. "You lie. Look into your heart, Duncan."

"I have looked into my heart." And up until this moon phase, he'd thought it incapable of any sort of emotional depths.

"Bastard." Her soft voice was filled with hatred.

"So I'm beginning to believe," he muttered and turned, walking out of the house and away from its crazy occupants.

He stopped on the veranda and watched the storm. The snow had eased, but the wind hadn't, and the day was still bitingly cold. Not the sort of day you wanted to be out in.

Not the sort of day you wanted to find yourself unconscious in.

For one second, he froze. Then he swore and dove into the storm, running as if the hounds of hell were after him. He didn't feel the tempest blowing around him. Didn't feel the cold. Didn't even feel the pavement pounding under his feet. All he could feel was an odd sort of numbness, creeping slowly through his body, as if his strength was being sucked away by an unknown force.

Only it wasn't truly unknown. It was Neva, siphoning his strength to bolster hers.

He'd never truly feared before, but he did now. For her. For them.

Because if she could do *that*, then this thing between them went far deeper than he'd thought, far deeper than just a moon dance.

Wouldn't it be the mother of all ironies if, in a matter of days, he'd managed to destroy the one thing he'd spent half his life searching for?

More than eight blocks separated Betise's house and Neva's. He crossed them in record time, slowing only as he reached her house. He opened the gate, then hesitated, looking at the windblown whiteness to his right. She wasn't home. She was down there, somewhere.

He didn't question his certainty. Didn't dare. He swore again, a growl of sound the wind quickly snatched away, and hurried forward. The sullen gleam of a streetlight became visible, indicating that he was approaching another road. He stopped on the corner, glancing to his left.

And saw her huddled against the curb, looking like little more like a brightly-colored bundle of snow-covered rags than a woman. His gut twisted, and for a second he couldn't seem to breathe. Then he was beside her, stripping off his gloves and slipping his fingers under her woolen ski mask, feeling for a pulse. It was there, nice and steady. He checked her ears, then her fingers and her feet. All were well covered. All were warm. Relief slithered through him. Hypothermia didn't appear to have struck yet.

He stripped off his coat, then his sweater, rolling it lengthways and carefully placing it around her neck. As improvised cervical collars went, it wasn't the best, but it was a hell of a lot better than risking moving her without it. He carefully turned her over. No blood. That might be good. Might be bad.

"Neva?" He lightly tapped her cheeks. Her color was good, and he could feel the warmth of her skin through the mask.

Her eyes fluttered, and a smile touched her lips. A care-free, easy sort of smile that did strange things to his heart's rhythm.

Neva?

She giggled, and he raised an eyebrow in surprise. It sounded for all the world like she was drunk. *Are you okay?*

Okay? No. Perfect? Yes.

Her words made him smile. She *was* perfect, in almost every way imaginable. He picked up his coat and tried to wrap it around her, but she slapped his hands away with a laugh. It was such a carefree sound he almost laughed with her, despite the concern swamping him.

What happened? He managed to avoid her hands and finally wrapped the coat around her.

A truck happened. Clipped me.

She seemed to be moving all right, and he could no longer sense pain in her mind. Still, he'd better get her to the hospital, just to be sure.

No. Take me home. Please.

Her mind speech was a little indistinct, yet he could smell no alcohol on her breath. *You need to go to the hospital. There might be internal injuries.*

No! Her words might be slurred but the alarm in her voice was clear and forceful. *I'm okay. My parents are there. I can't talk to them yet.*

She touched a gloved hand to his cheek, her bright eyes catching his. Her pupils were slightly dilated, but not with desire. He suspected she'd been drugged. But with what? And could he risk not taking her to the hospital when she might have been overdosed?

"Please." Her voice was soft. Imploring. "Just trust me and do as I ask."

He closed his eyes and took a deep breath. He was a fool for even risking a compromise, but he opened his eyes and said, "I'll take you home and check you over. If I think you should go to the hospital, you'll go, okay?"

Her relief slithered through him, flame bright. "Okay."

He picked her up, cradling her close. She rested her cheek against his shoulder and sighed almost contentedly.

"Home, James," she murmured, in a ritzy sort of way.

Her warm breath caressed his neck and breathed life into the embers of desire. Moons, simply holding her felt so good. So damn right.

He kicked open her front gate and hurried up the steps. Her front door was unlocked, and he shook his head, unable to believe any woman living alone in this day and age could be so trusting. Even a relatively small town like Ripple Creek had its fair share of creeps.

And she had probably cast *him* as one of them.

He pushed the thought away and headed up the stairs to

her bedroom. Thankfully, she'd left the heat on, and the house was warm.

"I like your thinking," she said, as he placed her on the bed. "No better way to warm up a cold body than a good bout of sex."

He squatted in front of her and carefully took off her boots, then her woolen socks. Her feet and toes were warm. "You know this for a fact?" he asked, glancing up with a smile.

She sniffed and lifted her nose, her expression haughty but green eyes twinkling. "I have been told," she said in the best impression of snobbery he'd ever heard.

"Extreme physical activity is not good for someone who might have hypothermia." He rose and unwound his makeshift collar, then undid her coat and discovered another one underneath. No wonder she was so warm.

"I haven't got hypothermia."

No, thankfully she didn't. He tossed her coats to one side and started undoing her shirt. "But you have been hit by a car, and you're probably under the influence of some sort of drug." He doubted she'd be in such a playful mood otherwise. Not after what he'd said only an hour or so earlier.

She touched a finger to his face, running it gently down to his lips. It was a touch that burned right down to his soul.

"How about we try some extreme physical activity right now?" Her voice was low and so damn sexy heat shot to his groin.

He ached to do just that. It might still be the afternoon, and the moon might be on the other side of the world, but right now he wanted her as fiercely as he'd ever wanted anyone during the moon's rush. But as much as he wanted

her, he didn't want to take advantage of her. Not any more
than he already had. Her shirt joined her coats, followed
quickly by her bra.

"See anything you like?" She leaned back, all but thrusting her wonderful breasts in his face.

Everything. But he resisted the urge to bury his face in
her bountiful flesh and twined his fingers through hers,
gently tugging her upright. "Where did you go after I left?"
He released her, but she swayed slightly, and he quickly
touched a hand to her waist to steady her.

She wrapped her arms around his neck and gave him a
happy sort of smile. "What does it matter?"

He kissed her nose, then began undoing her jeans. "Tell
me."

She yawned, then said, "Betise's hair salon. Had to ask
her some questions, remember?"

He'd forgotten he'd asked her to do that. "I didn't order
you to go out in the middle of a snowstorm."

He hooked his thumbs around the waist of her jeans and
panties and pushed them down. She stepped free then
flopped back onto the bed, arms and legs akimbo.

"Come here," she said, patting the bed beside her.

He again resisted the desire to do just that. "Roll over
onto your left side."

She raised her eyebrows and did as he asked. "Planning
a little side-on adventure, are we?"

"Maybe." A doozey of a bruise was beginning to appear
on her rump, but there were no skin lacerations, and she
seemed to be moving her legs without flinching. He carefully checked the rest of her, but could find no other signs of
injury. "Did you drink anything at Betise's?"

She sighed. "I don't want to talk about her."

"Neither do I, believe me. Did you drink anything?"

"Coffee." She reached up, grabbed his shirt and dragged him close, green eyes dancing with devilment as they searched his. "Kiss me."

"Love to." And he did. Long and slowly. Tasted her, savored her, until he knew every inch of her mouth as intimately as he knew the rest of her. When he finally broke away, his breathing was harsh, and the desire to take what she was so freely offering pounded through his veins.

"How much coffee?" he asked hoarsely.

She gave him a vixen smile and trailed her fingers down his chest. "Not even half a cup."

If Betise had put something in the coffee, at least Neva hadn't taken all of it. She was probably safe from an overdose, though he'd certainly have to keep an eye on her for the next couple of hours. He flipped back the bed covers. "Climb in. I'll make you some hot chocolate."

"I don't want some hot chocolate."

She brushed her fingers up and down the front of his jeans, teasing, but not quite touching his erection, which seemed to press even more painfully against the restriction of the denim. A shudder ran through him. Right then, he didn't want any hot chocolate, either. He patted the pillow. She sighed and climbed rather gracelessly under the covers.

"Care to join me?"

"Yes. But later." He tucked the blankets around her. "Did Betise say anything of interest?"

The amusement fled her face, and her eyes searched his. "She told me you were soul mates. She told me you refused to acknowledge it."

Anger flashed through him, warm and bright. The

woman was more delusional than he'd thought. He knelt down beside Neva and touched a hand to her cheek. "Betise is not my soul mate. We shared one dance, nothing more." He paused, staring into Neva's beautiful eyes, trying to make her believe him. Trying to make her see. "I have no fear of acknowledging my soul mate."

Tears touched the green depths, but she blinked them away. "Then why—"

He put a finger against her lips. "I don't know why. And right now, I don't care." He hesitated. "What else did she say?"

"She lied about my dad."

That he'd discovered for himself. "And?"

"She gave me a brief description of the man who attacked her. It's no more than what we already know."

No surprise there. He very much suspected Betise hadn't actually been attacked, but rather had been playing a game in wolf form that got a little too rough for her liking. Why else would she refuse to give them a proper description? She must have seen her attacker—she had scratches on her face. Scratches that had come from either fingernails or claws, not teeth, like the other victims.

"Nothing else?"

She shook her head and yawned yet again.

"I'll get the chocolate. You stay here."

Her sigh followed him down the stairs. By the time he'd made them both some hot chocolate and carried the mugs back up the stairs, she was asleep.

He stopped in the middle of the room, his gaze on her face, and his heart doing weird things in his chest. He finally acknowledged what he'd known the minute her pain had echoed through him and she'd begun siphoning his strength. This was more than just the power of the moon and the need for the dance. Far more.

He placed both mugs on the bedside table closest to her, then tossed teddy bears off the nearby chair and dragged it closer. Propping his feet on the bed, he picked up a mug and sipped at the drink slowly as he let his gaze rest on her serene and beautiful features.

He hadn't lied to her. He had no fear of acknowledging his soul mate.

What he feared more than anything else in the world was that she would refuse to acknowledge him.

Eleven

There was a madman in her head. A madman with a big hammer, continually bashing away at her skull. Neva groaned softly and rolled onto her back. Pain flared in the region of her rump and curled up her side.

The truck, she thought. Then she felt the caress of cotton sheets against her skin and realized she was no longer lying in the snow but in bed. Her bed, if the tang of citrus in the air was anything to go by.

She opened her eyes and looked toward the window. It was dark outside, and the storm no longer raged. Snow continued to drift past the glass, the flakes briefly glistening silver as the lamp near the window caught them with its light. She reached out for her watch, wincing slightly as her side protested the movement. It was six o'clock. Four hours had slipped by. Four hours she couldn't remember.

Frowning slightly, she eased upright. Duncan had been in her room, but not in her bed. The air carried his warm, woody scent, but it didn't linger on the sheets. Two cups sat on the bedside table. She picked one up, sniffing it lightly. Chocolate. She certainly couldn't remember drinking it.

Her last memory was of the blue truck swiping her and sending her sprawling. She frowned, trying to reach past the haze in her mind, sure something important had happened between that point and now. Vague memories of being stripped rolled through the fog in her mind, followed by the flush of remembered passion. Yet, they hadn't danced. Of that she was certain.

Neva? Her sister's voice winged into her mind, warm but concerned. *You okay?*

I think so. She climbed out of bed and realized she was completely naked when the warm air caressed her skin as gently as a lover's sigh. She grabbed her robe and quickly put it on.

What happened last night? I tried contacting you, but you were off on another planet.

I'm not sure what happened. I got swiped by a truck coming home from Betise's and can't remember much after that. She hesitated at the top of the stairs. Though the hall was dark, light peeked out from under the kitchen door. If the delicious aroma beginning to drift upwards was anything to go by, Duncan was cooking dinner.

Savannah's sharp gasp echoed down the mental lines between them, and Neva winced.

Are you okay? Why aren't you in the hospital?

It barely touched me, and I didn't want to go to the emergency room. Not that she could actually remember saying that. *Have you arranged twenty-four seven protection, like I asked?*

Yes. And we pulled several hairs off that doctor's coat you found in the trash can. They match the hair we found at two of the murder scenes.

Black hair?

Black hair, Savannah confirmed softly.

Neva sighed. No wonder her sister was so convinced it was a Sinclair—they might not be able to lay sole claim to the silver coat, but they *were* the only pack in Ripple Creek with black hair. And while there were quite a few humans living here who also had black hair, none of them would get anywhere near the mansion during the phase of the full moon let alone be able to overpower a wolf.

Then the murderer was definitely coming after you. Maybe you were closer to something than you'd thought.

Maybe. Savannah's doubt echoed down the line between them. *Tell me about the truck that hit you. I'll have Steve and Ronan look out for it.*

Your deputies have more important things to do. Besides, the storm was a bitch, and the driver probably didn't even see me. Yet she remembered the sound of laughter and wondered if that was true.

He would have felt the bump as the truck hit you.

He didn't hit me that hard, so I doubt it. She hesitated. *Have Mom and Dad been in to see you yet?*

Yeah, and dad's furious. He didn't say anything, but I think he knows you were up at the mansion. I'd avoid him for the next couple of days and give him a chance to cool down.

That would take weeks, not days. She rubbed a hand across her eyes and turned tail, heading into the bathroom to grab some painkillers. After she'd taken them, she told her sister everything she'd learned over the last couple of days. It didn't take long, because she hadn't really learned that much.

I'll send Ronan over to Betise's place. I wish the damn fool had reported the attack immediately. We might have been able to pull some connecting evidence off her gown. She hesitated. *If you're right about lovers being the targets, we'll have to convince the brothers to give us a list and arrange protection.*

I suspect that's now being handled within the pack.

Probably. And just so you know, we've got a warrant to search the Sinclair mansion, and we'll be requesting hair samples from everyone who's there. You'd better make sure you stay away tonight and tomorrow.

I can tell you now it wasn't René behind the last attack, and it certainly wasn't Duncan.

I'm not saying it's one of Zeke's get.

No, she wasn't. But she wasn't really considering anyone else, either, and Neva had a suspicion they were all playing into the murderer's game-plan, whatever that plan was.

Give me a reason to suspect someone else and I will, Savannah chided. *Right now, I can only work with what I've got.*

She could remember a time when Savannah had worked with nothing more than guesswork and intuition. But all that had changed after she'd come home from an extended break five years ago. Neva wondered again what exactly had happened to so completely change her sister's method of policing, but now was not the time to ask.

I hope you're not planning to be up at the mansion running the whole shebang.

Savannah's mental snort was derisive. *Goddamn doctors won't let me get out of bed. Threatened to tie me down if I tried to leave. I should have the lot of them thrown in jail and see how they like being confined.*

Neva grinned, though she could easily imagine her sister following through with her threat. *You need to rest, Sav. Push it in a couple of days, when you're feeling stronger.*

Savannah sighed. *I guess you're the one person I can't lie to.*

Exactly. If I uncover any other information, I'll tell you. In the meantime, catch some sleep. And make sure Steve checks who's coming in and out of the room rather than flirting with that pretty young nurse.

How did you know it was Steve at the door?

Elementary, my dear. You said you'd send Ronan out to Betise's. Bodee is usually home by now looking after the kids, and you can't stand Ike. That leaves Steve.

Ike's got the midnight shift, Savannah grumbled. *I told the nurse if he so much as twitches my way, she's to beat him over the head.*

Neva's grin grew. It was a well-known fact that Ike had been lusting after her sister ever since his transfer to Ripple Creek. He was nice, in a boring sort of way, and just the sort of man their parents would approve of. Savannah's method of dealing with his lust was to simply ignore it, but all that seemed to have done was inflame his determination.

I have no intention of ever again mixing business with pleasure, Savannah said. *And no, I'm not going to explain that statement right now.*

Damn.

The warmth of her sister's smile spun through her. *Remember, don't go near the mansion tonight. I'll talk to you later.*

Don't let the bedbugs bite. Or Ike, as the case may be.

Savannah made the mental equivalent of a rude gesture and closed down the link. Still grinning, Neva made her way down the stairs.

Duncan looked around as she entered, and she noted his shutters were back in place. Odd. For some reason, she'd half expected to see them gone. What on earth had happened between them last night? What couldn't she remember that she *should* remember?

"Hope you like pumpkin risotto." His voice was neutral,

almost careful, but his gaze swept down her body—a heated touch that wasn't, and one that left her tingling all over.

"Never tried it." She walked over to the drawer to grab some cutlery to set the table. The silk of her gown caressed her skin as enticingly as a kiss, and suddenly she was all too aware of the amount of flesh she was exposing as she walked and that she wore nothing beneath it.

His quick intake of breath suggested he was just as aware of that fact. "Then you haven't lived."

No, she hadn't. Not until she'd stepped into his world and had been forced to acknowledge the wolf within. A wolf she no longer wanted to keep fully leashed. Not when he was around, anyway.

She set the table then walked over to the refrigerator. "You have the fine choice of soda, homemade lemonade or water."

"I'll chance the lemonade."

"A wise choice. The soda's open and probably flat." She poured them both a drink then sat down as he brought over the two bowls of creamy rice. She picked up her fork and tasted a bit. "Hmmm," she murmured appreciably. "Delicious. Where'd you learn to cook like this?"

He shrugged. "I got bored cooking steak and eggs every night for dinner, so I bought myself some cookbooks."

"What, no scrumptious little wolf hanging around to cook for you?"

He studied her for a moment, expression totally unreadable. "Occasionally," he said after a moment. "But mostly I was alone."

She picked up her glass and took a sip as she considered him. His mood was restrained, subdued almost, and yet there was an undercurrent she couldn't quite pin down. And like her, he had his shields fully up, which was really no surprise, given what she'd done to him earlier.

Speaking of which . . . "Why did you really say those things about my parents? Especially if you knew they had no bearing on the case?"

"I still don't know if your mother's past has any bearing on this case. I suspect it might, though I don't think your mother is actually involved."

That wasn't exactly the answer she'd been searching for. "How would an attack on the Bitterroot Sinclairs over thirty years ago be connected to the murders happening here now?"

"When I discover the connection, I suspect I'll discover the murderer." He hesitated. "How are you feeling this morning?"

She had a suspicion the question wasn't asked out of concern for her health, but rather something else. "I've got the mother of all headaches and a sore butt, but other than that, I'm fine. Why?"

"Are you up to a little breaking and entering?"

Her heart skipped then began to race. "Where?"

"Betise's hair salon."

Surprise flitted through her. "Why?"

"Because I suspect she slipped some sort of sleeping tablet into your coffee this afternoon. I want to see if she left the cup lying around."

"I put it down beside my chair, so she could have missed it." She frowned. "But why would she bother? Even if she's decided she doesn't like sharing you, what point would there be in drugging me?"

"For the last time, she and I have never exchanged promises, nor did I have more than one dance with her." His

voice was tight, and anger flicked briefly behind the shutters. "And you could have died if I hadn't found you so
quickly."

His anger burned her skin and made her throat go dry.
Lord, it would be so easy to believe he actually *cared*.
Which was ridiculous. He was a lone wolf—a man who
enjoyed the dance and wanted nothing more from a relationship. "So how did you find me?"

"I was lucky." He pointed his fork at her barely touched
meal. "Now eat, before it gets cold."

She ate, but could only get halfway through the huge
bowl he'd given her. She pushed the rest of it away and
leaned back with a sigh. "Thank you."

He nodded and rose, collecting both bowls and taking
them over to the sink. She watched him walk away, admir-
ing the way his faded jeans clung to his butt and wishing
she had the courage to actually admit out loud what she
really wanted right now. The wolf within might be free, but
she wasn't totally courageous. Not yet.

"What else do you hope to find at the hair salon?" she
asked, more out of a need to fill the heated silence than any
real curiosity. "Because if she did drop sleeping tablets in
my drink, they probably came from her handbag. I doubt
she'd keep something like that at the salon."

"No. Which is why I want to head on over to her house
afterwards." He handed her a cup of coffee and sat back
down.

She wrapped her fingers around the mug and frowned. "I
think her mother is living with her. I doubt she'd leave to
head up to the mansion, even if Betise does."

"No. But she might head out to a dinner invitation with
an old friend."

Neva raised an eyebrow. "I didn't think Iyona had any friends—old or new."

"According to Neeson Jones, she has two. Neeson's helped me arrange a little get together tonight at the *Blue Moon*."

The *Blue Moon* was the bigger of Ripple Creek's two bars and usually packed with partygoers when the full moon was rising. "You were lucky to get a table."

"Called in a favor. The owner's an old friend of mine."

She leaned back in her chair and sipped her coffee. His gaze drifted down her body, lingering on the folds of silk covering her breasts. Anticipation tingled across her skin, and the deep down ache sprang to life.

And all because of a look. It was almost scary just how attuned she was to this man.

"Why do you want to search Betise's house? What do you hope to find?" She stretched out her legs, her feet touching his. Warmth sprung between them, prickling up her leg.

"I don't know. Something strange is going on with that pair, not the least of which are the lies she's spreading about me. A clandestine search might uncover a few handy secrets."

"You don't think she's linked to the murders, do you?" She ran her toes up the long lean length of his foot. She'd never found feet arousing before, but just touching his was doing strange things to her breathing. As was the sexy smile that tugged at his lips, daring her to be bolder.

"At this point, no, though Iyona obviously hates my pack. It's always possible she does know something."

She slipped her foot up his leg, enjoying the contrasts of soft denim and taut muscle under her toes and half wishing those powerful legs were entwined around her. She reached as far as his muscular thighs but couldn't go any further without slipping off the chair. "Have you asked her about the Bitterroot incident?"

"Yes."

He reached under the table and began to knead her instep with his thumb. A tremor shot up her leg, jumping her pulse into a triple-time dance.

"She claims she wasn't there," he continued, his rich voice deeper by several notches, and as seductive as the moon itself.

She closed her eyes, enjoying the gentle but insistent press of his hand against her skin. "You don't believe her?"

"No."

"I could get Savannah to check it out, if you want."

"I already have a friend checking it out. He should be calling back soon." He wrapped his hand around her foot, his fingers so warm against her flesh it felt like she was being held by hot iron. "Are you ticklish?"

Her eyes flashed open. His grin radiated enough heat to melt the snow drifting past the kitchen window, and devilment shone in his dark eyes. Her heart did an odd tumble. She had a feeling she was seeing a side of him so very few did. "No, I'm not." She tried to jerk her foot away, but he held her tight.

"Really?" His ran a finger lightly down the sole of her foot, and she bit her bottom lip, fighting the urge to laugh.

"Really. Now let go."

"I don't think so."

He flicked a fingernail across her instep and the laugh escaped. She squirmed on the chair, an odd flush of trepidation and desire running through her.

He raised an eyebrow. "For someone who's not ticklish, that sounded suspiciously like a laugh."

"Well, maybe I am a *little* ticklish."

He ran his finger across her foot again. Laughter bubbled through her and broke free. He stopped, dark eyes a heated mix of desire and amusement.

"Okay," she said breathlessly. "Maybe I'm a *lot* ticklish."

"Just on the foot?" His fingers slid enticingly up her calf, and pinpricks of desire fled across her skin, leaving her hotter than she'd ever thought possible.

"Yes." Her reply was little more than a pant of air.

"You sure about that?"

No. "Yes."

"So you're definitely not ticklish behind your knee?"

His fingers teased her skin as he spoke, and she couldn't contain her laughter. He stopped again, his grin as delicious as the look in his eyes. "Shall we explore where else you might be ticklish?"

"Not in my lifetime." Grinning, she ripped her leg from his grasp and jumped up from the table, bolting for the stairs.

He caught her in the hall and she laughed, halfheartedly fighting his hold on her. He pressed her back against the wall, his hands on either side of her body, neatly corralling her. His masculine odor filled her every breath, and the desire that scorched the air between them left her breathless and aching.

He leaned close, his gaze all but devouring her. "I never could resist a challenge."

His mouth brushed hers, a tender caress that left her lips tingling and her wanting more. But before she could react in any way, his hands had slipped to her waist and she was being tickled unmercifully.

She laughed, long and loud. Laughed until her knees felt as if they were going to give way and tears were streaming down her face.

"Stop, stop," she begged between gasps for air.

He did, bracing his hands on either side of her again. "I think we can safely say you're ticklish all over." His grin was boyishly cheeky.

"You think?" she managed to say.

"I think." He leaned a little closer, and his cheeky grin melted into something far more dangerous, far more luscious. "We can't risk heading out to Betise's for another hour or so. Any idea what we should do until then?"

She hesitated, her pulse zooming, the need to give in to desire warring with the instinct to keep safe and keep her distance—emotionally, if not physically—from this man.

"We could go back to the kitchen and finish our coffee." But her voice came out with a betraying huskiness, and the heat singeing the air became a tempest that blasted them both.

His smile faded, but his dark eyes burned bright in the hall's semidarkness. "We could. Or you could tell me what you really want."

She could. But she wouldn't. The wolf within might be free, and it might want him with a fierceness she'd never felt before, but she suspected if she openly admitted that, she might also be forced to admit other things. Like how much she *didn't* hate him. Or, how she was beginning to fear the thought of him walking away at the end of this moon phase.

"Tell me." He dropped one hand and began undoing the knot at her waist.

A tremor of anticipation ran through her. "No."

"I can taste your desire on the air, little wolf. What harm is there in admitting it?"

"Plenty."

The knot fell away and her gown slipped apart. The warm air caressed her even warmer skin, and her breath caught, then quickened. But he didn't touch her. Instead, he caught the left edge of the gown and gently flicked it back and forth across one erect nipple. The sensation was like nothing she'd ever felt before—erotic, arousing, torturous.

"Tell me," he said softly.

She swallowed, but it didn't seem to ease the dryness in her throat or the trembling in her belly. "Why do you care? I'm yours for this phase, no matter what I do or don't admit."

"Is that what you want? For me to just take you any time I want? Right here and now?"

She licked her lips, and his gaze jumped to her mouth. Pinpricks of sweat danced across her skin. She needed him so badly she ached to scream, *Yes*. But she'd sworn not so long ago never to admit her needs to this man, and for the sake of sanity, for the sake of her heart, she had to stick to that vow.

"Does it really matter what I want?"

"Would you believe me if I said yes?"

"No."

"Why not?" He switched his attentions to her right nipple. She all but moaned at the sweet sensuality of the silk snapping across her skin.

"Because it's just another game. Just another way to destroy me."

His pause was brief, but nevertheless there. "Would it make any difference if I apologize?"

She briefly closed her eyes. He sounded sincere, and she so desperately wanted to believe that he was. But in the end, it didn't really matter, because he was still leaving once the murderer was caught, and she'd still be left here alone to clean up the mess. "An apology won't rectify the damage you've done."

"Perhaps if I explained—"

"Oh yeah, that'll work." Her voice was sharp with sarcasm. "Tell my dad I went to the moon dance for the sole purpose of seducing you to gain entry into the mansion. That'll surely make everything all right."

He leaned forward, brushing another sweet kiss across her mouth. "I wasn't intending to tell him that."

His warm breath tingled across her lips. She breathed in as he breathed out, until it seemed as if the spicy taste of him was filling every pore. She swallowed heavily. "I wouldn't tell him anything. If he sees you right now, he's likely to run for the nearest gun."

He raised a dark eyebrow. "I didn't think your dad believed in that sort of thing."

"He's a wolf, and I'm his little girl."

"And I'm nothing but trash taking advantage of you." There was a hint of bitterness in his voice that suggested he'd heard that sentiment more than once.

Part of her ached to deny the words, to tell him that he was so much more than his reputation had led her to believe. But she didn't. Salvation and survival lay in silence. He was a lone wolf who didn't want anything more than this moon dance. Except, perhaps, for an admission that she *did* need, just as badly as anyone else at the mansion, despite all the high ideals of her pack.

"It doesn't matter what he thinks," she said softly.

"No," he agreed after a moment. "But it matters what you think."

Why? That's what she ached to ask. Especially when he had already admitted he wanted nothing from her but the next few nights. "Right now, I don't want to think." She just needed his touch—on her skin, and deep inside.

"Then tell me what you *do* want," he whispered, bringing them right back to square one.

He stopped teasing her breasts with the silk, but before she could murmur her disappointment, he dipped his head, his tongue circling the dark ring of one nipple, teasing but not touching the oversensitive center.

Every inch of her trembled—ached—with expectation. She closed her eyes and leaned her head back against the wall, enjoying his touch and the sensations storming through her.

"Not that," she said after a moment. Because as much as she was enjoying it, the moon and she both knew she wanted a whole lot more.

"No?"

The liquid touch left her skin as he shifted his attention to her other breast. This time, he nipped, drawing her nipple deep into his mouth, sucking on it hard. She gasped, her knees almost collapsing at the rush of unexpected pleasure.

"Nor that," she somehow said.

"Then perhaps this?" His tongue teased her skin again, and slowly, tormentingly, he worked his way down her belly. Goose bumps scurried across her sweat-beaded skin, and her heart hammered so loudly its beat seemed to echo through the silence.

When his tongue finally delved into her moistness, she moaned, and had to fight to keep her knees locked and her body upright. His fingers pressed against her thighs. Trembling, she widened her stance, allowing him greater access. His tongue delved deeper, and pleasure flowed like liquid fire through her veins, until her whole body quivered and throbbed to the tune of that gentle yet insistent touch. A touch that quickly created a tide threatening to overload her senses.

But at the precise moment she needed that touch the most, it left her. She groaned and opened her eyes, wondering what weird, tortuous game he was playing now. His gaze caught hers, seeming to delve deep into her soul. The intent, the hunger, so evident in his dark gaze assured her this was no game, but a carefully controlled seduction. Not only of her senses, but of her mind.

And perhaps, if she wasn't very careful, her heart.

Holding her gaze, he slowly, almost leisurely, stripped off his jeans and shorts and tossed them to one side. He was as hard as she was wet, and the sight of him made her throat go dry. Moons, how she ached to feel that hardness deep inside.

Placing his hands on either side of her again, he leaned forward and claimed her mouth. He tasted of lust, of love, and of her, and it stirred her in ways she never thought possible. When he finally pulled away, she could barely even breathe, and the throbbing ache was so fierce she thought she'd die.

"Tell me what you want," he said, voice soft but as fierce as his gaze.

She swallowed but could no longer deny the need pounding through her veins. "You."

Elation winged through the darkness of his eyes. "How do you want me?"

His touch slid through her slickness and delved deep. She moaned, arching into his hand but wanting so much more.

"Like this?" he asked, his voice little more than a husky growl.

She shook her head, too consumed by the sensations of pleasure shooting through her to do anything more.

"Then perhaps we'll try this." The heat of his flesh, the heaviness of his desire, pressed hard against her, until all she could smell was the spicy mix of man and lust, and all she could feel was the pounding of his heart through her breasts and the pulsing of his need against her belly.

"Tell me what you want, Neva. Admit it."

She could do little else. Not when his gaze was so intense, his body so close, and her need so high. "I want to feel you deep inside."

Her voice was little more than a croak of sound, but a fierce and victorious look shone in his eyes. Then she was in his arms, and he was inside of her, thrusting so deep, enveloping her in a heat that was basic. Pure. So very powerful, and so very, very right.

His mouth found hers again, and their tongues caressed as the pressure built. His powerful body stroked fast and hard into hers, driving her insane with need. She writhed against him, matching his rhythm, matching his urgency. The sweet pressure built until it felt as if she would explode.

Then she did, and the force of her climax damn near blew her mind. He came with her, his roar echoing across the silence, sounding as if he was howling her name to the moon. As their orgasms ebbed and sanity returned, he claimed her mouth and kissed her hard.

When he allowed her to breathe again, she opened her

eyes and stared into the ebony recesses of his. The shutters were down, and what she saw there scared her. Because what she saw was caring. Deep caring.

It had to be wishful thinking. It couldn't be anything else, not with a wolf who had once sworn never to share his life or his heart with another.

He kissed her again, soft and lingering. "I think—" He stopped, his gaze hardening as he glanced toward the door.

In that instant, there was a sharp rap against the wood. She jumped, grabbing the edges of her gown and quickly tying them together.

"Who's there?" she called.

"Me. Open up, Neva."

She closed her eyes and took a deep breath. Of all the people she *didn't* want to see right now, her father had to top the list.

The confrontation she didn't want, and wasn't really ready for, was about to happen.

Twelve

Duncan swore softly. Neva's father couldn't have chosen a worse time to come visiting. The smell of lust and sex sat heavily on the warm air, and Neva's warm skin still glowed with the aftermath of their lovemaking. It wasn't something either of them could deny and would only further fuel the old man's anger.

Not that Duncan was worried about himself—just Neva. She loved her parents, and he didn't want the situation to get any messier than it already was, but he had a feeling it would.

She whirled and grabbed his jeans and shorts, thrusting them into his hands. *Go into the kitchen and get dressed,* she ordered. *Sit at the table and make like nothing is happening.*

He gently brushed a sweaty strand of hair from her cheek. *He's not stupid. It's very evident what we've been doing.*

Her eyes flashed at him. *I know, but I don't intend to rub his face in it.*

Neither did he. Not this time. But he didn't intend to leave her alone to face her father's wrath, either. Especially when that wrath was mostly *his* making. He threw on his clothes but didn't retreat, and she made an exasperated sound before moving to turn on the light and open the door.

"So it's true." Though Levon's voice was soft, it was filled with anger. Rich with contempt. "You didn't leave Ripple Creek after all. You lied to me, and you lied to your mother."

Her hurt swirled through Duncan, as bright as a flame. Yet none of it showed in her voice as she said, "Would you have felt any better if I'd told the truth?" She stepped back, opening the door wider. "Are you coming in, or are we going to discuss this on the doorstop for all the neighbors to hear?"

Levon's gaze ran past her, meeting Duncan's. "Oh, I'm coming in all right." He stepped inside and thrust a hand deep into his pocket.

Duncan saw the bulge. Knew a weapon was hidden there. And while he had the strength to wrest the gun from the older wolf's grip, he wasn't about to risk it with Neva standing so close. Accidents happened, and he didn't want it happening to her.

He crossed his arms and leaned against the wall, feigning indifference as she closed the door. "I never figured you for a man of violence, Levon."

She shot him a quick, confused look, then her gaze darted to her father, and she made an exasperated sound. "Do you really think he's worth going to jail over?"

Even though Duncan had half expected her to say something like that, her words still cut. But declarations of caring, after everything he'd done to her, weren't in the cards right now. Maybe they never would be.

"I'd keep that gun in your pocket," he drawled softly. "Because I know from experience you wouldn't enjoy jail."

A muscle in the old man's jaw throbbed. "Do you know what they're saying about her in the hospital?"

"Don't talk about me like I'm not here," she cut in. "And what does it matter what people are saying about me?"

Levon shot her a furious look. "It matters to me. It matters to your mother."

"And my feelings and needs don't?"

"You're my daughter," Levon said fiercely. "And I will not have your reputation sullied by a man like *this*."

Neva's expression was an endearing mix of anger and amusement. "Duncan's not the first man I've danced with, Dad, and he probably won't be the last."

"He will be if I have anything to say about it." Levon drew the gun out of his pocket and, with a trembling hand, pointed it at Duncan.

Duncan didn't move. Just tensed, ready to dive away should the older man's finger so much as twitch on the trigger.

Neva swore and stepped between them. "Don't be so damned ridiculous." She hesitated, sniffing the air. "You've been drinking."

Damn it, Neva, Duncan said. *Step out of the line of fire.*

No. He won't shoot me.

That was a risk Duncan wasn't willing to let her take. He reached for the power of the binding. *I order you to step away.*

She shot him a furious look and clenched her fists, her whole body trembling. But she didn't move. Duncan wasn't sure whether to admire her courage or be angry at her stubbornness.

"I'm not drunk," Levon said into the silence

"No, you're just insane. How's threatening Duncan going to help me or my reputation?"

For someone who wanted to avoid this confrontation at all costs, she was doing a fine job of fighting it without help. He very much suspected this battle had been building for some time now, and his actions had just made it happen sooner rather than later.

"He leaves." Levon's voice was sharp. "Now. Tonight."

"And as I asked before, how is that supposed to help my reputation?"

"One moon dance is an aberration that will quickly be forgotten, as long as he leaves quickly."

Neva raised an eyebrow. "And if it's not an aberration?"

Levon shot her a furious look. "It is. You deserve far better than a man of his ilk."

"Yeah, right," Neva said, voice flat. "It's not for me you're demanding this, is it? You're here to protect *your* reputation and *your* image."

Levon glared at her. "I'm not—"

"Aren't you? So why haven't you stopped to ask if this is what I want? Why haven't you bothered to ask how I feel about Duncan? Did you ever stop to consider that this *might* be more than just a dance?"

Levon's gaze darted between the two of them, and his face went pale. Duncan wasn't sure if it was the shock of having his daughter finally standing up to him or the horror of possibly having *him* as a permanent member of the pack.

"You can't be serious," Levon muttered. "Surely you know what sort of reputation—"

"I do. And right now, I don't care."

"But . . . but . . ." Levon stopped and scrubbed a hand across his rough jaw. "You *can't* be serious about a man like him."

She reached out, wrapping a hand around the barrel of the gun and wresting it easily from her father's grip. "Right now, I'm not sure that I am. But I have the right to discover what I do and don't feel. I'm not a teenager any more, so please don't treat me like one."

"I'm only trying to protect you."

"I know, but right now, you're smothering me."

Levon's gaze met Duncan's again, and in the rich green depths he saw both anger and fear. "You deserve better than scum like—"

Even from where he stood, Duncan felt the flash of her fury. "You will not call him scum in *my* house," she said, her voice soft but shaking with anger. "Get out."

"I'm only trying—"

"Until you—and Mom—are willing to listen to what I have to say, I don't want to talk to you." She strode past him and opened the door. "I said get out."

"Your sister—"

"Was willing to listen to me and understands what I've done. You and Mom aren't even willing to listen."

"It's just that we're disappointed—"

"Yeah? Well, so am I. In you. Where are all those pretty words of tolerance now?" She waved her hand at the open door. "I mean it, Dad. If you want to stay, you apologize to Duncan. If not, leave."

Levon turned around and walked to the door. There he hesitated, meeting Neva's gaze for several seconds. Duncan saw her face go pale and found himself clenching his fists again, ready to step in and defend her even though he had no idea what Levon had just said to her.

"I mean it, Neva," Levon said out loud.

"I know you do," she replied and slammed the door shut behind her father. It was a sound that echoed through the sudden silence.

She remained where she was, staring at the door and breathing deeply. He wanted to go to her and wrap his arms around her, but he knew she wouldn't appreciate it.

"What did he say to you?"

"Nothing." Though her voice was carefully controlled, he could feel the pain in her.

"Then why are you so upset?"

"It's pack business," she shot back. "And none of *your* concern."

He took a deep breath and released it slowly. "Neva, I'm sorry if I caused—"

She rounded on him, green eyes blazing. "If you *ever* try to make me do something against my will again, I'll fry your brains so badly you won't be able to shit without help."

While he had no doubt she meant what she said, he couldn't help the slight smile tugging his lips. She was so damned beautiful, even when angry. He let his gaze drift downwards, watching the rise and fall of her breasts as she breathed. Watching her nipples peak with renewed awareness. "I was only trying—"

"To control me. The same way my damn parents have been trying to control me. I won't stand it from them anymore, and I certainly won't take it from you."

He pushed away from the wall and walked towards her. "I was only trying to protect you."

She licked her lips and backed away from him. With the door behind her, she couldn't go far. "Well, how about trusting me instead? The damn gun wasn't loaded. It never has been."

Her back hit the door, and she stopped. Desire widened her pupils, darkened her green eyes, and he was so damned hard for her it was painful.

"You can't know that for certain," he said, reaching again for the silk tie around her waist.

She swallowed heavily. "The firing mechanism is stuffed. Dad bought the weapon ages ago when there was a

rash of break-ins. He figured he could use it to scare intrud-
ers away."

And had obviously figured it would scare *him* away, too.
Which would have been a fair assumption in his younger
years, when all he'd wanted was a good time with no strings
and no problems. But that wasn't the case with Neva. The
tie came loose and the silk fell away, once more revealing
her golden curves and luscious triangle of soft hair. A triangle he couldn't wait to lose himself in again. He took the
gun from her and dropped it into the pocket of one the coats
on the coat rack near the door. "Why didn't you just tell me
that?"

"Because I didn't want you taking it off him. He
deserved a little more dignity than that."

"Even after what he said?" He slid a finger under the silk
and skimmed it up to her shoulder, gently dislodging the
gown.

She quivered under his touch, her breathing quick,
uneven. "Even after. He's still my dad."

He slid his finger across her warm flesh to her other
shoulder, sliding the rest of the gown off. It shimmied to the
floor, puddling around her feet. Her desire spun around
him, a warm rich scent that stirred his senses and thrummed
through his blood.

The moon was rising. And so was his need to bury himself deep inside her.

"You can't," she denied, voice soft, husky. "We have to
get to Betise's."

"We have at least half an hour to fill in, if not more." He
stripped off his clothes, tossing them on the floor next to her
gown. "And I intend to spend that time dancing with you."

The pulse at her neck was little more than a wild flutter,

her nipples so hard they were pebbles pressing into his chest. Her gaze searched his for a moment, then a teasing, sensuous smile touched her lips. "How?"

He kissed her sweet mouth—softly, seductively. "What I intend," he whispered, his lips so close to hers he could taste every quick breath, "is to turn you around and spread you against the door, caressing your entire body as I take you from behind until the heat overcomes us and we howl our pleasure to the moon."

Anticipation flared in her eyes, and the scent of her arousal got stronger. She opened her mouth, panting softly, as if she couldn't suck in enough air.

"And then?" Her voice was a husky whisper that damn near exploded his control.

"Then I intend to carry you upstairs and continue with a more leisurely seduction in the shower as we wash the smell of sex and lust from our skins."

"The moon certainly has a strong effect on you Sinclairs, doesn't it?"

It did, but right now it wasn't the moon, it was the woman. "I want you," he whispered against her lips.

"Then take me."

He did.

Neva shivered and wished she'd taken the time to put on her extra coat. Even though the wind had dropped, the night was still bitterly cold. Her breath fogged, hanging on the air, mingling with the silvery snowflakes that danced through the night.

Through the hush of darkness, music throbbed, a bass-heavy beat that stirred her blood almost as much as the man standing in front of her. The *Blue Moon* was only a couple

of blocks away, and she half-wished she and Duncan were
there now, laughing and drinking with the other patrons.
Doing ordinary things, enjoying themselves in ordinary
ways. Being an ordinary couple.

Only they weren't a couple and were never likely to be.
Especially if her father had his way.

She smiled grimly. While her father's edict that she leave
Duncan after the full moon or she'd no longer be considered
part of his pack made her madder than hell, in many ways it
was also ironic. Especially considering her time with
Duncan was limited to this moon phase anyway.

She crossed her arms and shifted her weight from one
foot to the other. *How long does it take to open a damn
window?*

Though he didn't look around, his amusement spun
through her. *I spent time in jail for being drunk, not breaking and entering. Don't expect any speed records here.*

She sighed impatiently and looked around. They were
standing in the small alley that ran the length of the block
behind the row of shops. Around them were Dumpsters
loaded to overflowing, and the powerful smell hung on the
crisp air. Behind them was a row of houses, and the warm
glow peeking past blinds indicated most of the occupants
were home. They had to be quiet, and they had to be careful.

She wished she was home. In bed. With Duncan.

Her gaze drifted past the snow-capped rooflines to the
snow-filled sky. The moon was lost to the night, but she
didn't need to see it to know it was rising high. The power
of it thrummed through her veins. Made her ache to be
touched, to be loved.

By one man, not many.

She bit her lip and wished she could reach out to

Savannah and discuss the confusion of her feelings. But she couldn't, not when they were about to break into Betise's salon. Sister or not, Savannah would send her deputies around to stop them.

There was a soft click, and Duncan sighed in relief. *I'm glad I was never forced to be a thief. It's too damned difficult.*

He opened the window, then cupped his hands. She stepped into them and grabbed the sill, pulling herself through and landing on the floor on the other side in an ungainly heap.

You okay?

Yep. She picked herself up and stepped to one side, dusting off her jeans as she did so.

Duncan quickly joined her. *Looks like we're in the back storeroom.*

We are. She walked out the door and headed across to the chair she'd sat in earlier. *The cup is gone.*

Thought it might be. He shrugged and began opening drawers.

She watched him for a minute, her hands on her hips, then said, *What are you looking for?*

Don't know. But I'm sure she's up to something. I'm just not sure if it's connected to the attacks. Searching through her stuff can't hurt.

It could if any of the rangers happened past. She glanced around for a second then headed over to the reception desk and sat down. The computer was off and turning it on was too much of a risk, especially if they had to get out in a hurry. The last thing they wanted was to leave a brightly-shining calling card in the form of a glowing computer screen. She opened the drawers and shuffled through them.

There wasn't much to find, beyond the usual stationary items and a couple of masks in the last drawer. She leaned back in the chair, staring at shelves lined with hair products. Faces stared back at her. Plastic faces. "Wigs," she said into the silence.

Duncan looked up. "What?"

"Wigs. On the shelf." She rose and walked over.

"So?"

She plucked the black one free and rubbed the hair between her fingertips. "Savannah said they'd found black hair on several of the victims. Why couldn't the killer have been wearing a wig?"

"Are the wigs made of real hair?" He stopped beside her and felt the wig, his fingers brushing hers and sending little shocks of electricity up her arm.

"They feel like it."

"Perhaps you should pluck a few hairs and get your sister to compare them."

She glanced at him. "Betise doesn't own the only salon in town."

"No. And if the killer is wearing a wig, he's probably got one of his own. I doubt he'd be using one of these. But we've got nothing to lose by taking the chance."

She plucked a couple of hairs, then carefully replaced the wig and went into the back to find a plastic bag while Duncan continued his search through the rest of the drawers.

"Nothing," he said after a few moments.

"That's not really surprising," she replied, walking back into the main room. "If she is up to something, she wouldn't be stupid enough to leave evidence of it lying around here with people coming in and out all day."

"No." He sat on the edge of the desk and flicked through the appointment book. "Looks like the victims were customers of hers."

She frowned. "No, they weren't."

He glanced up at her, one eyebrow raised. "Their names are in the book. The last victim saw her two days before she died."

She looked over his shoulder. The name was there in black and white. "She told me she didn't know any of them."

"Then she lied. I wonder why?"

"Maybe she didn't want the hassle of dealing with the rangers."

"Maybe." He leaned forward and brushed a kiss across her lips, his eyes bright with the same hunger that stirred her blood. "I think we'd better head on to her place and do a little more investigating."

It was last thing she wanted to do, especially when his taste still lingered so enticingly on her mouth. Her wolf was definitely off the leash, and she suspected there was no going back to the way things had been before she'd foolishly walked into the mansion thinking she could control both the moon and her own responses. In the space of a couple of days, just about everything had changed, and she wasn't sure whether to be happy about that or not.

She stepped away, allowing him to brush past. They climbed out the window then Duncan slid his knife along the edge, knocking the catch back into place again.

"What about our footprints?" she asked, staring at the deep imprints they were leaving in the snow.

He grabbed the snow-laden lid off the nearby trash can and dumped the snow onto the telltale prints near the window. Then he kicked the bin over, scattering the rubbish around the door, covering the rest of them. "Let's get back to the—"

He stopped. Across the night came the sound of car engine drawing close. Neva met his gaze. "You don't think . . .?"

"We can't take the chance that it's not. Shift shape and jump the fence."

She did, barely clearing it, her belly scraping across the rough top edges. Leaping from a standstill had never been one of her fortes. She was too small to get any great height. She landed lightly and padded along the fence line until she found a gap in the wood. Lights speared the darkness, twin beams of brightness that lit the alley and highlighted the rubbish hiding their prints. A red car cruised into sight, stopping close to the salon's back door. Betise climbed out, cursing softly and kicking away a soda bottle as she headed for the entrance.

Duncan stopped beside Neva, his silver coat blending with snow. *I'm surprised she's not already at the mansion. The dance has been going for a good two hours.*

Maybe she's not going to the dance.

Betise is an addict. I doubt she can stop.

She looked at him. He was as powerful in wolf form as he was in human, and his eyes glowed like black glass. *Are you an addict?*

Once, he admitted. *But no more.*

Why?

He shrugged. *I grew tired of the chase. Tired of much-used flesh.*

That's not a very nice thing to say.

His amusement spun around her. *But true.*

So you chased me because I was new to the dance?

Yes.

So I could have stood there fully clothed, and you still would have come after me?

Yes.

Damn. Wish I'd known that.

I'm glad you didn't. It's not often I get to enjoy the sight of a nubile nymph playing in the fountain.

And it's not a sight you're likely to see again. That water was freezing. She glanced toward the salon as Betise came back out. She appeared to be carrying something small, but from this angle, Neva couldn't see what it was.

I can't see it, either.

She glanced at him. *It could be the masks I saw in the drawer.*

Maybe, he commented. *But it might be worth following her, just to see what she's up to.*

What about searching her house?

We can't risk going there until we know she's going to be gone for a while.

She's likely to notice a car tailing her.

But not a pair of wolves. In this snow, she can't go very fast, so we should be able to keep up.

Maybe you can, she grumbled. *I've got shorter legs, remember.*

He grinned, and in wolf form, it was a fearsome sight. *Legs I wouldn't mind wrapped around me right now.*

That conjures some weird damn images when we're in wolf form.

I don't care what form you're in. You're beautiful either way.

She studied him a little warily. *Okay, what are you after? You're being entirely too nice all of a sudden.*

His amusement spun through her mind, as warm as sunshine. *I'm a wolf and the moon is rising—what do you think I want?*

You can get that without being nice.

He gave the mental equivalent of a shrug. *Maybe you're just seeing the real me.*

Yeah, right. If the man was basically nice, he wouldn't have the reputation he had.

People change, Neva. My reputation was earned a long time ago. His mental tones were flat, but the air burned with the flash of his anger.

But you've more than lived up to it with me, haven't you?

He didn't say anything, and the swirl of his emotions died. Had he been in human form, she very much suspected the shutters in his eyes would be up again.

Betise started her car and cruised off slowly. Duncan stepped back several paces. *Keep close.*

He leapt the fence, clearing it easily. She followed, scraping her belly a second time. She'd be bruised in the morning for sure. They loped after the car, keeping it in sight easily enough. Duncan had been right—Betise wasn't able to drive very fast with all the snow coating the road.

The car headed east along Main Street until they'd reached the outer limits of Ripple Creek, then it turned south into Mayflower Street. It was a back road, rough and narrow, and the wash of warm light from the streetlights behind them quickly gave way to darkness. Houses were few and far between out here, and the silence was almost eerie. A shiver rippled across her skin. Anyone coming out to this wild and lonely section of town at this time of night was surely up to no good.

From up ahead, mingling with the purr of the engine,

came the bubbling rush of Hunter's River, the biggest of the two rivers that flowed though Ripple Creek. This road crossed it then took a long loop back to Main Street. Where in hell was Betise going? And why?

Neva lolled out her tongue, trying to catch more air as she concentrated on running in the tire tracks, where the going was easier. Loping long distances was all well and good when you had long legs and were fit, but the longest distance she'd ever run was between the diner and home last year when she was late for a date. A date that hadn't been worth the effort of getting ready, let alone running.

Which was basically the story of her dating life—at least until she'd decided to seduce Duncan. And while they weren't dating, they were certainly dancing. She had to wonder how she was ever going to find a man who could do to her the things Duncan had done to her. A man who could make her feel the way he'd made her feel.

But what, exactly, did she feel? And did she really want to acknowledge those feelings, given the fact he was leaving? Perhaps it was better not to know. Not to examine too closely. Otherwise she might just end up getting hurt.

The sound of bubbling water got stronger, and the car's bright lights picked out the old wooden bridge from the surrounding darkness. Betise slowed, easing the car onto the narrow bridge before stopping in the middle.

Stay here, behind the car, Duncan ordered. *I'm going forward a little to see what she's doing.*

Be careful. I don't like the feel of this.

Neither do I.

He padded forward, his silver coat blending with the snow, making him difficult to see. A second later there was a small splash, then the car began to creep forward again.

She's thrown something in the water, Neva guessed.

That she has. I'm going in to retrieve it. He hesitated. *You want to keep following her? We can't afford to lose her right now.*

Will you be all right? The water is freezing.

In wolf form I won't feel it as much. Go, before we lose her. Just make sure you keep out of sight.

Like she needed to be told that. Biting back her annoyance, she loped over the bridge and followed the tire tracks.

Betise made her way back to Main Street, turned left, then headed back to the undoubtedly of town. When she turned right onto Bunting Street, a sick sensation ran through Neva. She had a horrible suspicion she knew where Betise was headed.

Her place.

She swore softly, though it came out little more than a rumble of sound. She leapt the nearest fence, taking a short-cut across her neighbor's backyards, and shifted shape as she ran for her back door.

She thrust it open, kicked off her shoes and shucked her coat, then slammed the door shut and raced for the stairs. Lights gleamed through the living room windows as a car pulled into her driveway. She raced up the stairs, stripping as she went, throwing her clothes in a heap in the hallway before racing into the shower. Thrusting on the taps, she wasted a few precious seconds waiting for the water to warm up, then jumped in.

A second later the doorbell rang. She got out of the shower but left the water running, grabbed a towel and padded down the stairs. "Who is it?" she called, dripping water everywhere as she tucked the towel around her breasts.

"Betise."

The other wolf's voice sounded slightly surprised, and a shiver traveled down Neva's spine. It was almost as if Betise hadn't expected her to be home—and that would only be the case if she'd suspected they'd been following her.

Neva opened the door. Betise's gaze slid down Neva's body, and her lips twitched as if in amusement. But it was an amusement at odds with the anger in her silvery-green eyes.

"Hope I'm not interrupting anything," Betise said, her voice warm, her eyes cold.

"Well, actually, you are. What can I do for you?"

"Is Duncan here?"

Neva clutched the door handle tightly. "Yes. Upstairs, having a shower. Why?"

"It's personal. Perhaps I should wait?"

"I really don't think—"

"It's important I speak to him. I'll wait in the kitchen, if you like, while you two finish your . . . showering." She hesitated. "Unless, of course, you think my presence here might disturb your relationship with Duncan."

Neva wondered what in hell was going on in Betise's mind. As much as she'd first believed the older wolf's statements about her affair with Duncan, his contempt and loathing of her went too deep to be anything but true repulsion. One thing was obvious—whatever these two had been, they most certainly weren't soul mates.

"Duncan and I don't have a relationship, so I have nothing to fear." *And certainly not from the likes of you.* Which was an extremely bitchy thought, but one that was certainly true. "But we could be a while showering. Why don't I get him to phone you once we finish?"

"This is urgent." Betise crossed her arms, the anger and suspicion deeper in her silvery eyes. "Why don't you just go upstairs and tell him I'm here? I'm sure he'll come down to see me."

"Given the choice, I certainly wouldn't." Duncan's dry comment came from the top of the stairs. "What the hell do you want now, Betise?"

Neva's heart leapt in her chest, but she hid her relief as she looked over her shoulder. Duncan was standing at the top of the stairs, a towel wrapped around his hips, his skin gleaming and as wet as hers. The smile that touched his lips curled her toes, and though the shutters were up in his eyes, she could feel his amusement. And his anger—at Betise, not her.

Betise all but glared at him. "I thought you might like to know about an interesting conversation I overheard at the Blue Moon."

Neva shared a glance with Duncan. *Has Betise really been at the Blue Moon? And if so, why there rather than the dance?*

It'll be easy enough to check, Duncan said. *The Blue Moon has lots of security cameras. I'll get Rai to check them.*

And here I was thinking the 'good friend' you mentioned was male. I really should have known better. Her mental tone sounded as catty as her words, but she just couldn't help it.

She's married.

That didn't stop you in Denver.

He didn't answer. He didn't need to, when his anger damn near sizzled her mind. His gaze went past her. "What did you overhear?"

Betise stepped inside. "One person, male, talking on a cell phone. About René."

He crossed his arms, his eyes little more than black slits. "Are you going to spit it all out, or do I have to come down and shake the rest of it out?"

The suppressed hostility in his voice left Neva in no doubt he'd do it. The sudden flash of uncertainty she got from Betise suggested she had no doubt either—and yet that uncertainty was mixed with an animosity that matched Duncan's. What was going on? None of the emotions she was catching from Betise made any real sense. On the one hand, there was love and a deep belief in destiny. On the other, a far-reaching anger. And while she knew it was more than possible to feel both for the same person, there seemed to be something else here, as well. Something that left a bad taste in Neva's mouth.

"He was talking about going after your brother," Betise said coldly. "Tonight, while the dance was on."

Duncan didn't react in any noticeable way. Nor did he move. "Did you see this man?"

"No."

"Would you recognize his voice if you heard it again?"

Betise hesitated. "Probably."

"Did he say when or how?"

"No."

The phone rang shrilly. Neva jumped, then glanced up at Duncan.

"Answer it," he said, voice clipped.

She did. "Neva Grant speaking."

"May I speak to Duncan, please?"

The voice was cultured and rich and reminded her very much of an older version of Duncan. She glanced up at him. "For you."

His gaze went to Betise for a second, then he walked down the stairs and took the phone from her hands. Neva rubbed her arms, but it didn't ease the goose bumps fleeing across her skin.

Duncan listened to the caller for several seconds, his expression never changing, then put the phone down. But his black eyes gleamed with fury as his gaze met hers. "That was my father. René's been shot."

Thirteen

Duncan took a deep breath, trying to control the anger pounding through his veins. The need to protect the pack and all its members was a natural instinct to a wolf—and something he'd failed to do.

Neva placed a hand against his arm, her fingers warm against his skin. He shook off her touch and spun around, ignoring the flash of her hurt as he stalked towards Betise.

Though her eyes widened slightly, the smell of her anticipation and desire spun through the air. He wrapped his fingers around her neck, resisting the urge to squeeze tight but holding her still none too gently.

"If I discover you have had anything to do with René being shot, I'll kill you."

Her expression was fear-filled, yet he could taste her emotions as clearly as he smelled her arousal, and fear played no part in them.

"This is the thanks I get for coming here to warn you?"

"We both know you're up to something."

"I'm up to nothing more than trying to get promises made to me fulfilled."

"I never made any promises to you, Betise, and I very much doubt René did, either." He thrust her backwards, sending her sprawling into the soft snow. She landed in an ungainly heap, flashing bare thighs and a thatch of golden hair. His gut turned. "Take your lies, and your much-used flesh elsewhere from now on. We don't want you at the mansion anymore."

He slammed the door shut on the rush of her fury and turned around. Neva was staring at him, her arms crossed and her expression a mix of relief and worry.

"That might not have been the wisest move, particularly if she is somehow involved with the killings."

"Right now, I don't particularly care." He had a suspicion time was running out, and the killer had just upped the ante. He took the stairs two at a time and walked into the bedroom, crossing to the still-open window he'd climbed through earlier. He closed it, then grabbed his clothes and began dressing.

Neva stopped in the doorway. "You never mentioned how René is."

"That's because I don't really know."

"Then he's not dead?"

"No."

"You're going up there now?"

"Yes." His voice was slightly clipped, and the growing tide of her annoyance washed around him. He ignored it and pulled on his boots. Right now, he didn't have time to waste. He had to get back to the mansion to help his father. "Are you getting dressed, or are you going like that?"

"I thought you'd class this as pack business and not suitable for outsiders."

She was no longer an outsider, even though she'd yet to acknowledge him or her feelings. Even if she never did. "If Betise is somehow involved in these killings, I'd be a fool to leave you here alone, especially after I've just tossed her out of the house."

"I can take care of myself."

"I'm sure your sister thought the same thing." He saw the glimmer of hurt in her green eyes and took a deep breath, releasing it slowly. "Just get dressed. I haven't the time to argue right now."

"Fine. Don't argue. But I'm not going."

"Listen—"

"No," she cut in. "You listen. If Betise is up to something, it's important we keep an eye on her."

"If she is involved, she's probably just raised the stakes. I don't want to risk you getting hurt."

She crossed her arms. "You have no say over what I do or don't risk. You and I are sharing a moon dance, nothing more."

He met her gaze. Saw her uncertainty and her determination. Realized then that she was still seeing him as the man he had been rather than the man he now was. And that was something he could not combat—not with words, and not in such a short amount of time. "Are you sure of that?"

She hesitated. "Yes."

"Well, I'm not."

Her eyes widened a little. "What do you mean?"

"What I said." He picked his coat up off the floor and walked towards her. She didn't back away, but the uncertainty in her eyes grew. As did the scent of her arousal.

He stopped so close her peaked nipples brushed his chest with every breath she took. Heat sparked the air between them, fierce enough to draw sweat from his skin and hers. The desire to take her, to bury himself in the warmth of her willing flesh and let the rest of the world take care of itself, burned fiercely. But duty and his pack had to take priority. For now.

"I don't like the thought of you going after Betise alone."

"I'll keep my distance."

"Make sure you do." He wrapped an arm around her

small waist and crushed her against him. Kissed her hungrily, fiercely, claiming her mouth as completely as he'd
claim her body later, when they had more time.

The sound of a car starting forced him to pull away.
"You'd better hurry and get dressed," he said. "Or she'll slip
away. Keep in contact with me."

She nodded and spun away, her hips swaying enticingly
as she walked into the bathroom. He took a deep breath
and forced his feet towards the stairs. Light swept across the
windows as Betise backed her car out of the driveway. He
headed for the back door, ensuring it was locked before he
stepped into the night's snow-filled darkness.

Then he shifted shape and ran for the mansion.

Neva padded through the white-cloaked darkness, following the red gleam of taillights. She'd half expected Betise
to head for the mansion despite Duncan's warning, but it
was clear she was headed home. Which was a little surprising, especially given the heat of the moon. An addict
did whatever they needed to do to ensure the supply of
their drug, didn't they? So why wasn't Betise out hunting
a mate?

She pricked her ears as the sound of another engine
rolled across the night. It came from behind her, but was
headed her way. She leapt off the road and made for the
trees, weaving her way through the trunks as the gleam of
headlights flickered across the night.

Ahead, Betise turned into the driveway of her house and
stopped in front of the garage. Neva paused, her tongue
lolling as she battled to catch her breath. If there was one
thing she was going to do when this was all over, it was get
into shape.

Betise climbed out of her car and glanced back toward the road. The roar of the engine drew closer, then lights swept across the strand of trees where Neva hid. She didn't move, hoping the shadows and the surrounding pines would hide her golden coat.

The lights swept past, then a truck pulled into the driveway and stopped behind Betise's car. A chill ran through Neva. A blue truck. Just like the one that had hit her.

Maybe her accident wasn't an accident after all.

Iyona climbed out and spoke to her daughter. Though the night was hushed, Neva was too far away to hear what they were saying. And she didn't dare move, just in case either woman spotted her.

After a fierce, somewhat animated conversation, Betise and her mother headed inside. Lights shone in the kitchen, and a few seconds later, gleamed from the windows at the far end of the house.

Neva retreated through the trees and back onto the road, following the tire tracks down the driveway so she didn't leave any paw prints. When she reached the truck's tailgate, she hesitated, flicking her ears forward. There was a lot of movement inside the house. Hurried movement. Frowning, she crawled under the truck and out the other side. There she shifted shape, and in human form followed the footprints up the stairs.

When she reached the window, she stopped, flattening her back against the wall before peering carefully in. Through the gap in the curtains she could see Iyona throwing things into cardboard boxes. Neva raised her eyebrows. Were they leaving? And if so, why?

She watched a moment longer, then ducked past the window and jumped off the veranda. She walked the length of the house, keeping to the shadows so her footprints wouldn't be so noticeable. The house was on a slope, so by the time she reached the room Betise was in, the window was higher than her head, and she couldn't see in. But if the sound of things being thrown around was anything to go by, then Betise was either having an almighty temper tantrum or, like Iyona, she was packing. Neva leaned back against the wall and waited. After a few minutes, Iyona appeared, marching toward the truck with a large box.

Neva shifted shape again and hunkered down, the snow cold against her belly. Iyona dumped the box in the truck then went back inside. Several more minutes passed, then Betise came out, backpacks slung over either shoulder and bags in both hands. The lights went off, then Iyona reappeared, carrying another box.

"You got everything?" Iyona's voice was sharp with anger and perhaps a little contempt.

"Yep. Rang the rangers, too, just to let them know we'll be away for a few days." Betise's smirk was easy to see, even from where Neva lay. "They said they'd come by and check the house for us."

Iyona snorted. "That's kindly of them."

"I thought so."

Iyona dumped the box in the back of the truck then paused, glancing toward her daughter. "You sure you want to do this?"

"They owe you. And he owes me."

Iyona nodded and climbed into the truck. Betise followed suit, and the truck was quickly backed out of the driveway. Neva took a deep breath then bounded across the snow covered lawn and began following them again.

*

The mansion was ablaze with lights by the time Duncan got there. There was a ranger stationed at the main gate, and the guards his father had hired were manning the other two. Duncan backtracked and slipped in through one of the tunnels, making his way through damp and rarely used passageways to the medical rooms.

He shifted shape as he neared the entrance and hit the switch. The door swung silently open, and Duncan stepped through.

Martin jumped and spun around. "You damn near frightened the life out of me," he grumbled, turning back to the sink to wash his hands. "You'd think those doors would have the decency to squeak and at least give an old man some warning."

"Is René okay?" Duncan left the door open, just in case he had to make a fast retreat. He couldn't smell anyone else close except the doc and his brother, but that didn't mean the rangers weren't nearby. Or even outside the door.

"He's lucky. The bullet hit him low in the shoulder and looked a lot worse than it was. Wouldn't be surprised if the killer thought he'd scored a true hit."

"Does he have to go to the hospital?"

Martin nodded. "I'm not set up to deal with that sort of surgery anymore. I've patched him up the best I can and stemmed the bleeding, but that's about all I can do."

"Can I talk to him?"

"Quickly. We called for an ambulance ten minutes ago, so it should be here any minute."

"Where are the rangers?"

"Down in the main ballroom, interviewing folk and taking samples from pack members." Martin shook his head. "The damn fools even insisted on getting a sample from me."

He raised his eyebrows. "Were they already here when René was shot?"

Martin nodded. "Lucky, too. With the snow still falling, they might not have found the footprints and tire tracks otherwise."

Both were evidence that could be used in court, but was the attack on René linked with the attacks on the women? That's what they had to discover—and fast, he suspected.

"You'll let me know if the rangers come back?"

"The surgery door is locked, and these old bones don't move all that fast."

Duncan smiled and headed into the next room. René was lying on the bed closest to the wall, stripped to the waist, and he had a huge swathe of bandages around his shoulder and left arm.

"I think I should give up the moon dance as a lost cause this cycle," René said without opening his eyes.

"At least he or she didn't shoot your vitals."

René snorted. "I guess there is that to be thankful for."

Duncan stopped at the end of the bed and crossed his arms. "So what were you doing when it happened?"

René opened his eyes, a smile twitching his lips. "What do you think I was doing?"

"And your mate?"

"Frightened, but okay." He grimaced. "I doubt she'll ever dance with me again, though. Reckons I'm dangerous to be around."

"You're dangerous to be around even when you're not getting shot."

"True." Amusement touched his mouth but quickly fled. "I never heard them approach. Never smelled them."

"Which means they probably had a long range rifle. Where were you when it happened?"

"In the summer house."

"Where, exactly?"

"Sitting on the seat, back to the outside fence, with a wet and willing wolf sitting snugly on my lap."

The shooter had to have been in the trees beyond the wall. If he'd been in one of the trees close to the summer house, René would surely have heard him. Or, at the very least, smelled him. "Martin told me they found tracks."

"Apparently. I was pretty out of it for a while there, so I can't really tell you much of what went on after I was shot."

"Then tell me what was going on between you and Betise."

Contempt was evident in René's dark gaze. "That bitch is nothing but trouble."

"She claims you made promises you've failed to live up to."

His brother snorted. "The only promise I've failed to keep was the threat to knock her out if she didn't stop harassing me."

"So you've done nothing more than dance with her?"

"Three times. Which was two times too many, I've since discovered."

Duncan frowned. "What do you mean?"

"The woman's certifiable. After the second dance she was talking like we had a future together. By the third, she was acting territorial and talking about having kids."

"You never gave her reason to believe you might have cared for her?"

René snorted. "Care for her? Good grief, have you smelled the woman?"

"So why go back a second and third time?"

"Because my brains lie in my little head, not my big one." He shrugged. "She was there, she was willing, and I've never been particular."

None of them were, and one way or another, it had gotten them all into trouble. "Was last night the last time you danced with her?"

"Yes. And that's when I told her she was delusional." He hesitated and frowned. "You know, she said something weird."

That didn't surprise him. Betise had been saying a lot of weird things lately. "What did she say?"

"She said the Sinclairs owed her mother, and by the end of this moon phase, she intended to take what was promised."

Duncan frowned. What did they owe Iyona? As far as he knew, she'd never been to any of the dances here. "Is that all?"

"All I heard. I must admit, I tuned out before I walked away."

Someone rapped against the outside door. "Coming, coming," Martin called, then stuck his head through the doorway. "If you don't want to be seen, you'd better leave."

Duncan nodded and glanced at his brother. "I'll make sure Zeke provides protection while you're in the hospital."

René raised his eyebrows. "You really think that's necessary?"

"Until we know what's really going on, yes." He spun on his heel and headed back for the tunnel. After he'd ensured the door was closed, he made his way towards his father's rooms. Zeke wasn't there, but that wasn't surprising. As head of the pack, he'd have to be present while the rangers were interviewing and taking samples.

Duncan picked up the phone and quickly dialed Lance.

"Wilton residence." His friend's cheery tones came through loud and clear.

"Lance, Duncan."

"Hey! I was just about to call you."

"You found something?"

"Oh yeah. Discovered who else was in that little raiding party over in the Bitterroot reservation. Would you be surprised if I said one of the others had moved into Ripple Creek just over a month ago?"

"With what has been going on, no."

"Well, if everything I've dug up is true, this woman has a pretty big axe to grind. Apparently, when she was barely a cub she was promised to Tray Sinclair in a deal that was supposed to strengthen business and blood ties between the silver and golden packs over there."

Duncan raised his eyebrows. Arranged marriages had gone out with the Dark Ages, mainly because very few worked. It was extremely rare for such a couple to be soul mates, and for most wolves, commitment to anyone other than their true mate was almost impossible.

"When Tray turned eighteen," Lance continued, "he decides he can't stand the woman and reneges. To say she didn't take his rejection kindly is an understatement."

In many respects, she had every reason to be angry. But burning down the mansion and killing innocents went beyond anyone's idea of fair retribution. "So she led the raiding party to the mansion?"

"Along with half a dozen drunken buddies, yes."

"Did she get jail time?"

"Oh yeah. They threw the book at her. Got out after ten years on good behavior, and apparently she is a very nasty piece of work."

"She got a name?" Not that he really needed to ask, as he had a damn good idea who the woman was.

"She's now known as Iyona Myna. Got married some ten years ago, divorced two years later. I believe she has a daughter from a previous relationship who's also living in Ripple Creek at the moment."

"Betise."

"That's the one."

Duncan rubbed his hand across his jaw. He now had a possible suspect—two actually. Except for one thing. The wolf attacking the women was silver.

"Don't suppose you know what coat color she was?"

"No. But she's from the golden pack, so you'd presume gold."

Logic would predict so, but nothing in this case was going the way logic said it should. "Any idea who Betise's father is?"

"A couple of the gossip magazines suggested Iyona was pregnant when Tray rejected her. They also suggested Tray wasn't the father. I haven't found anything to confirm or deny this yet."

The timing was about right for Betise to be that child. "Don't suppose you found any interviews with Tray?"

"He died the night of the fire."

So Iyona had gotten her revenge, even if she had killed many innocents in the process. "Let me know if you find anything else."

"I will."

Duncan hung up and leaned back in the chair. If Betise

was indeed Tray Sinclair's daughter, then her comments about the Sinclairs owing both her and her mother made a little more sense. But if she was after some form of blood recognition or compensation, why not go through a DNA test to prove paternity? What she was doing now—trying to hook a Sinclair through marriage—was surely going the long way around things. And while none of Zeke's get were related to the Bitterroot Sinclairs, there were others in the pack who were. Moons, if she wasn't careful, she could very well end up mating with a half brother, though he suspected it wouldn't really bother her.

He glanced at the time and wondered how Neva was doing. Was she keeping her distance like she'd promised? He frowned and rose, walking to the window. The snow was still falling, the night's chill evident through the glass. He hoped she wasn't still out in it. Hoped she was warm and snug in bed.

He closed his eyes and reached for her, but there was nothing in the mental lines beyond a buzzing warmth. Wherever she was, she was too far away to hear him. Worry snaked through him, and he half wished he'd followed the desire to demand she stay put in the house and not run after Betise.

The door behind him opened, and Zeke stepped in. "Thought you might be here," his father said. "Martin handed those samples he took from Betise over to my friend in forensics. I suggest you mention them to our head ranger when you talk to her."

"I will." Even though the mere fact they'd taken samples wasn't likely to impress Savannah.

"You talked to René yet?" Zeke asked.

"Yes. And I've talked to Lance."

"Then you know about Iyona?"

"Yes." Duncan closed the curtains then turned around and leaned back. The chill of the glass was still evident through the thick material. "Did you get anything of interest out of Detrek?"

"Not much more than what Lance probably told you. Apparently, Betise and Tray had a huge argument several days before the night of promising. Detrek had no idea what the argument was about, and from what I gather, really didn't care. He didn't like Iyona and said he was sorry he ever promised his son to her."

"Did he say anything about Iyona being pregnant?"

Zeke nodded. "He said the bitch had been trying to pass off a pup as Tray's, but he'd sent her packing."

"Surely Iyona could have proven it with DNA tests."

"She could have, and the fact she didn't even try speaks volumes, in my book. Fact is, Tray was sterile. It was apparently something they'd discovered only a few weeks beforehand."

"You'd have to hazard a guess that's probably what they argued about."

"Probably."

Zeke moved across to the bar and poured himself a drink, then raised the bottle in query. Duncan shook his head.

"I suspect Iyona or her bastard are probably responsible for the attack on René, but what about the murders? Do you think they're related?"

Though he'd never seen Betise's alternate shape, she certainly had both the height and the wide shoulders to suggest she'd be big in wolf form. But having the right body type didn't make her a murderer. "The biggest problem is the fact that the murderer is a male—"

"That's only being presumed," Zeke cut in. "No one knows for sure."

"Savannah might." After all, she'd survived an attack by the killer, and she'd obviously seen something, or the killer would not have gone after her in the hospital.

"Our head ranger isn't likely to tell us anything, especially when she considers our pack the main suspects." Zeke paused, black eyes glimmering with sudden amusement. "Of course, she has a twin, and the golden tribe share an extremely powerful psychic connection. It's very possible your Neva experienced her sister's attack and saw what her sister saw."

Your Neva. The words seemed to echo through Duncan, and he had to curb a smile, because in reality, there was no reason to smile. She was his nothing until she looked deep into her heart and acknowledged what lay between them. And right now, she was too scared of his reputation to even dare try.

"I hadn't thought of that," he admitted. "I'll talk to her when I see her again."

Zeke took a drink, then said, "If your connection with her is strong enough, you might be able to touch her mind and share her memories."

"That takes trust."

Zeke's half-smile was sympathetic. "Many bridges to mend, huh?"

"Maybe a lifetime's worth." There was no bitterness in his voice. With the benefit of hindsight, he did regret his actions. And yet he knew, given the same circumstances, the same information, and the chance to do it all again, he'd probably make the same choices.

"What do you intend to do?"

He knew his father was talking about Neva rather than the murders. He shrugged and moved away from the chill of the windows. "I really don't know. I'm committed for at least another two months in Eagle. I can't walk out on Dave without giving him time to find and train a replacement, and I need to find myself another job."

"You have the ski lodge your mother left you. You could always return and manage that. And I've heard that they're thinking about setting up a search and rescue team here in Ripple Creek."

He nodded. He'd heard the same from Dave. "I'll worry about it when I have our current problem solved. I'm heading over to the hospital to talk to our head ranger, then I'll see if Neva remembers anything. I'll let you know if I get anywhere."

"I gather Neva didn't warn you about the rangers' raid tonight?"

"No." Nor was he surprised. Her allegiance lay with her sister, not with him. Maybe one day that would change, but not today, or tomorrow or even next week.

Zeke took a long drink, then said, "I don't know why Savannah's so damn convinced it's one of us."

"Because they found black hairs on several victims. It wasn't a human who killed those women. It was a wolf, and we're the only pack with black hair."

"And silver coats. If the murderer was in wolf form when he attacked, how could the rangers find black hair?"

"Why didn't they find prints? Why were there no scents to track?" Duncan shrugged. "Who knows. Maybe they changed shape to gloat."

"The bastard behind this is certainly sick enough to do that."

"That they are." He frowned. Why had he said they rather than he or she? "Are you arranging a guard for René at the hospital?"

"Tye, Kane and I will be taking it in shifts. Right now, we don't dare trust anyone else. Just in case."

Duncan nodded. "I don't think you'll have to do it for long. I have a feeling this thing will be over with in the next day or so."

"I hope you're right. And I hope we can avoid any more damn killings." "Amen to that," Duncan said and headed back to the tunnels.

Neva lost the truck halfway down Main Street. By that stage, her legs were aching, her lungs felt as if they were on fire, and the snow she'd gulped down hadn't done a thing to ease the dryness in her throat.

She padded along the street, following the truck's tire tracks and hoping the snow didn't decide to fall any heavier, because then she'd certainly lose them.

The *Blue Moon* came into view, an oasis of warmth and energy in the cold night. Music pumped, beating through her blood like fire, and she momentarily wished she was inside, dancing and laughing with everyone else.

But not alone.

She sighed. *Admit it*, she thought. *The damn man has gotten under your skin.* And had she felt this deep an attraction to anyone else but Duncan Sinclair, she would not be dithering about her feelings for him. But she couldn't change years of conditioning, and he was everything she'd been taught to avoid.

And while she should undoubtedly be doing as Ari had advised—screwing that beautiful man's brains out and letting the future take care of itself—she just wasn't built that way.

Yes, her wolf might be free—but her wolf loved Ripple Creek, loved working at the diner, and as much as she'd toyed with the idea, really had no hankering to explore the world. Her sister was the wild child in the family, not her. And Savannah was probably a more suitable match for Duncan than she'd ever be.

So why did the thought of him leaving tear at her so?

She didn't know.

Didn't want to know.

Coward, an inner voice whispered.

But better a coward than holding out her heart to a man who'd long ago vowed to remain a lone wolf.

The tire tracks led her to the far edge of town then veered left onto Heather Creek Road. Neva paused, trying to catch her breath as she listened to the sounds of the night. Beyond the pounding music and happy laughter coming from the *Blue Moon*, there was little noise. If the truck was moving anywhere near, she couldn't hear it.

She shook off the snow that had settled on her coat and continued on. She'd head down the road a mile or so, but if the tracks went on after that, she was going home. The night was too cold, and her legs were too tired to go any farther. Besides, Heather Creek Road eventually made it all the way down to Dillon, and there was no way in hell she was traveling that distance. Not on foot, anyway.

The glow of lights from Main Street faded, and the darkness and the snow seemed to close in. Unease slithered through her. She didn't know this area all that well, but knew there were very few people living out this way. A few ski lodges, a house or two, but that was it. If she got into trouble, she'd find no help close by.

The thought made her pause. Through the silence, she heard the sound of an engine—one that seemed to be stationary rather than moving. Unease prickled down her spine, raising the hairs along her backbone. The urge to run away was so great she half-turned. Only the knowledge that more people might die if she didn't keep going made her head forward again.

Lights glimmered ahead. Red taillights, gleaming in the night like a mad wolf's eyes.

She shivered and padded forward more cautiously. It was a blue truck ahead. Iyona's truck. Halted in the middle of the road, lights on, engine running. Neva stopped and sniffed the air. She could smell oil and gas fumes from the exhaust, but couldn't pick up Betise's sharp scent, or Iyona's slightly off aroma. There was no sound other than the idling engine.

And no way in hell she was going closer. It looked like a trap, and right now, the safest thing she could do was high-tail it out of there. She could always come back later—in the safety of the car and with Duncan by her side.

She retreated. But she'd barely gone three steps when the night blurred, and she suddenly found herself under the snarling weight of a silver wolf.

Fourteen

Duncan's footsteps echoed as he walked down the hospital corridor toward Savannah's room. The young officer stationed at her door watched him warily, his hair gleaming carrot red under the harsh lights, and his hand drifting toward the gun at his side.

Obviously a ranger who was new to Ripple Creek, otherwise the youngster would have known who *he* was—if not by sight then by reputation. Duncan held up his hands and stopped. "Duncan Sinclair. I wish to talk to Savannah, if possible."

The ranger leaned around the doorway to speak to her. Duncan shook his head. The fool was obviously *very* new, because turning your back like that was *not* a good idea. Savannah must have said something along those lines, because when the young ranger looked back, his face was almost as red as his hair. "You can go in."

He held back his smile. "Thanks."

The carrot-topped ranger nodded, his hand still near the gun and a watchful look in his blue eyes. Duncan walked into the room. Savannah was sitting up in bed, her face still swathed in bandages, but overall looking a whole lot healthier than she had yesterday.

"What can I do for you, Mr. Sinclair?" Her voice held none of the warmth so evident in Neva's.

He dragged a chair up to her bed and sat down. "I believe we might be able to help each other."

A smile touched her lips. "Oh yeah? You come to confess?"

"Are you interested in hearing what I have to say, or are we going to dwell on a past I can do nothing about?"

She studied him for a moment, and he wished he could see her eyes. He had a feeling that, like Neva's, they would be extremely expressive.

"You hurt my sister," she said in that same flat, no-nonsense tone, "and I'll bust your balls from here to kingdom come."

He smiled faintly. "Fair enough."

She nodded. "Then talk."

He did. She said nothing, listening intently, nodding every now and again. When he'd finished, she said, "There's one problem with the idea that Iyona or Betise or both might be involved with these murders—"

"The black hairs found at the murder scene?"

"How did you know about them? Neva?"

"Yes."

"Then she trusts you."

With knowledge, but certainly not anything else. Yet. "She came after me at the mansion because even *you* think I'm not the murderer."

"That doesn't mean the rest of your pack isn't. Betise or Iyona might be working with one of them."

He reached into his jacket pocket and pulled out the plastic bag he'd fished out of the river earlier tonight. "Try matching this with those hairs you found." He placed it into her hands.

She felt through the plastic. "A wig?"

"A black wig. We were following Betise earlier and saw her throw it into Hunter River. I fished it out."

"We? You and Neva?"

"Yep. So you've got a believable witness as well as me."

The smile that touched her lips held true warmth and in many ways reminded him of Neva, which wasn't all that strange, considering they were twins.

"A wig doesn't make her the murderer. It's a silver wolf attacking these women, not a golden."

"But both Betise and Iyona have a better motive than anyone else. My pack aren't saints, but none of us are behind these murders. I'll guarantee it."

"Well, a guarantee like that is certainly going to go a *long* way in a court of law." But she said it with a smile, and he took no offense.

"Has anyone seen Betise's coat color?" he asked. "If she *is* the child of one of the Bitterroot Sinclairs, she might very well be silver."

"Possibly." Savannah's voice was noncommittal. "I'll have this checked out along with the samples we took tonight. Hopefully, we'll get an answer."

"We have something else you might be interested in, too. Martin took skin and blood samples from under Betise's nails the night she was attacked. They're currently being analyzed at the forensics lab."

"Any samples not taken by us under controlled conditions won't be accepted as evidence in court."

"Perhaps. But it may provide a link to the women who were killed. Once you have that link, you can concentrate on collecting evidence that is rock-solid."

"Maybe." Her voice was noncommittal.

He hesitated, then asked, "Can you remember anything of your own attack?"

"No. It's all still a blur."

"Have you asked Neva?"

She was silent for a long moment, then swore softly. "I didn't even think of it."

At least he wasn't the only one. He rose and put the chair back. "She was there with you in spirit."

"She's the reason I'm alive," Savannah said softly. "The only reason. The wolf was big—very big. And that's all I remember."

"But it may not be all Neva remembers."

"No." Savannah paused. "You intending to ask her yourself?"

"Yes."

"Don't try taking the law into your own hands, Sinclair. Not in my town. And if you find anything, you bring it to me to deal with."

"Right." After he'd found that bastard or bitch behind this and given him—or her—a beating or two.

"I mean it. Or the threat I made earlier will apply."

He didn't reply. Didn't get the chance to. Neva's fear slammed into his mind and, hot on its heels, her pain. The force of both, one on top of the other, hurled him back against the wall and left him gasping.

"Neva!" Savannah's cry sang through the air, through his mind, and was filled with fear for her sister.

He shook his head, trying to free himself from the haze of Neva's pain and terror to reach for her mentally. Nothing. She was too consumed by whatever was happening to her to hear him.

He pushed away from the wall and staggered to the door. He had to find her—fast. The young officer had rushed in at Savannah's cry and was near her bed. There were quick footsteps coming toward the room, and then nurses came

through the doorway. He pushed past them and thundered
down the hall.

You heard? Savannah's surprised thought cut through
his shields and arrowed into his mind.

Yes.

Oh Moons . . . does she know?

*No. Nor will she, until she is ready to acknowledge it for
herself.*

*Can you find her? I can't get any sense from her—I have
no idea where she is.*

I can find her. He didn't need to feel her thoughts for
that. All he had to do was follow his heart.

Do you need help?

No. Because if anyone had hurt her, he'd kill them. And
he didn't need rangers as witnesses.

Run swiftly.

He didn't answer. Just ran.

It was Savannah's attack all over again and, for one second,
Neva froze. All she could smell was the other wolf's putrid
breath, all she could hear was the rumble of its growl. All
she could feel was the drip of saliva against her face as the
gleaming white teeth slashed through the air, headed toward
her throat. She twisted desperately, and the teeth tore into
her foreleg instead. Pain ripped through her, burning away
the fear.

Savannah had beaten this bitch—but only because she'd
siphoned Neva's abilities at the last moment. There would
be no last moment here. As she'd told Duncan, she was far
from defenseless.

She reached for the fear singing through her veins and
flung it back at the other wolf, smashing through her foe's

shields and forcing it deep into her mind. A mind that was crazy with the moon's heat. Crazy with hate. For her.

The mad, yellow eyes went wide, then the silver wolf cowered away, whimpering and shivering. Neva scrambled upright and ran. With every step blood flew through the air, glistening with black fire as it splattered across the pristine snow.

Air stirred, arrowing towards her. Another wolf, coming from the right. Out of the corner of her eye she saw the blur of gold rising high as the wolf sprang. She slammed past this second wolf's shields, filling her mind with the terror and hatred she was still feeling from the first wolf. The golden bitch dropped, trembling and whimpering with fright. Neva kept on running, though her lungs burned and the warmth of blood pulsing down her leg became a tide.

Lights beckoned brightly through the darkness ahead. She ran onto Main Street but didn't stop, too fearful that if she did, those wolves would catch her. She couldn't hear them behind her, but that didn't mean they weren't. Warmth and music pulsed through the night, but she didn't head for the *Blue Moon*, even though she would be safe enough there. There was only one place she wanted to be right now—and he was close. She could feel him. In her mind. With her heart.

Neva? Savannah's thought was as sharp as glass. *Are you okay?*

Fine, she lied, not wanting to panic her sister any more than she already had. *I'll come and talk to you soon.*

She saw Duncan a second later—a sleek silver shadow exploding out of the snow-filled night. She shifted shape as he shifted shape, and all but fell into the warmth of his arms.

Trembling, shivering, she wrapped her arms around him and held on tight. Breathed deep the spicy, foresty smell of him, letting the sense of warmth and security and strength he exuded wash over her. Calm her.

The arms that held her so protectively were taut, and his heart was a rumble of rapid thunder in the ear she pressed hard against his chest. His anger was a cloud of red that burned her mind and stung the night, but behind it was fear. For her. The knowledge made her heart do a weird little dance.

She didn't know how long they stood there like that, holding each other in the middle of Main Street as the snow danced around them. She didn't really care, because she'd never felt so safe in her life. When he eventually pulled away, he caught her chin, directing her gaze to his.

"Was it Betise and Iyona?"

She nodded. "I doubt that it could have been anyone else, if only—"

"Tell me about it later," he cut in. "Right now, you need to get to the emergency room." He bent, swinging her up into his arms.

"I don't—"

"No arguments." His voice was almost savage. "That arm needs stitches."

She glanced down. The sleeve of her coat was ripped to shreds, and blood covered her arm and fingers. "It's not as bad as it looks."

"Maybe. But who knows what you can catch from a bite from a bitch like Betise?"

A smile played across her lips. "A rather nasty thing to say." Though as nasty comments went, she was thinking far worse.

"Right now, I'm feeling particularly nasty." He glanced at her. Though his black eyes were as unreadable as ever, something in his expression made her tremble. "You're mine, if only for the rest of this moon phase. No one attacks anything of mine and gets away with it."

His words seemed to echo through her, doing strange things to her pulse rate and her heart. Moons, it would be so easy to believe he cared. But that was something she dared not do, because it would be all too easy to fall.

If she hadn't fallen already.

She closed her eyes. No. It was the moon and the power of the man himself. Nothing more. She couldn't fall for a man like Duncan. He was everything she'd *never* wanted.

He strode through the night, not saying anything, just holding her with a tenderness that suggested she was precious cargo. Tears prickled her closed eyelids. She wouldn't think that. Couldn't think that. It wasn't safe.

"Safe isn't always what it's cracked up to be," he said softly. "Safe can be horribly lonely."

Which she'd discovered over the years, so why was she holding on to it so tightly? She didn't know, and that scared her almost as much as exploring what she might feel for him. She let her gaze rake the face she knew would haunt her dreams forever. "How could a relationship between us ever work?" Especially given her father's edict? "You don't want to come back to Ripple Creek, I don't really want to leave. I want a family. You want nothing more than a good time."

"All relationships must compromise to survive."

"But not all relationships are worth the effort. It's just the moon that binds us, nothing more. I can't help what I feel."

"You haven't explored what you feel." He paused as the

doors to the hospital swished open. "Let's discuss this when we're alone."

"There's nothing to discuss." And there would be no later. Not for them.

Because of who he was. Because of who she was, and the way she'd been brought up. She was willing enough to shake the shackles of her parents' beliefs and rules, but she didn't want them completely out of her life. She was a wolf, and family was everything. She couldn't walk away from her parents—not forever—and if she wanted Duncan in her life that's what she would have to do. Her father had made it clear he'd forgive the moon dance, but he would not forgive a continuing dalliance with someone like Duncan.

If it came down to a choice, there really was none. To keep her family in her life, she had to stick to her original plan and walk away from him. No matter what she might feel.

No matter how much it hurt.

Duncan paced the confines of the emergency waiting room. He itched to be a part of the posse Savannah was arranging to go after Betise and Iyona, but his first priority was Neva and her safety. But once he had her tucked securely away, he was going after the two bitches. No matter how forcefully Savannah had ordered him away.

And yet even as he paced he knew the anger that burned him was not so much the need for revenge, but rather annoyance at Neva's continuing insistence that this was nothing more than a moon dance. Because of who he was. Because of what he'd done. And because of her parents.

His mother had once told him that fate had a way of catching up and making you pay. He'd thought jail time had been his punishment, but this was far worse than anything he'd faced in the few days he'd spent in jail. He'd once been sure there was never going to be anyone out there for him. To actually find her and hold her, and yet be faced with the knowledge that she might never admit to what lay between them, was surely a punishment that far outweighed any of the crimes of his past.

But as he'd told Savannah, the past was something he could do nothing about—beyond regret it. It had shaped him, had helped make him what he was today, but it wasn't *who* he was today. Surely time would make Neva see that. If she'd give him time. Right now, he doubted she would.

Footsteps echoed down the hall. He looked up and saw a nurse wheeling Neva towards him. Her face was pale and she looked tired, but the smile that touched her full lips made his blood surge.

"The doctor says I have to take it easy with my arm for the next day or so." Her green eyes twinkled mischievously. "Looks like you're going to have to do all the work tonight."

He fell into step beside the wheelchair as they headed toward the exit. "I was under the impression I was doing all the work anyway."

A slight blush crept through her cheeks, and she cast a sideways glance at the nurse, who was grinning with delight. But if Neva was at all worried about what the nurse might be thinking, her next words belied it.

"And who approached whom to start with?"

"Ah yes," he said softly, his gaze meeting hers. "An amazing experience I shall never forget."

The bloom of heat in her cheeks grew. But so did her smile. "Well, there you go. Having done all the hard work to begin with, I deserve to sit back and enjoy it for a while."

"Then I shall endeavor to see that you do." He swung her
out of the wheelchair and into his arms, kissing her briefly
but passionately before glancing at the nurse. "Thanks."

Still smiling, the nurse nodded and retreated back inside.
He glanced down at Neva. "Ready?"

"That depends on what I'm supposed to be ready for."

Her voice was low and sexy as hell, and heat shot to his
groin. She smelled so good, so damn desirable, it was all he
could do not to take her right there and then.

He forced his feet to move down the pavement. "To go
home, witch."

"If that's all you're offering, then I guess so."

He couldn't help smiling. In a couple of days she'd gone
from a reticent lover to an all too willing participant. She was
amazing. Totally amazing. "Let's get out of the snow first."

"I've never done it in the snow," she said thoughtfully.
She was running her fingers up and down his arms, a gentle
caress that burned deep.

And making it damn hard to walk. "It's cold."

"But romantic."

Her breath was warm and sweet against his neck, and the
smell of her arousal stirred his senses and made him hunger.
Half a block had never seemed so far away. "Hypothermia
is never romantic."

She raised an eyebrow, eyes glimmering with green fire
in the darkness. "You only get hypothermia if you're out in
the cold a long time."

"I plan for it to be a long time."

"With the moon rising high and the urgency I feel beating through your skin? Doubtful." She paused and looked
around. "This is not the way to my house."

"No, it's the way to mine." Luckily, the lodge was down

the other end of the street from the hospital, otherwise he'd be calling a cab. She might want to make love in the snow, but right now she was beginning to shiver.

She frowned. "I don't want to go to the mansion."

"Good, because we're not going there."

Her surprise rippled around him. "You own a house here in Ripple Creek?"

"Sort of."

"What's 'sort of' supposed to mean?"

"That I own it, but it's not a house."

She gave him a long look that was filled with annoyance. "Then what is it?"

"It's Snowflake Lodge. My mother left it to me when she died." And he'd already called ahead to ensure one of the cabins was open and ready for them.

"Really? I thought the Harpers owned it."

"They manage it on my behalf. I doubt Betise and Iyona would think to look there, as it's one of the smaller lodges and definitely middle range."

"And the Sinclairs are well-known for their deluxe tastes."

"Exactly. You can stay there until I get this all sorted out."

Fear touched her eyes, and the warm caress of her fingers against his skin stopped. "You keep saying I rather than we. You're going after them, aren't you?"

"Yes. They have to be stopped."

"Savannah and the rangers will stop them."

"I intend to be there as backup." Not that he distrusted the abilities of Savannah's team. He just suspected Betise and Iyona would not be so easily caught. Not if they'd been planning all this for a long time.

He walked down the lodge's driveway, past the main lobby entrance and through the terraced gardens. The cabin they'd been assigned was at the rear of the property and extremely private.

"You're leaving once they're caught, aren't you?"

He hesitated. "For a while."

"So this could be our last night?"

He didn't answer. Didn't dare, lest he blurt out exactly what he was feeling. She wouldn't believe it. Not until she'd reached deep inside and discovered the truth for herself.

He placed her gently on her feet then opened the door and had a quick look inside to ensure all was ready. The room was warm, lit by the golden light of the fire burning in the huge stone fireplace. Two sofas and a couple of well-padded chairs corralled the fire, and on the other side of the room, there was a TV and a bar. The bedrooms and bathroom were upstairs. It wasn't much, but it was comfortable.

"After you, my lady," he said, turning around.

Only to discover she'd stripped. For one brief second, he allowed himself the pleasure of simply looking at her, letting his gaze travel down the long length of her neck, taking in her small but perfectly formed breasts, watching their peaks harden with desire. Her breathing was quick and sharp, every intake seeming to shudder through her entire body. Her desire stung the air, a rich scent that called to the wildness in him and made him harder than he'd ever thought possible.

But the full moon was too close, and if he started loving her, he might not want to stop. And she was injured, and he had villains to catch.

"Neva—"

"No." She stepped into his arms, her words hot and

breathy against his lips. "Just dance with me. Right here, right now."

He took a deep breath and puffed it out. "It's better that we don't—"

"Don't what?" she murmured saucily, her fingers cool against his chest as she slipped her hands under his sweater.

He pulled her hands firmly away. "You need to rest."

"I need to dance." Her gaze searched his, eyes gleaming in the darkness. "Are you going to take me up on the offer, or shall I go find someone who will?"

Even a saint would not be able to resist such an invitation—and he was a long way from sainthood. He crushed her close, his mouth finding hers almost savagely. She wrapped her arms around his neck, holding him tight, matching his urgency. Desire shimmered between them, but even a heat so fierce was not enough to stop her shivering. He picked her up and carried her inside, kicking the door shut before making his way across to the sofa nearest the fire. Once he'd placed her on her feet again he stepped back and quickly stripped. The musky scent of her desire grew stronger, fueling the need already raging through his veins. But rather than pulling her close and claiming her as he ached to do, he reached out, running his hand down her neck. She trembled, her pulse galloping beneath his fingertips.

"I don't want to dance," he said softly.

Her gaze swept down his body, and a smile teased her kiss-swollen lips. "Well, certain parts of your body are belying that statement."

"That's not what I mean. I want to make love to you."

Confusion flickered through her bright eyes. "They're the same thing."

"No. Dancing is for pleasure. Making love is something more." And he ached to show her what he dared not say.

She ran her tongue across her lips. He had to resist the sudden urge to follow that moist trail with his mouth.

"In what way?"

Though her voice was calm, panic gleamed in her eyes. She understood all too well what he meant. He let his hand drift past her throat. Her already puckered nipples seemed to become harder, as if straining for his touch. "If you wish to discover the answer, you have to play the game."

He brushed his fingers across the top of her breasts, circling but not touching the dark centers. She took a deep, shuddery breath. "What game?"

"Pretense."

"Which is?"

"Let's pretend we are lovers. Let's pretend it's the night before the full moon, and we are about to promise our souls to each other."

She studied him for several heartbeats, her expression a mix of confusion and alarm. "Why?"

"Because I've never had a true lover, just dancers."

She hesitated. "I'm not sure this a game I can play."

"Why not?" He gently plucked one nipple.

Goose bumps fled across her skin, and her pupils dilated, almost swallowing the new-leaf green of her irises. "Because I don't see the point of it."

He shifted his touch to her other breast, this time rolling the firm nub between his fingertips. "It's not the night of promising, Neva. No harm can come from pretending."

"Can you be sure? The magic might lie in the ritual itself rather than the night."

"Have you ever heard of the ritual being performed on any other night but the one before the full moon?"

"No, but—"

"No buts. Just yes or no."

Neva took another deep breath. His gentle touch shuddered through every fiber of her being, and though she wanted him with a fierceness that was almost painful, she feared to pretend what lay between them was anything more than just a dance. Because such pretense might lead to the examination of feelings she'd managed to avoid up until now. "What if I say no?"

"Then you go to bed and rest as the doctor ordered."

"That's sexual blackmail."

"No, that's honesty. This one time, I want more than just a dance."

She closed her eyes. It was a risk. She knew in her heart it was a risk because no one truly knew any more if the magic of promising was confined to the one night. And because, deep down, she knew her heart was already on the line, and this might tip it over the edge and down the hill toward heartbreak.

But could she let him walk away tomorrow or the day after without knowing what it might be like to be truly loved by this man?

He raised a hand, cupping her cheek. It felt like he was branding her skin for eternity. "Your answer?"

No. "Yes."

He smiled, his dark eyes filled with a heat that caused a meltdown deep inside her. He caught her hand and tugged her onto the rug near the hearth. The thick fur pressed against her toes, and the warmth of the flames caressed her skin but seemed oddly cool compared to the fire burning inside and out.

He pressed her fingers against his chest. The heat of his body and his warm, woody scent washed across her senses, stirring her in ways she'd never thought possible. And the wild beat of his heart under her fingertips only fueled her desire to greater heights.

"Does my lady know what night it is?"

His voice was little more than a stroke of sound, yet it seemed to sing through every part of her. She took a deep breath and released it slowly. His question was the start of the ritual. If she replied, if the magic *could* be raised on nights other than the one before the full moon, she could bind herself for eternity to a man who did not love her. Because once begun, there was no retreat. Not unless the participants were familiar with the paths of magic.

But if she didn't reply, if the magic *couldn't* be raised on any other night, she'd miss the chance to know what it might be like to be the woman he loved enough to commit to.

Pretense, he'd said, *nothing more*. She could pretend she loved him. Pretend that he loved her. Even if it broke her heart.

"It is the night before the full moon. The night of promises." She briefly closed her eyes against the sudden sting of tears. Deep down, part of her wished that this was real. That the words were real. That he truly did love her.

He stepped closer. Her breasts were pressed against his warm bare chest, and the heat of his erection scorched her stomach. "Or the night of destiny."

The air seemed to stir around them. Or was it merely his breath stroking her mouth with warmth?

"You are my heart, my soul." And knew even as she said the words that she shouldn't have started this. Couldn't pretend, because she did care, as much as she'd tried *not* to admit it.

"I can't do this," she added. "Let's just dance."

He didn't hear her. Or maybe he chose not to hear her. "Kneel with me."

"We can't do this." Because she didn't want to pretend when part of her ached so fiercely for it to be real.

His eyes were black fires of determination that burned through her soul. "Kneel with me," he repeated and tugged her down in front of him.

"Duncan—"

He stopped her with a kiss that was both ferocious and passionate. One that left her mind reeling and her body aching.

"Dance with me," he said, voice so husky, so damn sexy, chills ran across her skin. "This night and the rest of our nights, for as long as the divine light shines in the evening skies. For as long as we live beneath it."

The air seemed to thrum, to burn, at his words. Magic, or her imagination?

"No," she choked, trying to pull away.

His touch slid past her hip to cup her rear, holding her in place, his grip gentle but firm. "Pretense," he whispered, brushing a kiss across her lips. "That's all it is."

This was more than pretense. Something was happening. Surely he could feel it. Surely the tingle in the air wasn't just her imagination.

He caught her chin, raising her gaze to his. His eyes were ebony pools she wanted to lose herself in forever.

"I feel nothing more than desire. Want nothing more

than to love you as you should be loved. Pretend with me."

She closed her eyes and shifted her stance. "Under her light, I offer you my body."

Desire and something else, something more ethereal, shimmered between them, warming the night. Warming her. His rigid heat slid deep inside, until it felt as if he was claiming every inch of her. He began to rock. It felt so good, so right, a moan escaped her lips.

"Under the divine light of the moon," he said, "I offer you my heart."

It felt like her own heart was snapping tight, ready to shatter. "Under her light, I offer you mine."

The sting in the air was becoming stronger. Sweat skated across her skin. *Pretense*, she told herself fiercely. *Nothing more.*

His grip on her rump grew stronger, holding her steady as the tempo of his thrusts increased. "Under the divine light, I offer you my soul."

Deep down the tremors were beginning, spreading through her body like a wave. She gripped his shoulders, digging her nails into his flesh, fighting the sensations rippling through her, fearing the burning in the air. Fearing the fact she could not stop the words flowing from her lips.

"By her light, I offer you mine."

He was thrusting deep and hard. The world seemed to be spinning, and every fiber of her being was tingling with magic. Burning with the need for release.

"Then let our souls become one as our bodies have become one." "Let the moon bless and rejoice in this union," she somehow gasped. "Do you accept the gift of my seed?" he growled. "Do you accept the promises of the night and the moon?" "Yes," she cried. "Yes."

He went rigid against her, the force of his release tearing her name from his throat. Heat seemed to explode around them, through them, and her climax came in a rush of power that stole her breath, stole all thought, and swept her into a world that was sheer, unadulterated bliss.

For a long moment, neither of them moved. She rested her forehead on his chest, desperately trying to catch her breath, desperately hoping the ritual hadn't worked. But the air still hummed, her skin still tingled, and he was still so very hard inside her.

After a while, he lifted her chin, his lips seeking hers, his kiss a lingering taste of passion.

"What the moon has joined, let no wolf break." He brushed sweaty strands of hair from her forehead, then kissed her again. Sweetly. Gently. But it wasn't his kiss that sent goose bumps fleeing across her skin. It was the caring in his dark eyes. The gentle, almost loving smile touching his lips. "May the moon bless this union and grant us life."

Energy seemed to flow through every pore of her being. For one moment, it felt as if the moon itself was blessing her. Blessing them. She fought the sting of more tears and closed her eyes. Thankfully, the moon *couldn't* bless this union with life. Not when Duncan had been given the fertility control injection.

"By the moon's divine light, let us now celebrate this union." Though the words were the last in the ritual, they were also what she wanted. All she wanted.

All they did, through the remainder of the long night. By the end of which she truly knew what it felt like to be loved by a man like Duncan.

But did she dare believe it?

*

A distant ringing stirred Duncan from slumber, but it was a sound that stopped almost the minute he woke. He swore softly and looked around. The morning's light peeked past the bedroom curtains, indicating dawn had come and gone. He hadn't meant to sleep so long. Hadn't meant to love Neva so long. Hadn't meant to do a lot of things.

But he regretted none of them.

Especially not binding Neva to him heart and soul.

He smiled and splayed his fingers across her belly, pressing her close against him. She was his, and there was nothing on this Earth that could separate them now.

While it was supposed to have been nothing more than pretense, the minute he'd said the first words of the ritual and felt the stirrings of magic in the air, he'd known what was happening. And there was no way in hell he'd been about to stop—or let her stop. Neva was his, and the ceremony ensured that, from this point on, she could no more turn to another wolf than he could. It wasn't playing fair, wasn't giving her the choice, but in all honesty, he didn't care. He'd spent more than half his life looking for his soul mate, and now that he'd found her, he wasn't about to let her go. Wasn't about to sit back and watch her walk into the arms of what her family might consider a "more suitable" mate.

Because he very much suspected that was what she might do. Family was everything to a wolf, to Neva more than most, and this break with her parents was killing her. And while he was responsible for that, he had no intention of walking away to mend the rift. And the ceremony had given him the time he needed to convince Neva and her parents, that his intentions and his feelings were both honest and true.

The ringing started again, soft but insistent. It seemed to be coming from downstairs . . . his cell phone, he realized. It was still in the pants he'd discarded in the living room. Neva stirred, and he brushed a kiss across her shoulder.

"Sleep," he said, using the power of the moon binding to make it an order. She'd probably fry his brains when she woke and realized he was still using that hold on her, but right now, he didn't care. She needed the rest.

She murmured something that sounded suspiciously like a curse, then drifted back to sleep. He kissed her again, this time on her cheek, then climbed out of bed and padded downstairs, finding his pants and pulling out the phone. "Hello?"

"There's been a fire at the hospital."

His father's voice was flat, devoid of any emotion, and Duncan's gut began to churn. "René?"

"Is missing. Kane was found unconscious but alive in one of the stairwells. Looks like he'd been trying to stop the kidnappers."

"He's okay?"

"Nothing more than a bruised ego, and a mighty bump on the back of the head."

"I gather it was Betise and Iyona?"

"Yes. Apparently Betise let him chase her into the stairwell, where Iyona jumped him."

Duncan took a deep breath and released it slowly. "What about Savannah and the other patients?" Neva would want to know her sister was okay, even though she would surely have known if something bad *had* happened. The link between the two of them was strong.

"They're fine. The fire was in the basement, used merely as a distraction."

"You're heading up a hunting party?"

"Tye's on his way to join me and Kane. Savannah's given permission for us to be included in the official party."

Probably because she knew they'd form a hunting party of their own if she didn't. "Do you intend to join them?"

"Yes. If only because if I find those two alone, I might be tempted to kill them. The Sinclair name has taken enough of a beating these past few weeks. We don't need to add murder to our crimes."

Duncan glanced around for his sweater. "I'll be there in five minutes."

"We're meeting over at the rangers' office."

"I'll be there."

He hung up and quickly dressed, then bounded up the stairs. He knelt by the bed, kissing Neva's lips gently, feeling the stirrings of passion in the sleepiness of her response.

"Sleep well, my love. I'll be back soon." He brushed the hair from her eyes, kissed her nose, then left.

The phone rang again as he was walking towards Main Street. He pressed the receiver and said, "Don't tell me, the location's changed."

"It certainly has."

It wasn't his father on the phone. It was Betise. His knuckles went white with the force of his grip. "If you've hurt him, bitch, you're both dead."

Betise tsked. "Such anger."

"Just tell me what you want."

"My mother is waiting in front of the hair salon for you. I'm not sure where you are, but you have two minutes to get there and get into the truck. We hear, see, or smell the rangers anywhere near, and René is a dead man."

"This is not going to achieve anything."

"Promises were made. Tonight they will be fulfilled."

The bitch was definitely crazy. He hit the "end" button, then dialed his father's number as he ran. "Betise just called me," he said, the minute his father answered. "She wants me in front of her hair salon, alone, within two minutes."

Zeke swore. Duncan didn't give his father the chance to say anything else. "Follow the truck's tracks," he said. "And don't get near enough for them to see or smell you, or René's dead."

He hung up, sped around the corner, and saw not one waiting truck, but two. Out of the corner of his eye, he caught movement, and something sharp plunged into his arm. He swore and swung around, fist flying. Betise laughed and danced out of the way. He glanced down. A dart had been buried hilt deep into his forearm.

"Do you really think I'd trust you to sit back like a good little wolf while we take you to René?" she taunted. "I may be well-used flesh, Duncan, but I'm not stupid."

He lunged for her. But it felt like he was moving through glue, and his feet were extraordinarily heavy. Betise laughed, capering just beyond his reach. The dart must have been drugged. He cursed her and lunged again, but suddenly found himself falling face first onto the pavement. Then the darkness rushed in, accompanied by harsh, almost maniacal laughter.

Fifteen

Neva woke to the nagging sensation that something was wrong. Frowning, she lay still in bed, listening to the silence haunting the cabin. Duncan wasn't there. His smell was little more than a lingering tease of wood on the air, and there was no sound of footsteps or breathing. Maybe he'd joined the hunt for Betise and Iyona.

She glanced toward the window. The light filtering past the curtains was soft, almost muted, as if the day had come and gone, and dusk was almost over. Surely she couldn't have slept that long.

Neva? Savannah's thought was abrupt, and the feeling of wrongness increased.

What's happened? She swung out of bed, shivering a little as the cool air caressed her skin, and padded downstairs to find her clothes.

Plenty. Savannah's mind voice was grim. *There was a fire at the hospital, which we've since discovered was little more than a cover for René Sinclair being snatched. Duncan then got a phone call stating he'd better meet Iyona in front of Betise's hair salon if he wanted to see his brother alive.*

He wouldn't have gone to such a meeting alone. Surely he wasn't that stupid.

He was given little choice and little time. But he did call his father. By the time we got there, the trucks were gone. We followed the tracks, but the damn snow came down again, and we lost them.

Neva cursed the unseasonably late onslaught of snow, though no doubt the skiers still lingering in Ripple Creek were rejoicing. *I'm coming to the hospital.*

I'm not there.

What? Savannah—

I'm fine. I'm being careful. But I'm a ranger, and I'll be damned if I'll lay on my back in bed while these bitches run around killing and kidnapping people.

Neva moved across to the window and looked out. It was no longer snowing, and the moon was rich and yellow and almost full as it began its ascent in the darkening sky. She stared at it for a moment, remembering Betise's words. Remembering her conviction, her certainty, that she and Duncan were soul mates. *She's going to perform the promising ritual.*

What?

Betise believes she's Duncan's soul mate. She grabbed her coat, swept a set of keys off the coffee table and ran for the door.

Impossible, when you— Savannah's thought cut off abruptly. *It doesn't matter, does it?*

No. It's the night of promising. The magic can be raised whether it's your soul mate or not. God, how she wished their pretense last night had been real. While she might then have bound herself to a man who did not love her, she'd rather that than Duncan being fettered to a murdering fiend like Betise. *Have you searched down Heather Creek Road?*

We did last night, after they'd attacked you, but we found nothing. And the truck tracks didn't head that way tonight.

Well, that's where they are. Why she was certain, she couldn't say. And if she was wrong, Duncan would pay.

Where are you?

Just coming out of Snowflake Lodge.

I'll meet you on Main. Be there in five minutes.

Savanna was there in two, and she didn't come alone. There was a convoy of four trucks in all. Neva climbed into the first one, relieved to see Ronan at the wheel. Her gaze swung left to meet Savannah's. The main bandage had been removed from her sister's face, but there were still dressings on her right cheek and over her left eye. "I'm a little surprised to see you in the back seat rather than the driver's."

Her sister's good eye twinkled brightly in the shadows. "I may be stubborn, but I'm not a fool." Her voice was dry. "Besides, I can't see well enough to drive just yet."

"Mind you," Ronan commented, a smile touching his gray eyes as he glanced at Neva, "it took the threat of a revolt to lose that foolhardiness she claims *not* to have."

"Why am I not surprised?" Neva slammed the door shut and buckled up her seat belt as Ronan took off. Lights swept through the rear window, briefly setting Ronan's russet hair aflame as the trucks behind fell into line.

"Probably because doing stupid things runs in our family," Savannah replied.

Neva met her sister's gaze. "That it does." Things like deciding to seduce the most dangerous man in the Sinclair pack, or pretending to perform the promising ritual. One had led her heart into danger, and the other had forced her to confront what she'd been trying to ignore—the fact that in a mere couple of days she'd fallen in love with Duncan.

She pulled her gaze from Savannah's and stared out the window. "It doesn't matter," she said softly.

It does if you love him.

I love Mom and Dad, too. I won't give up my family for the sake of a man. No matter what I feel for him.

Savannah didn't say anything. There was nothing she *could* say, because they both knew the truth of the words.

Ronan turned the truck onto Heather Creek Road, and they quickly left the lights of Ripple Creek behind them. Under the cold light of the rising moon, the land became a vast expanse of black and silver. It was stark, oddly beautiful, but also eerie.

Neva stared out the window, her gaze roaming across the lustrous landscape without really seeing any of it. They were closing in. She wasn't sure how she knew, but the sensation was similar to what she shared with her sister. It was as if somehow Duncan had become a part of her, as if he was reaching out for her, not only psychically but physically. She could feel him, not only in her mind, but on her body. Almost as if he were caressing her, trailing his fingers across her skin, sending little tingles of electricity through every nerve ending. She was attuned to him. Totally attuned. She briefly closed her eyes, too afraid to confront the reason why that might be. Because confronting it wouldn't change the facts. Wouldn't change her parents' opinion. Wouldn't change her refusal to walk away from them completely.

She bit her lip, her gaze moving past the trees and spying a flicker of gold in the darkness. "Stop," she said quickly and was out the door before Ronan even touched the brake.

"Neva, wait," Savannah cried.

She stopped on the verge of the road. She wasn't a fool. If Iyona and Betise could overpower someone like René, what hope would she have against them?

The night was cold and still, the snow beyond the road powdery light, glittering brightly under the moon's harsh light. The nearby trees cast deep shadows, and the smell of pine and balsam was rich in the air. She sniffed deeply. Behind those two scents was another. A warm, woody aroma that sent the blood pounding through her veins. Duncan was here somewhere. And so were Betise and Iyona, even though she couldn't smell them.

The other trucks pulled to a halt behind them, and men poured out. Savannah stopped beside her, sniffing the air lightly. "I can't smell them."

"Duncan's here. Betise will be, too."

Savannah looked past her, and Neva followed the direction of her gaze. Zeke Sinclair walked towards them, his stride long and powerful, his angelic face expressionless, and his dark eyes shuttered. For one moment, he looked so much like Duncan her heart ached. Behind him were two shadows who were just as potent, but who were hiding their anger less skillfully. Tye and Kane.

Zeke stopped in front of Neva. The sense of his power, the sheer force of his masculinity swept over her, and yet didn't stir her. She glanced at her sister and saw that Savannah was similarly unmoved. Which was a good thing, but odd, given the night and the moon.

"Where?" His voice was sharp. Abrupt.

Neva pointed to where she'd seen the brief flicker of light, and mentally passed the image and the information on to Savannah. "About half a mile in." How she'd managed to see the light from such a distance she didn't know. Nor did she care. Not if it freed Duncan.

Zeke looked at Savannah. "How do you want to do this?"

"Neva suspects Betise will try to perform the ritual of promising. If that's the case, they'll more than likely be in a clearing. We need to get René free first, then we'll surround the clearing and get Duncan out." She hesitated, her green eyes narrowing. "No accidents, Zeke. I want these two women alive."

Zeke raised his hands. "We have no weapons."

"A wolf doesn't need a weapon to kill."

There was nothing warm in Zeke's sudden smile. "I will protect my sons, Ranger, no matter what your rules say."

"You can protect all you want. Just don't kill."

Zeke's gaze flickered to Neva, studying her so intently she shifted uncomfortably. After a moment, his smile became warmer. "Perhaps I won't need to. There are other emotions, and other players, here tonight."

Heat touched Neva's cheeks. She had a horrible feeling this man saw far more than normal men, and in her case, that he saw the feelings she was trying hard to ignore. She pulled her gaze from his and glanced at her sister. "You want me to lead?"

"You take Ronan and the Sinclairs and head to the right. The rest of us will head left."

As she nodded she glanced at the sky. The moon was bright, and magic was beginning to stir the night. If they didn't hurry, they'd be too late.

She shifted shape and lunged forward through the soft snow.

It was the cold that woke Duncan. It surrounded him, filled him. He frowned but didn't move, allowing awareness to surface fully as he listened to the night. Someone breathed close by, someone whose scent was all too familiar, and relief surged. René.

He cracked open an eye. They were in a small cave. Warm shadows danced across the walls, flickering shapes that indicated a fire was close. Naked, his brother leaned against the opposite wall, his eyes closed, though he wasn't asleep. The tension riding René's bruised and cut shoulders told Duncan that much. René's hands and feet were tied with chains that gleamed silver in the night, and the bandages over the gunshot wound were bloody, an indication that the wound had opened again.

Anger surged through Duncan, but he thrust it away. Right now, anger wasn't going to help either of them. He glanced down at himself. He was also naked, though he couldn't have been undressed for long, because he could still feel his fingers and toes. Hypothermia was a ways off yet. But he had a fair idea why they were both naked, and what Betise intended to do. Tonight was the night of promises, and that mad bitch was undoubtedly going to try to raise the magic.

Worse though was the fact he was also tied with chains, and if the warmth against his skin was anything to go by, those chains didn't just look silver, they *were* silver. Which meant neither of them could shift shape until the chains were off, as silver was the one metal immune to magic of all kinds. He moved his arms, trying to find some give in the looped chains and work them loose.

"I wish you luck," René said quietly. "Because I certainly haven't had any."

Then the two women had been less careful about tying him, because the chains weren't as tight as they had been.

"Are you all right?" Though Duncan asked the question softly, his words seemed to echo in the cave, and outside, someone stirred.

"Yes. Though I have to say the moon dance is not much fun when you're just a body and not a willing participant."

"It could be worse, Brother." And probably would get

worse, unless he could find a way out for both of them. He very much doubted that René had been taken just as a hostage. There were two women and two of them, and this was all about revenge. Revenge for past wrongs. Revenge for promises never made.

And what better revenge was there than to bind yourself to a man who hated you?

A shadow loomed across the wall, shifting from wolf to human shape. He craned his neck to the left and watched Betise enter. Like them, she was naked. Oddly enough, her body was covered with a white powder, and he couldn't smell her. He couldn't smell Iyona, either, though she was undoubtedly just as close.

Betise's gaze met his, green eyes glowing like ice in the darkness. "The time has come to keep your promises, Duncan."

"Tell me first why you killed those women." Not that it really mattered now. He just needed to buy more time. Time to loosen the chains some more. Time for his father and brothers to track them down.

She shrugged. "Kill the competition, give the dance a bad name, and my chances of catching a Sinclair mate rise, don't they?"

Only a crazy woman would believe that. "So why make it look like they were raped?"

"To confuse the rangers. Worked like a charm, too, didn't it? They were so convinced it was one of you Sinclairs they didn't even bother looking for other possible culprits."

"So why attack yourself?" It was a guess, but a reasonably safe one.

"Neva told me her sister was waking. I knew if the ranger remembered the attack, she'd know it was a female who attacked her, not a male." She shrugged again. "I was hoping it would throw everyone off, but it didn't. You suspected me, didn't you?"

"Yes." Though not of the killings. Not at first.

She nodded. "I smelled you in my hair salon, you know."

"Is that why you got rid of the wig?" Surprise flitted across her face, and he smiled coldly. "I fished it out of the river, Betise. Savannah has it."

"You lie."

"It doesn't matter if he's lying." Iyona stepped out of the shadows, a rifle held steadily in her hands. A rifle that was aimed straight at René. "The time of promising has come."

"I made no promises to Betise. I never will."

"You will if you want your brother to live to his time of promising."

His gaze flicked to hers. Where Betise's gaze was crazy, Iyona's was hard. Intent.

"This will gain you nothing."

"You're a Sinclair, and the Sinclairs owe me."

"My pack had nothing to do with what happened to you."

"You're all Sinclairs. I don't care which pack pays me what I am owed."

"And what the hell are you owed, Iyona?"

"A name. A child. A comfortable lifestyle."

The woman might not look mad, but she was every bit as insane as her daughter. "Neither René nor I can give you a child. That's taken care of every moon dance."

Betise snorted. "You taking bets on that fact?"

He stared at her, a sick sensation in his gut. "What are you saying?"

Betise's smile was contemptuous. "That I tampered with

one box of injections. Twenty, in all, I think. The good doctor keeps meticulous records, and I knew René was being done early. But if I'd known you were coming back, I would have tampered with yours, as well."

Relief slithered through him. At least he didn't have to worry about Neva being pregnant. They might have performed the moon ceremony and, for all intents and purposes, be married, but right now, they did not need a child. Not when they were still very much strangers, and she was still wary of both him and her feelings.

"The surgery is locked. How could you possibly get in?"

Betise arched an eyebrow. "Through the tunnels, of course." She glanced at René, a cold smile on her lips. "You really should work on your shield, you know. Your mind is such an easy read when you're dancing."

René didn't even bother opening his eyes as he said, "I will never give you a child."

"My dear boy, you probably already have," Iyona commented dryly. "And not only Betise, but me and your other half dozen partners as well."

"I wouldn't bet on it." René's voice was cold. Harsh. "Martin is not the fool you think him to be. He saw the box had been tampered with and got rid of them."

Betise stared at him. "You're lying."

René opened his eyes and looked at her. His dark gaze was as hard as the rocks behind him. "Am I?"

Betise studied them both for a second, her eyes gleaming moon bright in the night. "Get up, both of you."

If they were ever going to escape, it had to be now, when the two women were overly confident and before the ceremony was performed. While he could not get caught by the promising ritual, René could. And he knew René would say the words and link himself forever with a bitch like Iyona, if it meant saving Duncan's life. He glanced at his brother's set face, eyebrow raised in question, and saw the barest nod of agreement. He pushed back against the wall and struggled to his feet. "The promising ritual won't work, Betise."

"If you don't say the right words, René is a dead man."

"Better a dead man than being bound to dead-smelling flesh," René commented as he struggled upright.

"Dead flesh that you will be bound to for eternity," Iyona snarled.

"Over my lifeless body."

"Or your brother's." The sound of the safety clicking off seemed to echo ominously in the cavern. "We're not overly fussy about which one we kill. All we want is a child, so we can claim our share of the Sinclair fortune."

Duncan couldn't help the harsh laugh that escaped his lips. "Do you really think our father will acknowledge any child you two bear?"

"Blood is blood, and everyone knows Zeke is an old-fashioned wolf. He'll support the get of his sons." She stepped to one side. "Now move, both of you."

Duncan shuffled forward until he'd moved up alongside his brother. They shared a brief glance, and as one, walked clumsily forward. The chains around their legs clinked softly, the bell like sound covering the noise Duncan made as he slid the loosened chain from his arms and caught them in his hand.

In that same moment, awareness surged through his mind. Neva was close. He couldn't smell her, but he could feel her—in his heart, with his soul.

Neva?

Here. So is Savannah, as well as your father and brothers.

How far away?

Not far. Why?

Hurry. He didn't tell her why. Didn't have the time, because they were too close to the two women. If they shuffled forward any farther, Betise would see his hands were no longer tied. Tension emanated from René, telling Duncan his brother was ready to move.

"Dive low," he said and swung the chain, lashing it around Iyona's face and neck as René hit her low and hard, sending her sprawling backwards. Her scream was a high-pitched sound of pain and fury that got lost in the sound of a gunshot.

René grunted, but Duncan had no time to see if his brother had been hurt, because a snarling fury hit him hard and sent him sprawling backwards.

Teeth tore into his shoulder and arm. He hissed and thrust his hands between them, grabbing Betise by the throat and forcing her back, away from his neck. Saliva dripped from her huge jaws, splashing across his chest as she snarled and snapped and twisted, her strength almost as great as his own. Her nails tore into his bare stomach and cut down his side as she scrambled to gain purchase against him. Her eyes gleamed with malevolent fire, and he had no doubt that she intended to kill him. Not because she hated him, but because she loved him. Because he wouldn't—couldn't—love her.

He thrust her back with all his force and lunged sideways. The rush of howling air told him she was closing in again. His nails dug into the cold dirt floor as he wrapped his fingers around a rock. With a grunt of effort, he swung around, smashing it across Betise's snarling snout, beating her away. Her growl became a yelp of pain as she leapt out of his reach. He let go of the rock and reached desperately for the chains around his feet. He had to work them free so he could move. Could change. Claws scrambled against dirt and stone behind him, then air rushed over him. He threw himself sideways, punching upwards at the silver form that flew overhead. His fist sank deep, but she didn't seem to feel it, twisting in midair so that she landed facing him. With one bound, she was on him again.

He thrust his hand out, his fingers digging into her thick neck, his whole arm trembling with the effort of keeping her snarling, snapping canines away from his throat.

Warmth flooded across his skin, and a golden haze of energy covered her form as she shifted shape once again. He bucked, trying to get her off him, but she screamed, a sound so high-pitched it hurt his ears. Then her knee found his groin. Pain flooded him, an all-consuming red haze, and suddenly it was all he could do to even breathe. Energy rolled across his skin again, then she was on him in wolf form, tearing into his shoulders and chest.

Somehow he forced his arms between them and pushed her back. Her teeth sank deep into his forearm, a sharp pain that battled the deep ache in his groin. He swore and thrust two straightened fingers deep into her throat. She coughed but didn't release her hold, worrying at his flesh like a dog with a bone.

He swore again and punched her across the ears. She shook her head, sending saliva and blood flying, but she didn't let go. Just kept tearing and gnawing at his arm.

From out of the night came a flash of gold that hit Betise broadside and sent her flying. The two wolves tumbled beyond his line of sight, their growls mixing with the sound of snapping teeth and tearing flesh. He swore and sat up, hurriedly undoing the chains from his legs before surging to his feet.

He swung around, saw the two wolves, silver and gold, at the back of the cavern. Neva was on the bottom, but her teeth were deep into Betise's throat, and blood gleamed on silver fur.

He shifted shape and arrowed toward them, hitting Betise and sending her rolling off Neva, who scrambled to her feet and spat out a huge chunk of hair and flesh.

Are you all right? Her mind voice was rich with concern and caring.

Yes. Just seeing her made everything all right, though he knew it wasn't.

You're bleeding. She licked his wounds tentatively, then a rumble rose up her throat, and she nudged him sideways, taking the full impact of Betise's leap.

He swore as he hit the ground, though it came out little more than a harsh growl. He rolled to his feet, saw the two wolves tearing at each other near the cavern's entrance. Felt the sharp caress of electricity in the air, a sensation that built and built until every hair on his coat stood on end. It was similar but far stronger than the force he'd felt building in the kitchen the night Neva had slammed deep into his mind and assaulted him with her fear and pain.

Shield. Neva's warning blasted him, and he thrust up his shields immediately.

A heartbeat later, the force in the air seemed to explode, and Betise was torn from Neva's body and flung out the cavern entrance.

He shifted shape and walked towards Neva as the changing haze rolled across her wolf shape. He stopped beside her and slid his fingers through hers. They were trembling, and as wet with blood as his own.

Betise lay ten feet away. She'd regained human form and was half curled up in fetal position, her bloody body shaking, her green-grey eyes wide and staring.

"I fried her mind," Neva said, voice flat, emotionless.

He didn't say anything, just wrapped an arm around her and pulled her close. She rested her cheek against his chest, and though she made no sound, warm tears slid down his skin.

Over the top of her head, he saw a russet-haired ranger holding a gun on Iyona as Savannah cuffed her. Watched his father and brother's kneel beside René's still form. Felt the surge of relief as his father looked up and nodded. His brother was okay.

"It's over," he said softly.

"Yes, it is."

He closed his eyes at the starkness in her voice. And knew that for now, it was.

Neva winced as the needle slid into her forearm.

"Sorry," the doctor said, much too cheerfully. "But I can't do much about it. Tetanus shots are never pleasant, no matter how careful we are."

She nodded vaguely, her attention more on what was going on in the other room than what the doctor was doing to her arm. They'd been at the rangers' office for over an hour now. Because of the fire at the hospital, the emergency doctors had come to them, looking after her, Duncan, Iyona and Betise. Only René had gone on to the emergency room.

She hadn't seen Duncan since they'd come here, and she desperately needed to see him, to talk to him. Needed to make him understand why she'd come to the decision she had. Savannah was probably talking to him, as she couldn't see her sister, either. But Betise and Iyona were visible—the older wolf cursing and fighting every order, the younger wolf catatonic, not responding to anyone or anything. A living, breathing zombie.

Neva closed her eyes, not wanting to see what she'd done. And yet part of her didn't regret it. Betise had killed without remorse, and would have killed her and Duncan, and anyone else who got in the way of her mad scheme.

"Don't go lifting anything heavy for the next couple days," the doctor said. "And if there's any sign of soreness or infection, go straight to the emergency room."

She nodded and slipped off the table, walking into the other room. That's when she saw her parents. She stopped and met her father's gaze for a moment, saw the relief and worry haunting the green of his eyes. Her mother started towards her, tears on her face and one hand outstretched. Neva spun away, not ready or willing to talk to either of them just yet, and walked down the passage to Savannah's office. Her sister was there. So was Duncan.

Savannah rose and walked around her desk. "I'll leave you two alone." She placed her hand on Neva's good arm, and squeezed it lightly. Then she walked out and closed the door behind her.

Duncan rose from the visitor's chair. Neva let her gaze travel up the long, lean length of him, etching it into her memory. Though in truth, it already was. His left arm was in a sling, and there were scratches across his beautiful face.

He didn't step any closer, just reached out, cupping her cheek with his palm, letting his thumb brush warmth across her trembling lips. She briefly closed her eyes, breathing in the scent of him, battling the tears that suddenly threatened her control.

"You haven't changed your mind?" he asked softly.

"No." It came out little more than a tortured whisper.

He stepped closer, his dark eyes holding hers, shimmering with deep determination. And love. "I won't give up on us, you know that, don't you?"

"Yes." The word seemed to stick somewhere in her throat. She swallowed, but it didn't ease the burning in her throat. Didn't ease the burning in her chest. "I have no choice, Duncan, not with my father's ultimatum. I can't walk away from my family."

"Nor do I expect you to. But I intend to come back to Ripple Creek, and I intend to make your father see that we were meant to be."

"My father will never accept you."

"I won't give up," he repeated, his breath warm against her lips. "You are mine, Neva. You always will be."

He kissed her. Softly. Sweetly. Then he turned and walked out the door.

It felt like her heart had shattered. Pain unlike anything she'd ever felt before welled, and she raised a hand to her mouth, holding back the sobs. Holding in the need to cry out his name as the echo of his footsteps grew softer, until all that was left were the caress of his scent on the air and the taste of him on her lips.

A sob escaped. She closed her eyes and slumped back against the desk. Tears slid down her cheeks, and she swiped at them impatiently. She wouldn't cry here. Wouldn't cry in front of her parents. Heartbreak could wait until she was alone.

And alone was something she'd be for the rest of her life.

She bit her lip and pushed away from the desk. Savannah was standing next to their parents, and all three were standing near the exit. As much as she didn't want to talk to anyone right now, she had no choice but to approach her family.

The relief so evident in her father's expression had Neva clenching her fists.

"It is for the best," he said gruffly. "You deserve far better than a man with a past like his."

"Father, you have no idea what you're talking about," Savannah said, voice sharp and impatient. "Why don't you just get over—"

Neva touched her sister's arm, stopping her from saying anything else, and met her father's gaze squarely. "Did you marry your soul mate?"

He frowned. "You know I did."

"And don't you wish both Savannah and me the same happiness?"

"Yes, of course, but—"

"There are no buts, Father. And you've made me choose between my family and my soul mate."

And with that, she pushed past them and walked out the door.

Sixteen

"I'm really tempted to give the old bastard a piece of my mind," Ari said as she plopped down in the booth seat opposite Neva. "I mean, how dare he spout words of tolerance to the council when he's not even practicing it in his own backyard?"

Neva smiled as she swished the straw through the froth of her strawberry shake. "He'll fire you again."

Ari airily waved the comment away. "He's fired me three times this week already. We both know he can't afford to lose me. You and I are the only ones crazy enough to work for peanuts."

That was certainly true. She sipped her drink and glanced out the diner's window. Nearly two months had passed since Duncan had left, and spring had truly come to Ripple Creek. But the warmth hadn't touched her heart. And wouldn't. Not until he came back into her life.

And that couldn't happen soon enough. She blinked back the sting of tears and tried not to think about him. Tried not to think about the long nights of dreaming about his touch and waking to nothing more than loneliness and despair.

But at least not seeing or talking to him for so long had convinced her of two things. The first being the fact that she loved him, heart and soul, and wanted him in her life no matter what the cost. And the second being she was the biggest goddamned coward on Earth for letting him walk away from her that night. They should have confronted her parents together. Should have given *them* the ultimatum to accept their relationship if they wanted to be a part of her and Duncan's future.

But even when her heart had been breaking, part of her had still refused to believe love could happen so fast. Nor had she believed the ritual they'd performed was real— not until the next full moon, when the moon's heat did little more than make her ache for his caress. They were one, now and forever, committed to each other heart and soul.

And if her parents couldn't accept that, too bad. She had come to the point where she was more than willing to walk away—except when it came to Savannah.

A hand slid across Neva's, and her gaze jumped to her friend's.

"Your father is a fool," Ari said softly. "But I'm beginning to think you're a bigger one. If you love this man so much, go after him, babe. Your parents will come to their senses once they see how happy you are together."

Neva's smile was slightly bitter. "It's not quite as simple as that."

"Crap." Ari leaned back in the seat and crossed her arms. "Do you love him?"

"Yes."

"Does he love you?"

"Yes."

"Then what else is there to worry about? Go get your man, and to hell with your parents."

"My father swore an oath to the moon that I'd be evicted from the pack should I continue my relationship with Duncan."

Ari stared at her for a moment, then cursed softly. She knew, as Neva knew, that such an oath was binding to *all* members of the family. If she walked away to be with

Duncan, she'd never be able to talk to her sister again. And that was something she wasn't willing to lose.

"Moons," Ari commented. "What a mess."

"That it is." And she didn't see a way out of it. Not without putting Savannah in the middle.

I'll never be in the middle of it. The strength of Savannah's mind voice told Neva she was close to the diner. *Because I'm on your side, completely and utterly. You finally ready yet to do something about this whole situation?*

More than ready, Neva replied with a smile. With her twin by her side, all things were possible.

The bell above the door chimed as the door opened. Savannah walked in, dragging their mother in behind her. If the look on Nancy's face was anything to go by, she definitely wasn't here by choice. Neva glanced at the clock. No wonder. She was missing her weekly facial.

Nancy's scathing glance took them in, then swung back to Savannah. "What the hell are you doing?"

"What I should have done a month ago." The scar above her sister's left eye looked as angry as her expression. She thrust their mother into the booth next to Ari. "You move, Mom, and I swear to the moon, I'll shoot you."

With that she spun and marched toward the kitchen. Ari chuckled softly, a sound she quickly smothered as Nancy glared at her.

"This is your doing, isn't it?"

Ari's eyes were dancing with mirth as she held up her hands. "Nothing to do with me, honest. But you know, I'm damn glad someone is doing something. You and the boss seemed content to sit back and watch your daughter die of a broken heart."

"Ari—" Neva warned.

"You're fired," her mother said over the top of her voice.

"Yeah, right." Ari sniffed and crossed her arms.

Nancy slid out of the booth and pointed an imperious finger at the door. "Leave now."

Ari glanced at Neva, a smile playing around her lips. "Call me. And good luck."

"I'll probably need it."

Neva crossed her arms and watched her mother slide back into the booth, but she didn't bother saying anything. Even though she'd been back working at the diner for the last month, she'd barely exchanged a civil word with either of her parents since the night she'd let Duncan walk away. She saw no reason to change that until Savannah came back with their father.

Her mother obviously had no such inhibitions. "If you've ended up hurt, you have no one to blame but yourself."

"You're right," she bit back. "Because I let him walk away from me rather than having the courage to confront Father's edict with him by my side."

Her mother blinked. "Have you lost all the sense we bred into you? Why on earth would you think someone like Duncan Sinclair would ever make a suitable mate?"

"I don't know. Maybe the fact that we're soul mates?"

"Men like him don't have soul mates. They have lovers, and plenty of them. It's the sex that has you hooked, Neva, nothing more."

"If this is just sex, then I sure as hell can understand why the dance is so popular." Though her voice was flat, she had to thrust her hands under the table to hide the angry trembling. How dare they not trust her enough to know her own heart?

"Don't be crude," her mother replied stiffly. "A man with a past like his is not the sort of man we want—"

"And what of your past, Mother? Or has that been conveniently forgotten?"

Her mother's face went white. "What are you talking about?"

But the fear in her widening eyes suggested she knew exactly what Neva was talking about. "Dad doesn't know, does he?" she said, suddenly understanding.

"I don't know what?"

Her father's voice was sharp as he stopped in front of the booth and glared at the two of them. Savannah stood behind him, arms crossed and expression severe. Neva had a feeling she fully intended to stand there like that until this whole mess was sorted out.

"About mother's double standards," Neva replied. "About how it's all right for her to be given a second chance, and not Duncan."

"It all happened a long time ago," Nancy said, her face white, lips trembling. "I was only a teenager."

"So? Duncan wasn't much older. And nothing he has ever done has led to someone's death."

"What are you talking about?"

She met her father's stony glare and let the anger finally boil over. "We're talking about double standards. You stood up in front of the council yesterday and supported the Sinclairs right to the moon dance, stating no harm had ever come from it in all the years of it being here in Ripple Creek. Yet in private you state the dance is little more than a festival of whores, and you will not let your family participate."

"Decent people do not—"

"Decent people do and have. Half of Ripple Creek was up there the night I was there, and I'll wager many of them are on the damn council."

"That's beside the point—"

"That's *exactly* the point. You've always told me you should treat people as you find them, not as their past makes them out to be."

"Duncan Sinclair has a past longer than my arm, and he's not likely to change now." Her father's voice was a mix of patience and anger. "Sinclairs don't believe in commitment, Neva. Look at Zeke. A century under his belt and still dancing with every female that comes within range."

Neva crossed her arms, her fists clenched against her sides. "If we follow that theory, both Savannah and I should be drunken louts who run around burning houses and killing innocents."

Her mother's gasp filled the shocked silence. "How dare you—"

Neva thrust to her feet and leaned across the table. "How *dare* you! How can you look at Duncan's past and judge him unworthy when you have done far worse?"

Her father's hand came down on her shoulder. "You will not talk to your mother like that—"

Neva shook off his touch and swung around to face him. "And how dare you make me choose between the man I love and the family I love."

"I knew his mother," Levon said softly. "She was a good friend. I know the pain she went through watching the man she loved dance with others time and time again. It killed her, Neva. I'm only trying to save you from that."

"I'm old enough to choose my own destiny."

"But not old enough to understand the heartbreak to come. He will never commit to you."

She glanced at Savannah. Saw her sister's slight nod. Knew that her twin would walk when she walked. "That's where you're wrong, Father. Duncan has already committed. We performed the promising ceremony the night before he was kidnapped."

His face went as white as her mother's. "Impossible. The magic can't be raised except on the night of promising."

"Well, apparently it can, because we did."

"But . . . Why didn't you tell us?"

"I told you we were soul mates, and it didn't seem to make one goddamn bit of difference. Why would I think telling you we were promised would?"

"But . . . You can't. Not to him."

She sighed. "You know, I'm sick of arguing. I'm sick of trying to make you see. I've chosen my path. It's up to you to choose yours."

"And choose wisely," Savannah intoned. "Because I'm walking out that door with my sister, and I won't be back until you both come to your senses."

"This is stupid—"

"No, Father, this is the last straw. I don't want to live my life without Duncan in it, and if you can't accept that, then too bad."

She glanced at Savannah, and as one they walked out of the diner and down the street to the rangers' office. Neva took a deep breath and puffed it out slowly. "Well, that went better than I thought it would."

Savannah grinned. "But there were no fisticuffs. Where's the fun in that?"

Neva laughed and gave her sister a hug. "Thank you."

"No probs. Now stop worrying about our folks and go get that sexy man of yours. Either drag him home, or shag him senseless where he is so *I* can get a decent night's sleep."

Neva kissed her cheek. "That sounds like a plan to me." And was exactly what she intended to do.

Duncan leaned a shoulder against the windowsill and stared at the slowly rising moon. It was hard to believe that exactly two months ago he'd met Neva. Hard to believe he hadn't seen or heard from her for almost the same amount of time.

And while he hadn't really expected her to call, part of him had hoped that she might. Not that it mattered. In five days he was going home to Ripple Creek, whether or not he was given the job as head of the rescue team being set up over there. And he fully intended claiming what was his and making her parents see he was more than just his past.

Footsteps echoed in the hall beyond his office. He glanced over his shoulder and watched Dave Richards, the man in charge of the Eagle County search and rescue team, walk in.

"You want the good news, the bad news or the 'not-again' news?" Dave asked.

"I'm guessing the 'not-again' news would be another hiker getting lost." There certainly had been a rash of them lately. The latest influx of tourists didn't seem able to read a map and often panicked when darkness set in.

"You guessed that right." Dave handed him a piece of paper with the woman's details and last known position. "At least this one had a cell phone with her. She's up near Paddy's hut from the sound of it. I told her to stay put until you arrived."

"Let's hope she does." The last one they'd rescued decided to keep on walking and had almost walked off a damn cliff. "What's the bad news?"

"My spies over in Ripple Creek tell me you were passed over for the search and rescue post."

"I'm not entirely surprised." He may have the experience, but his reputation was shot to hell in Ripple Creek, and Levon was a strong voice on the council. He wouldn't willingly approve any action that would bring Duncan back home. "The good news?"

"Is that the head ranger caught wind of the decision and confronted the council. Apparently she told them that if they refused to pick the best man for the job, she'd hand in her resignation. When the rest of her team backed her up, the council backed down."

Duncan smiled. He'd have to remember to kiss Savannah when he next saw her. "When will it be official?"

"I'm told they'll be calling tomorrow."

"Good." At least he had a decent job to go back to when he went home. While he might own Snowflake Lodge, he had no intention of kicking the Harpers out to manage it himself. They were doing a far better job than he ever could.

He pushed away from the window and grabbed his coat off the hook. "I'll give you a call when I find our errant hiker."

"Do that," Dave said. "And good luck."

Duncan nodded and grabbed his gear on the way out. The night air was crisp and the sky above so full of stars it almost looked silver. He let his gaze drift to the moon, still hanging low in the evening sky. Two full moons without Neva were two too many, but at least the promising ritual had ensured neither of them suffered moon fever while they were apart. And yet he ached for her tonight. Ached with an intensity that cut through every part of him.

He shouldered the pack and headed up the mountain. Trees crowded in closer the higher he went, the various pines still hiding drifts of snow under their green skirts. He was almost at Paddy's hut when awareness surged, followed closely by a joy greater than anything he'd ever known.

Neva was here.

He walked on, not rushing, even though his whole body trembled with the need to grab her and hold her and love her. Through the trees ahead, flames flickered and danced. He smiled. His lost hiker had made herself at home.

He came into the clearing and shucked off the pack, tossing it toward the hut's door as he walked on. Neva was standing in front of the fire, her back to him as she stared out over the valley below. The warmth of the flames caressed her golden skin, so that she almost appeared to gleam like precious metal in the darkness.

She didn't turn around or acknowledge his presence in any way, and yet he felt her awareness of him through every fiber.

He stopped near the fire and took off his jacket. There was a sleeping bag at her feet, and a bottle of champagne and two glasses off to one side.

"I owe you an apology," she said softly.

"For what?" He pulled off his boots then stripped off his jeans.

"For not having the courage to ask you to stay two months ago."

"We were only together for four days. Confusion and doubt is allowed, I think." His shorts joined the pile of clothes. The night air caressed his skin but failed to cool the fever burning through him.

"You didn't doubt."

"But I have spent half my life looking for my soul mate. You were looking for nothing more than your sister's attacker."

"We found her."

"Together." He stopped behind her, not touching her, but so close that every breath held the warm citrus scent of her. So close that the heat radiating off her skin burned across his. "What of your parents?"

"That I don't know."

He ran a finger down the long line of her neck and across one shoulder. Her skin trembled under his touch, and her desire burned the air. "I'm sorry."

"Don't be. I have Savannah on my side, and that's all that matters for now. Time will change their minds. And if it doesn't . . ." She shrugged.

He let his touch slide down to her waist and across her stomach, pressing her back against him. She felt so good, so right, and all he wanted to do was turn her around and kiss her and make love to her. But there were still things that had to be said. A sigh escaped her lips. It was a sound he felt like echoing.

"Did you tell them we were soul mates?"

"I told them that I loved you. I told them that I didn't want to live without you. I told them that we performed the promising ritual."

"Ah." He brushed a kiss across her neck. She tasted warm and tangy, and far better than he remembered. Far better than she had in any of his dreams. "When did you realize the pretense was real?"

"Not until much later. How about you?"

"From the minute I said the first words. And I wasn't about to stop—or let you stop. I told you, you're mine, and I don't intend to share. Not ever."

"Good." She turned and wrapped her arms around his neck, her green eyes shining wickedly despite her stern expression. "Because neither do I."

He raised a hand to her cheek, brushing his thumb across her ripe lips. "So where does that leave us?"

She raised an eyebrow. "Long term?"

"Long term." Because he knew exactly what they'd be doing short term.

She considered him for a minute, her smile growing and love so evident in her bright eyes that it reflected through every fiber of his being. "I'm thinking at least six children."

He raised his eyebrows, feigning shock. "Six? Good grief, woman, do you want me working night and day to support you all?"

She rolled her eyes. "Oh, okay then. Four."

"A nice even number," he agreed, sliding his fingers down to her rump. "We'll have to buy a bigger house, though. Yours isn't big enough to house us all."

She raised an eyebrow. "You don't want to return to the mansion?"

"You wouldn't be comfortable living there."

"No," she agreed. "I wouldn't. But only because I don't think it's the best environment to bring up a pack of kids."

He cupped her rump and lifted her until he was able to slide deep inside. She felt so good, so wet and warm and ready, that he groaned. God, how he'd missed her. "A pack of kids? I thought we agreed on four?"

"Oh, yeah. So we did."

Her grin was pure cheek as she wrapped her legs around him and pushed him deeper. He groaned, his whole body trembling with the effort to remain still. Which she certainly wasn't.

"You do realize twins run in my family," she continued, rocking her body gently against his.

"You do realize if you keep doing what you're doing, in a matter of moments I'm not going to be able concentrate on anything you're saying."

"You want me to stop?"

"Not really."

"Good, because I wasn't intending to."

"Wicked wench."

"It's the company I keep." Her eyes twinkled at him. "Such a bad, bad man."

"I never thought you'd be the type to fall for a bad man."

"Neither did I. But I have. Hook, line, and sinker. There's no hope left for me now."

"None at all," he agreed. "Because that bad man intends to keep teaching you wicked things for the rest of his life."

"That sounds like a plan."

He smiled and kissed her nose. "So, we've discussed long term goals—what about short term?"

"Well, for the first hour or so, I plan to be ravished senseless, then I think we should drink some of that champagne before the ice melts. Then I think some more ravishing is in order."

"Now that sounds like a plan to me," he said and set about carrying it out.

Watch out
for the following titles by
Keri Arthur
now available
from
Piatkus!

Also available in Keri Arthur's
Ripple Creek *werewolf series:*

BENEATH A DARKENING MOON

Someone is murdering humans on the Ripple Creek
Werewolf Reservation, and the murders are eerily
similar to those Chief Ranger Savannah Grant witnessed
nearly ten years ago. Having once had the reputation
for being the wild sister, it seems her past has come back
to haunt her. Worse still, the man sent in to help with
the investigation is the one man Savannah had hoped
never to see again – the man who had taken her trust
and her heart, and smashed them both.

Cade Jones is in Ripple Creek to catch the killer who
escaped his noose ten years before. What he doesn't
expect to find is the woman who had also slithered from
his grasp. This time, Cade has ever intention of holding
her to the promises she made long ago. But, as the murders
continue, it becomes evident that the killer isn't murdering
at random. Suddenly, Savannah finds herself having
to trust the one man she'd sworn never to trust again.
But can Cade unravel the clues left from the past
and present in time to save them both, or will a killer's
need for revenge snatch away their hopes for a future
together yet again?

978-0-7499-0876-8

Titles available in Keri Arthur's
Nikki & Michael *vampire series:*

DANCING WITH THE DEVIL

Having grown up on the tough streets of Lyndhurst, Private Investigator Nikki James believes there is nothing left to surprise her. That changes the night she follows teenager Monica Trevgard into the shadows and becomes a pawn caught in a war betwen two very different men. One fills her mind with his madness; the other pushes his way into her heart. Nikki knows how dangerous love can be but, if she wants to survive, she must place her trust in a man who might destroy her.

For three hundred years, Michael Kelly has existed in the shadows, learning to control his vampiric death cravings. Nikki not only breaches his formidable barriers with her psychic abilities, but makes Michael believe he may finally have found a woman strong enough to walk by his side. Will his love be enough to protect her from a madman hell-bent on revenge? Or will the secrets they keep from each other prove to be the greatest threat of all?

978-0-7499-0894-2

HEARTS IN DARKNESS

Life has never been so insane for Private Investigator
Nikki James: a teenager is missing; a madman is
kidnapping the wealthy; she's got a vampire to contend
with; and her partner and best friend, Jake, is in the
hospital dying. And just when it seems like nothing else
could possibly go wrong for her, Michael Kelly returns.

The last thing Michael needs is a confrontation with Nikki
– especially when his control over his bloodlust is still so
tenuous. But when a kidnapper steps up his agenda to
murder, they are suddenly forced into a partnership. Soon
Michael discovers the biggest danger may not be from his
need to 'taste' Nikki, but from his desire to make her a
permanent part of his life – a life that is sure to get her
killed. Nikki is determined to make Michael see that life
apart is worse than death. But before she can make him
see the light, a spectre from Michael's past rises that could
destroy any hope she has of a future with him.

978-0-7499-0896-6

CHASING THE SHADOWS

Private Investigator Nikki James is in San Francisco at the request of her business partner and best friend, Jake. His friend's wife is missing, and he is determined to find her. The authorities believe the kidnapping is the work of a sick mind; Nikki knows it is something much worse. Vampires. Six of them. And they know who she is and why she's there.

Michael Kelly has just returned from a vampire hunting exhibition in his homeland. When he discovers Nikki's gone to San Francisco, he has no choice but to follow – not only to keep her safe from the vampire gang, but because he fears the psychic talents she's beginning to develop; abilities she should not have and cannot control. But as the body count begins to rise, so too does the danger. Soon Nikki becomes a target, but she has no intention of obeying Michael's demands that she leave. She's tired of playing it safe and wants him to realise it's all or nothing: she's either a full-time partner in his life, or she's out. Nothing, however, prepares Nikki for the price she has to pay for her stubbornness – the life of someone she loves.

978-0-7499-0893-5

KISS THE NIGHT GOODBYE

Private Investigator Nikki James wants nothing more than to pass the Circle's strict entry exams so she can begin to plan her wedding to Michael Kelly. But when one of the testers attempts to kill her, she realises buying a wedding dress is the least of her worries. Especially when Michael is shot and kidnapped.

The trail leads her to the ghost town where Michael once killed a murderer. She's not surprised to discover that Weylin Dunleavy, the brother of that long-ago sorcerer, has set out to raise his brother's spirit from hell. Nor is she truly surprised to discover that a barrier of magic surrounds the old town, leaving her to battle Dunleavy with only her wits, strength and the one psychic gift she cannot fully control. The one thing that does surprise her, the one thing she cannot accept, is the fact that Michael no longer remembers who she is . . .

978-0-7499-0897-3